I0831964

A Cord of Seven Strands

The sixth volume in
a collection of writings by

C.J.S. Hayward

C.J.S. Hayward Publications, Wheaton

1. Christianity--fiction. 2. Fantasy--cultures. 3. Culture and inculturation. 4. Literature.

ISBN 978-0-6152-0218-1

The reader is invited to visit CJSHayward.com.

Contents

I learned it all from Jesus

A gift does not need to be costly in order to be big. *A little child is worth God's time.* All who believe are brothers and sisters. *Be thankful.* Be the first to say, "I'm sorry," and the first to forgive. *Believing means clinging with your whole heart.* Clothe yourself in prayer. *Commune with God. Cry. Dance.* Don't judge. A respected pillar of the community can be two steps from Hell, and a prostitute can be two steps from Heaven. *Don't worry about tomorrow. Today has enough worries of its own.* Every blade of grass, every twinkling star, every ticklish friend, is a blessing from God. Cherish them. *Everything in the whole Creation tells us something about God.* Give someone a gift today. *God delights in you.* God has a sense of humor. *God is a friend who'll never, never leave you.* God is an artist. *God is everywhere, from the highest star to inside your heart. There is nowhere you can go to escape his presence -- or his love.* God is found, not in earthquake nor fire nor mighty wind, but in a soft and gentle whisper. *God is your Daddy.* God watches over even the little sparrows. *Heaven is very close.* He is risen! *He who sings, prays twice. He who dances, sings twice. He who laughs, dances twice. He who prays, laughs twice.* Hug your friends. *If you have to have everything under your control, trusting God may look as stable as a cow on ice skates. Trust him anyway. It's worth it.* If you want God to smile, tell him your prayers. If you want God to laugh, tell him your plans. *It's never too late to repent.* Joy comes from suffering. *Keep on forgiving.*

Laugh. *Listen to other people's stories.* Listen to the silence. *Love God with your whole being. Love one another. Love your enemies. Love your neighbor as yourself.* Make every action a prayer. *Make your prayers and your good deeds secret.* Play with children. *Prayers ascend like incense before God's throne.* Purity does not reside in the hands, but in the heart. *Respect the aged.* Rest. *Serve.* Sing. *Take time to be alone with God.* Tell God you love him. *Tell your friends that you love them.* The Heavens tell the glory of God. *There are miracles all around. You just have to be able to see.* Treasure God's smallest blessings. *We can bring little pieces of Heaven down to earth.* What you do for the least, you do for God. *Work is a blessing from God.* You are God's image.

Amazing Providence

My church in Cambridge asked students to share as Holy Trinity Cambridge said farewell to us. I ended up sharing this more than once.

Even before I left Wheaton, I had a disturbing amount of trouble. An employer broke its word, jeopardising my ability to pay. I was working on student loans for *six months*. They fell into place one business day before I left. And when I left I was gravely ill.

I arrived at Cambridge without a place to stay, and when after weeks I found one, I was barely able to work because I was so wiped out that my hardest efforts weren't enough for me to consistently work more than two hours a day. I went through treatments that could have killed me.

My studies suffered. I did terribly at almost everything during the schoolyear. Usually the people supervising me didn't even give me a grade--just advice on what to do next.

To say all this and *stop* would be very deceptive. In the end, I was bewildered, not so much by the sufferings I had been allowed to experience, but the joy. How has God blessed me?

Community, for starters. I've been held in a blanket of prayer by Christians here, in England, in other countries, Catholic, Orthodox, Protestant, all praying for me. I'm honored. There were times when I knew I should not have the strength to walk at all, but I was walking lightly, joyfully, on strength given by God. The Dean family helped me look for a place to stay, and I don't think I can even *remember* all the practical help they gave--but more than this, they welcomed me into their hearts at the time I felt most isolated and lonely. Holy Trinity is a warm place; a woman named Mary invited me over for a lavish meal that I don't think she can often afford to eat as a ninety year old widow. I believe my roommate Yussif was the reason why God closed so many doors in places to stay, and opened just one. He gave me this marvelous African shirt, and when I wear it I feel like I'm putting on regalia I have not earned. I've had visits: my father Came out to visit me, and later my aunt, uncle, and two cousins spent a day in Cambridge. We went on a small boat in the river Cam, and one of the people in the tour company lent my cousin Katie his hat. The tour guide looked at her and said, "It's a good thing you have that hat to protect you from the fierce English sun." I fear that especially here I must leave out much more than I can say; the Shepherd's Council will be annoyed if I talk for three hours.

God's transcendence has become more and more real to me. I've relearned that the God who lives inside our hearts is majestic and glorious, beyond the farthest stars. When I've attended Orthodox vespers, I've met God's transcendence.

Providence has been powerful. At the end of the year, my friend Dirk said he could move my possessions that evening to Colchester for storage. I e-mailed Michelle in Colchester and scrambled to get ready. After I arrived, Michelle said I had the luck of the Irish: one day earlier or later, she would not have been home. Among other things. This sort of thing had happened again and again and again, and when she later e-mailed me about my luck, I answered, "Not luck. Providence."

I've had all sorts of pleasures, small and great. I've improvised on my college's chapel organ. I've been able to take pictures of Cambridge and incorporate them into a game where you're running through a labyrinth, chasing a furball, looking at lovely Cambridge pictures, and answering icebreaker questions. (Don't worry. It's actually much stranger than it sounds.)

The academic environment is a real blessing. This may

sound strange, but academic theology often destroys students' faith. My faith has become both stronger and deeper. The tutorial system has been excellent, and things fell into place at the end of the year. I was able to work on my thesis when I was too tired to lift my head, and the day I turned it in, I told my Bible study I was realizing how God was not constrained by my limitations. Cambridge grades are based exclusively on the final, and I received e-mail from my tutor Thursday. I passed *everything*.

I've been learning about the link between God's transcendent glory, on one hand, and his loving providence on the other. What is it? In the Sermon on the Mount, Jesus said, "Which of you, by worrying, can add a single hour to his life?" Sickness is a good opportunity to realize that even a single hour is a gift from God. "Therefore I tell you, do not worry, asking, 'What will we eat?' or 'What will we drink?' or 'What will we wear?' For the pagans run after these things, and your heavenly Father knows that you need them. But seek *first* the kingdom of God, and his perfect righteousness, and all these things will be given to you as well."

It's not just that God doesn't need my help figuring out what's best for me. What I've learned is that what God, in his transcendence, in his mystery, in his glory, in his deeply hidden wisdom, ordains for me is much fuller, deeper, richer, more beautiful, more interesting, and more adventuresome than what I would choose for myself if (God forbid) I were in control...

The blessings continue after I've returned. My parents were given a sweetheart of a dog, named Jazz. Not ten minutes after I met her, Jazz climbed up on my lap and wanted to cuddle. Jazz is a seventy-five pound Laborador retriever and is a bit of a bull in a China shop. I trust that through her, God will give me furry companionship, aerobic exercise, and thicker arms. Please pray that I may rightly appreciate her.

Thank you *so much* for praying. It is said that Satan laughs at our plans, scoffs at our power, and trembles at our prayers. Please *persist in all of your prayers*, and if the Lord leads you, please let part of that include me.

Janra Ball: The Headache

The Original Cultural Context

> "When it comes to games, never try to understand the Janra mind."
>
> -Oeildubeau, Urvanovestilli philosopher and anthropologist

It is known that Janra sports usually last for at least half an hour, involve a ball, two or more teams, running and acrobatics, and animated discussion. Beyond that, neither the Urvanovestilli's logic nor the Yedidia's intuition are able to make head or tail of them. In general, the teams appear to have unequal numbers of players; the players often switch teams in the course of play; teams are created and dissolved; the nature of the activities makes sudden and radical changes; there is no visible winning or losing. There are occasionally times in the course of play when some intelligible goal appears to be being approached... but then, all players seem to be approaching it in a rather erratic manner (when asked why he didn't do thus and such simple thing and achieve the approached goal by an inexperienced anthropologist, one of the Janra said, "Technically, that would work, but that would be a very boring way to do it," and then bolted back into play: the extent to which game play is comprehensible heightens its incomprehensibility). Late in life, Oeildubeau hinted at having suspicions that, if the Janra believe that they are being watched, they will spontaneously stop whatever sport they are playing, and instead begin a series of activities expressly designed to give any observer a headache.

Rules

1. There is no winning or losing.
2. The game has one ball, which must be kept in motion at all times. If the ball ceases to move, nobody may speak or act except to move the ball.
3. *Il est interdit de parler en anglais au subjet de l'objet du jeu.*
4. Any player may give any other player a rule point, provided that there is no alliance or "You scratch my back, and I'll scratch yours" arrangement between them, at any time. Any player who has a rule point may spend that point in order to add, delete, or modify a rule in accordance with the spirit of the game.
5. Every player has a persona, or modus operandi, through which he is acting and answering questions. If any other player successfully identifies this persona or modus operandi, it must immediately be changed.
6. There is no rule number 6.
7. Each player must somehow touch another player before or during addressing him in speech.
8. No player may move from one point to another without using at least one acrobatic, dance, or martial arts motion.
9. Any use of a card deck or game board requires one change of rules for the card/board game per move.
10. Any rules disputes are to be resolved by no judge, until all involved parties come to a confusion which is more chaotic than in its initial form.
11. All players must wear one black sock and one white sock.

12. We're sorry, but rule number twelve is not available at this time. To leave a message, please rotate your telephone clockwise by ninety degrees, and simultaneously press 'q' and 'z'.
13. Any player who does not understand all of the rules, in their entirety, is immediately disqualified.
14. Any player who attempts to memorize all of the rules, or attempts to play the game by keeping its rules, is immediately disqualified.

FAQ list

Q: What is 'Springfield'?

A: Springfield is a game in which two people alternate naming state capitals, and the first person to name Springfield wins.

Q: What's the point of that?

A: The objective is to be the first person to say 'Springfield' as late as possible. The point is to see how far you can go -- and still be the first to say 'Springfield'. It's not a game of mathematical strategy. It's a game of perception.

Q: What is Psychiatrist?

A: Psychiatrist is a game in which one person, the psychiatrist, leaves the room, and all of the other players agree on a common delusion (such as believing themselves to be the person immediately to their left). The psychiatrist then enters, and asks the players questions, attempting to guess the delusion.

Q: What is spoon photography?

A: Very well known.

Q: What is Janra Ball all about?

A: Wouldn't you like to know?

Q: Why did you answer my question with another question?

A: How else could it be?

Q: What are the teams like?

A: Highly variable, and not necessarily mutually exclusive.

Q: How do I get ahead in the game?

A: Mu.

Q: Why won't you give me a straight answer to my questions?

A: Come, come. Aren't there much more interesting ways to grok the game?

Ingredients

Springfield, Monty Python, Calvin-Ball, body language, Harlem Globetrotters, sideways logic, Thieves' Cant, intuition, counter-intuitive segues, spoon photography, creativity, Zen koans, Psychiatrist, adrenaline, perception, tickling, urban legend Spam recipe, swallowing a pill, illusionism, modern physics, raw chaos, F.D. & C. yellow number 5.

Theology of Play

Most of Christianity that I've come into contact with has a well developed theology of work; sometimes called the Protestant Work Ethic, it is summarized in the verse, "Whatever you do, do it heartily, as if unto the Lord." (Col. 3:23). A mature Christian is characterized by hard work, and I do not wish to detract from that, but there is a counterpart to theology of work: theology of play.

It would probably be easier to defend a point of doctrine involving great self sacrifice - that a Christian should be so loyal to Christ that the prospect of being tortured and killed for this devotion is regarded as an honor, that a Christian should be willing to serve in boring and humiliating ways, that a Christian should resist temptation that takes the form of an apparent opportunity for great pleasure - but I will still state and explain this point: a Christian should be joyful, and furthermore that this joy should express itself in play and celebration.

When Paul describes the fruit of the Spirit, the first word he uses is love. Love will certainly apply itself by hard work. He goes on to describe it as patience, faithfulness, self-control. Patience, faithfulness, and self-control all have important application to hard work. But the second word is joy. If the fruit of the Spirit will yield hard work, it will also yield expressions of joy.

C.S. Lewis said that the greatest thing that the Psalms did for him was express the joy that made David dance. Doctrinal development is one of the reasons that God gave us the Bible, but it is not the sole reason. I would not by any means suggest that omitting Paul's epistles would improve the Bible, but there is a lot of the Bible that I read for the sheer joy and beauty as much as anything else. Psalm 148, one of my favorite, beautifully embellishes the word, "Halleluyah!" That alone is reason sufficient to merit its placement in the Bible. When the Psalms tell us that we should sing unto Yahweh, it is not telling us of a dreadful and terrible duty that we must endure because God says so. By contrast, it is encouraging an expression of joy. I try to show myself to the world primarily as a person of love, but I have also had a strong witness among the unbelievers as a person of joy; one of the stereotypes of a Christian that I have been glad to shatter is that of a repressed and repressive person. The stereotype says that a person who tries to live by the Bible's moral standards will have a somber life devoid of joy; I thus try to let the deep and inner joy "I've got a river of life flowing out of me..." that the Holy Spirit has placed in my heart show itself to them. Satan likes to take and twist pleasure into enticement for his evils; that does not make pleasure an evil thing. Yahweh made pleasure - the idea that Satan could imagine such a thing on his own is risible (for Satan cannot create; he can only mock) - and pleasure is intended for Christians to partake.

Celebration is something that can certainly come from things going well, but it is not a grave evil that is justified only by exceptional cause; it is a way of life. Some of celebration, some expressions of joy and thanksgiving, are in response to an event we are pleased at and thankful for, and rightly so, but celebration is not something to be reserved for rare occasions. I may be celebrating an event, but Christ is reason well sufficient for celebration; consequently, it is appropriate to celebrate, even when you can't point to an exceptional event. There is a time to mourn, but a Christian does not need extenuating circumstances as reason to celebrate.

I am not going to attempt to provide an exhaustive list of expressions of joy, and most definitely do not wish to provide commands which must be successively fulfilled to the letter and verified in triplicate, but I think that a few suggested variants of "stop and smell the roses" are in order:

Call a friend you haven't talked to in a while.

Read a children's book.

When it's warm, take off your shoes, close your eyes, and feel the grass under your feet.

Stop and remember five things you are glad for; thank God for them.

Drink a mug of hot cocoa. Slowly.

Go go a local art museum.

Hug a friend.

Climb a tree.

Close your eyes and imagine yourself somewhere else.

Sneak up behind a friend who is ticklish...

In addition to these that I've pulled off the top of my head, I'd like to look at three recurring, decidedly Biblical expressions of joy, and how many Christians have reacted to them.

- Singing. The Christian understanding of music is summed up in the words, "Make a joyful noise unto Yahweh." While it can also be solemn, music was created as a beautiful expression of joy. When Paul encourages the believers to sing to one another, he is not really appealing to a sense of duty, but rather encouraging a celebratory and joyful pleasure in this good gift of God. The jail warden was astounded to find that Paul was happily singing when he was imprisoned; this joy expressed itself in so powerful of a manner that it opened the warden's ears so that he, too, would gain this welling up of life, flowing into joy. Most Christians sing (even if some of the music has room for improvement); this is good. believe that Yahweh is pleased when he listens. This is Biblical.
- Dance. One of the expressions of celebration recorded in the Bible, as well as song, is dance.

In Exodus, after Israel passed through the red sea and Egypt didn't, Moses's song is followed after a couple of verses with the words, "Then the prophet Miriam, Aaron's sister, took a tambourine in her hand; and all the women went out after with tambourines and with dancing." In Samuel, it is asked, "Is this not David the king of the land? Did they not sing to one another of him in dances, 'Saul has killed his thousands, and David his ten thousands?'", and recorded, "David danced before Yahweh with all his might." The psalms jubilantly sing, "Let them praise his name with dancing, making melody to him with tambourine and lyre." and "Praise him with tambourine and dance; praise him with strings and pipe!" In Ecclesiastes, dancing is identified with joy: "...a time to weep, and a time to laugh; a time to mourn, and a time to dance..." Jeremiah issues words of comfort, saying, "Again I will build you, and you shall be built, O virgin Israel! Again you shall take your tambourines, and go forth in the dance of merrymakers." In Lamentation he also identifies dancing with joy, saying, "The joy of our hearts has ceased; our dancing has been turned to mourning."

It is not without reason that dance is a part of the worship services of Messianic Jews. It is not without reason that a song that has come to us from Africa states, "If the Spirit of the Lord moves in my soul, like David the victor I dance." The shaker hymn very beautifully states, "Dance, then, wherever you may be, for I am the Lord of the Dance, said he." Throughout, the hymn describes the walk of faith as a dance. Dancing is a good thing, an act of joy, that has been given to us by Yahweh himself for our good.

There are a few forms of dance that are essentially sex with clothes in the way, and should be avoided outside of a marital context. Because of the existence of these dances, some Christians have attacked dance as demonic; "Dance before Yahweh" necessitates an interpretation of "Dance alone before Yahweh."

This is silly. Celebration is meant to be enjoyed in community; its nature is not a selfish "I like this and I'm going to keep it all to myself," but a generous, "This is so good that I have to share it with you as well." This is the mark of a child fully enjoying a lollipop. When holidays and other times of celebration come, people want to be with friends and family, and it would be only a slight exaggeration to say that this is the whole reason that believers come together for worship services.

Dance, also, should be enjoyed in community.

- Proper use of wine.

In Judges, the vine refuses an offer to be the king over all trees, saying, "Shall I stop producing my wine that cheers gods and mortals, and go to sway over the trees?" The Psalms likewise describe material blessings by saying, "You cause grass to grow for the cattle, and plants for people to use, to bring forth food from the earth, and wine to gladden the human heart, oil to make the face shine, and bread to strengthen the human heart.", and Ecclesiastes, "Feasts are made for laughter; wine gladdens life..." The Song of Songs, in its description of the erotic, says, "Let him kiss me with the kisses of his mouth! For your love is better than wine... How sweet is your love, my sister, my bride! how much better is your love than wine...", comparisons that would mean little if wine were not understood to be a good thing. Isaiah accuses Israel of apostasy in the words, "Your silver has become dross, your wine is mixed with water." He Israel to a vineyard created so its master may enjoy its wine; elsewhere appear the words, "On this mountain Yahweh Sabaoth will make for all peoples a feast of rich food, a feast of well-aged wines, of rich food filled with marrow, of well-aged wines strained clear." Jeremiah contains Psalmlike words of celebration: "They shall come and sing aloud on the height of Zion, and they shall be radiant over the goodness of Yahweh, over the grain, the wine, and the oil, and over the young of the flock and the herd; their life shall become like a watered garden, and they shall never languish again." Hosea, in sadness at apostasy, makes it clear that wine is a gift from above: "She did not know that it was I who gave her the grain, the wine, and the oil, and who lavished upon her silver and gold that they used for Baal."

Going from the Old Testament to the New, it is seen that Jesus was accused of being a drunkard; for his first miracle, he turned water to wine, thus permitting a celebration to continue.

Now, it should be mentioned that alcohol is something that merits an appropriate respect and caution; consumed in excess, it is a deadly poison. It has been said that we should thank God for beer and burgundy by not drinking too much of them. Our culture has largely cast aside the virtue of moderation and the belief that a sin could be sin because it takes a good thing to excess (gluttony is not mentioned as a sin very often, and a great many people would be healthier to lose some weight). Not everybody thought this way. The ancient Greeks accorded moderation a place as one of the four cardinal virtues, and Paul named temperance and self-control as the final of the virtues listed as the fruit of the Spirit. Liquor, like most good things, should be consumed in a temperate, controlled, and balanced manner. And, like most good things, it becomes a bane if it is taken out of proper context. It was not without reason that Solomon wrote that wine is a mocker and beer a brawler. This country has age related laws pertaining to alcohol, and they should not be violated Granted that those laws be obeyed, it would be wise to consider to the advice to Jesus ben Sirach, who in his writing said, "Do not try to prove your strength by wine drinking, for wine has destroyed many. As the furnace tests the work of the smith, so wine tests hearts when the insolent quarrel. Wine is very life to human beings if taken in moderation. What is life to one who is without wine? It has been created to make people happy. Wine drunk at the proper time and in moderation is rejoicing of heart and gladness of soul." Elsewhere comparing wine to music, he regards wine as a good part of celebration.

There are many things that should be made manifest in the life of Christians; community, freedom, and celebration are important. Paul writes in Galatians, "For freedom Christ has set us free. Stand firm, therefore, and do not submit again to a yoke of slavery.", in Colossians, "Therefore do not let anyone condemn you in matters of food and drink.... If with Christ you died to the elemental spirits of the universe, why do you live as if you still belonged to the world? Why do you submit to regulations, 'Do not handle, Do not taste, Do not touch'?", and in I Timothy, "Now the Spirit expressly says that in later times some will renounce the faith by paying attention to the teachings of demons, through the hypocrisy of liars whose consciences are seared with a hot iron. They forbid marriage and demand abstinence from foods, which God created to be received with thanksgiving by those who believe and know the truth. For everything created by God is good, and nothing is to be rejected, provided it is received with thanksgiving; for it is sanctified by God's word and by prayer."

So let us enjoy the gifts that God has bestowed.

(scripture quotations generally NRSV)

The Metacultural Gospel

I want to tell you about my best friend, Nathaniel. When we were getting to know each other, Nathaniel told me that he was God come down in human form. I thought for a moment and said, "If that's true, you aren't doing a very good job of it." He laughed, and said, "You're probably right."

Where can I begin to describe him? Perhaps you've had this experience. When there's someone you don't know very well, it's easy to say "Yeah, I know him. He's that hockey player who tells the worst puns." But when it's someone you're close to, best-buddies intimate with, then words fail you. I could begin by saying, "Nathaniel was a construction worker," which would leave most people with two impressions. The first impression is that he was strong and had calloused hands, which is true. The second impression is that he wasn't much in the brains department, which is out-and-out false. He didn't have too much in the way of formal schooling -- stopped after getting his high school diploma -- but Nathaniel was absolutely *brilliant*. I still remember the time when I had him over at my place, reached on my shelf, pulled out the *Oxford Companion to Philosophy*, and read aloud the entry for 'aestheticism', and then began a devastating critique. I don't remember his whole argument, but the first part pointed out that there was an assumed and unjustified opposition between aesthetic and other (i.e. instrumental) attitudes, with an argument that seemed to challenge aestheticism by pointing out that there are other ways of viewing art. He asked if one would challenge the activity of working by pointing out the legitimacy of eating and sleeping. Nathaniel was the first kindred spirit I found in philosophy and other things; he challenged and stretched me, but he was the first person I met who had also thought things I thought no one else would ever understand.

I'd like to explain a little more about the conversation where I told him that if he was God come down in human form, he wasn't doing a very good job of it. How can I put this? It wasn't that he was inhuman -- certainly not the sort of thing usually conjured by the term 'inhuman', with some sort of indecency or cruelty or monstrosity. He *was* human -- he just challenged my conceptions of what it meant to be human. (I thought *I* was unusual!) Being with him was like realizing one had woken up in a different world -- in so many little ways. He fit in, but he wasn't like anybody else.

One of my first shocks came when I saw him chatting, naturally and freely, with some support staff at my office. At first I thought that they were for some reason old friends of his, but he disabused me of that notion. When we talked about it afterwards, I realized the extent to which I had treated support staff like part of the furniture. He seemed to be able to talk with *everyone* -- young (he's one of few adults I've known who could enter a child's world and really play), old, rich, poor, American, international, it didn't matter. He could enter the house of a Klu Klux Klansman for dinner and then leave and spend the rest of the evening with a follower of Minister Farrakahn -- being on friendly terms with both. He was very good at entering other people's worlds -- but he had very much his own world. And there were a thousand little things about it -- like how, in his letters, he always wrote 'I' as 'i' and 'you' as 'You'.

I was talking with him about Harold Bloom's treatment of cultures as caves (as per Plato's "Allegory of the Television, er, Cave"), when I came to the strangest realization. Nathaniel did and did not live in a culture. He did live in American culture in the sense that he spoke the language, literally and figuratively, enjoyed hamburgers, and couldn't handle chopsticks to save his life. You might say that he spoke the culture as would a foreign anthropologist who had given it a lot of study, but I wouldn't. He *owned* American culture. But at the same time, he didn't pick up any of its blind spots. I had given some thoughts to something I call metaculture -- something that happens when a kid grows up exposed to multiple cultures, or when someone is really smart and just doesn't think like anyone else does, and doesn't breathe his host culture the way most people do. I had been aware of something metacultural in myself, where I felt like I was a composite of cultures and eras, with something that wasn't captured in any single one of them. I was groping towards something from below, when he had it, all of it, from above. Where I started to climb up to the mouth of the cave, he descended from the world above and met me. I had thought about the phrase "the wave of the past" as an inversion of "the wave of the future", challenging the worship and even concept of modern progress, where each age gets better than the one before; I had been aware of something of real merit grasped by ages past that have been lost in our mad pursuits. And then Nathaniel showed me the wave of Heaven.

Nathaniel spent most of his life as a construction worker. He did a better job at seeming ordinary than I do at least; only his mother Camilla seemed to be able to even guess at who he really was. His family was visiting someone at Wheaton College, and -- before I go further, there's something I need to explain about Wheaton.

Wheaton College is a devout place, a religious Harvard if you will. And their approach to religion has its quirks. The temperance movement, which condemned God's creation of alcohol as evil, made a practice of having people sign a Pledge to abstain from alcohol. Wheaton College is one of few places where that practice is alive, and required of every member. Of course they say that they are not making a moral condemnation, but only a prudential measure, but their actions, even what they call their prohibition (which forbids most dancing as well), are deafening.

At the reception, they ran out of soda, and ran out of punch. Camilla kept tugging on Nathaniel's sleeve and asking him to do something. Finally he told them to fill a cooler with tap water -- then drew off a cup of the beverage and sent it to the administrator in charge.

It was champagne.

The champagne was dumped, the cooler rinsed out, and filled with water, and it somehow held champagne again. I was embarrassed enough to be drinking champagne (the best I ever tasted) out of a plastic cup. But the administration had a more serious embarrassment to deal with -- but I am getting off topic. I was impressed with their response -- they are better than their Pledge -- and Nathaniel was still welcome on their campus after that happened.

There are other cases where response to his eccentricities did not receive such a positive response. There was one time when we were visiting a really big church, and (after some really impressive instrumental music) the lights were dimmed, and an overhead projector began to display all sorts of computer graphics, and then there was a gunshot, and another, and another; the overhead image disappeared. The gunshots continued; someone turned on the lights, and there was Nathaniel, holding a powerful handgun, shooting the projector. (It was such a strange thing to see a pacifist holding a gun.) I think he emptied a total of about three clips into it, before putting the gun into his pocket. The people around him were cringing in fear, but not terror, or perhaps you could say terror, but not fear; they were afraid, but not of the gun. I think some of them were a little afraid of whatever would make a man angry enough to fire a gun in a church.

About that time, the pastor got over being stunned and glared at him and asked, "How dare you fire a gun in my sanctuary?" He glared back and said, "How dare you take God's sanctuary and making it into a circus? This is supposed to be a house of prayer and worship for all people, and you are making it into mere amusement, a consumer commodity. Is this church set up because these people do not have televisions, that they can flip on and be titillated? Church is a place to disciple men and conform them to God, not a place to conform religion so that it will appeal to spoiled brats. The reason that you are losing people to MTV is that you are doing a second rate job of being an MTV, not a first rate job of being a church. Cleanse this place of your vaudeville filth and make it a place where men are drawn into God's presence to glorify him and enjoy him forever. If not, much worse awaits you than bullet holes in your projector."

There was another time, when we were out of town for Easter and he came to the city's First Baptist. Everybody was wearing business suits and really nice dresses -- everybody but Nathaniel. Nathaniel was comfortably arrayed in bluejeans, a plain white T-shirt, and big, heavy, black steel-toed workboots.

There was an invisible stir, and about five minutes into the sermon the pastor stopped, and said, "Young man, I suppose you'd like to explain why the best you can give God on the holiest day of the year is clothing that teenagers wear to McDonald's."

Nathaniel, with perfect composure, said, "Yes, indeed. God is Spirit, and those who worship him must worship him in Spirit and in truth, not in this set of clothing or that set of clothing, nor in this or that outer form of worship or ceremonial observance, nor some particular style of music. You don't know who you are worshipping, if you think (because you can worship God by wearing nice clothes) that nice clothes are necessary for worship. The hour is coming, is indeed already here, when God seeks worshippers who will worship him beyond the external shells that their particular traditions have associated with worship. God is calling. Are you ready to answer?"

It was not long after that that we were out in a van, going to this camp. Duncan was driving; Duncan is a devout man, and a proud graduate of Jehu's Driving School. He was blasting down the highway, which was virtually empty, and everyone but Nathaniel was involved in a very intense discussion; Nathaniel (don't ask me how he does this) was in the back seat, with his head up against a pillow, sleeping. By then I noticed that a wind was rocking our car, and I realized why we were all alone on the road. There was a terrific thunderstorm going on all around, and as I looked out the window there was a flash of lightning, and several of us saw this big twister coming right at the van. I was barely collected enough to jump to the back of the van and shake Nathaniel awake, and asked, "Don't you care if we die?!?" Nathaniel seemed irritated at having been woken up, and asked, "What's the matter? Don't you have any faith?" Then he turned to the storm -- or the twister, at any rate, and said, "Peace!" And then, all of a sudden, *everything* stopped. The wind died down, the tornado dissipated, and within minutes we could see the sun shining. It was at that point that I wet my pants.

You have to understand, we were *more* scared after the storm stopped than before. Before then, we had a purely natural fear, the fear that we could quite possibly die. That was fear enough -- I don't mean to downplay it -- but afterwards we had a purely supernatural fear, the fear that stemmed from watching a ?man? issue commands to inanimate nature and be immediately obeyed. Vulgar and base fears are about what harm can be done. There is a deeper fear that is a kind of awe, the kind of fear we sometimes experience in diminished form when we enter the presence of someone we respect. And at that point we were absolutely terrified. I don't think we would have been any less scared had he already told us that he was God the Son, clothed in flesh just like you or me; at that point, it was as if a veil was lifted, and we got a tiny glimpse into the glory, the splendor, the light that were hidden in this friend who we ate with, who we talked with, and who could pin any two of us in wrestling. Tiny glimpse as it was, it seared our eyes; in retrospect, I'm surprised nobody fainted.

After Nathaniel let us have a couple of minutes to watch the storm dissipate and let us become properly terrified, he did one of the strangest things you could think of. He rebuked us for our lack of faith. At the time, I just sat there, stunned (so did everyone else), but afterwards, I began to have a glimpse into who he was, into his world, into the world that he invited me and invites you.

I am a metacultural, which means in part that I am able to think of my culture, and shift my own position in relation to it and other cultures. One of the things I had been thinking about is the strength of scientism in Western culture as it is now and has been for some time (not all of its history -- not by a long shot). Many cultures have been cultures in which people can see ghosts, even if they're not there -- they are open to the supernatural; it is real to them. American culture is a culture in which people can't see ghosts, even if they're really there -- we are closed to the supernatural; it isn't real to us. Contemporary American culture is the result of monumental efforts to shut out the tiniest glimmer of anything supernatural; this affects not only how people think, but on a more fundamental level what they are and are not able to do. And metacultural awareness, and conscious rejection, of the effects of scientism does not translate into an immediate freedom in one's emotions to believe in miracles.

The sobriety of a recovering alcoholic -- hard-earned, the result of swimming upstream -- is qualitatively different from the sobriety of someone who has never had a problem with alcohol. For the latter person, sobriety is something that flows easily, something that is almost automatic; for the former, it is something that is difficult, possible only as the result of vigilance. Something of the quality of this difference exists between many cultures of days gone by (and other parts of the world) and our own culture, with regards to belief in the supernatural. There have been places that have breathed the supernatural in ways that are not naturally open to us -- and Nathaniel was at least a step beyond that. Sometimes I wondered -- still do -- at the task before us -- as if we were recovering alcoholics, and he brought a bottle of 151, gave us each a shot glass, and said, "You are all going to drink some amount of this beverage and then stop, and not slip into drunkenness." That's something you do with people who don't have a problem with alcohol. It's not something you do with alcoholics. But then, it was just like Nathaniel to believe that we could do things we never would have been able to do by ourselves. And I trust him enough to believe that there was method in what seemed either madness or else the most profound naïveté: "C'mon. I as God incarnate can easily stop a tornado. Why could you possibly be afraid?" Over time, I have even been able to catch glimpses of the method to this divine madness. Beauty is forged in the eye of the beholder; when someone like that trusts you, he makes you worthy of his trust, even if you are not worthy of such trust to begin with.

Anyways, we got to the camp without (further) event, and went into a room; Nathaniel jumped up into the top bunk of the bed in the corner, and curled up so that he was sitting Indian style with his back in the corner, moving his fingers about as if he were playing a keyboard. (This is one of many facets of his private world that people who met him in public might never guess at, but he let his guard down around people who knew him. I'm not even going to try to document all his eccentricities; suffice it to say that this sort of thing was as natural with him as sitting on a chair.)

After changing my pants, I asked him, "What are you working on?"

He thought for a second, and said, "I'm trying to make a free translation of Bach's Little Fugue in G Minor into English. I think there's more of a connection between the muses than we think, enough so to make translation possible in some cases, if not nearly as easy or universal as translation between natural languages. Have you ever had a basic insight that could have found expression in different forms? I am not exactly trying to translate the finished product of Bach's fugue, as to express in language what Bach chose to express in music."

I asked, "What do you have so far?"

He played the theme and said, "Not much. I'm still trying to figure out whether to translate it as poetry or logic." He paused, and said, "What's on your mind?"

I said, "I was just thinking about church last Sunday. Most of the time I can ignore bad music, but this time the music was bad enough to be a distraction to worship. Why is it that most of the time-honored tunes we use to worship God were never intended to be sung sober, and most contemporary music does not reach even that standard? I don't want to impose a burden on people of 'You must appreciate highbrow music to worship here,' but it seems that there is already a burden of 'You must endure terrible music to worship here.' I know that good music does not make worship, but it seems to me that bad music can break worship. If that music were translated into words, the result would be poorly written and poorly thought out."

Nathaniel looked at me and said, "Sean, the brokenness of this world makes things goofy. I am setting something in motion that will rock the world. Until my work is consummated, until I have returned in glory, there will always be problems. You can see these things perhaps a little more readily than most people; you suffer from them too. You are right to be grieved; the same things grieve me. But you can still live in a world where worship is diminished, where there are laws punishing beggars for begging. The just have always walked by faith with a pure heart, regardless of how much vice is in the world around them. And they have never left my Father's care."

It was after that that we had a really good talk, and I viewed my metaculture differently after that point. I had seen it as a separation between myself and most of mankind; I started to see it as a way of being human, and a part of the catholic plan of salvation, even a part of the tools God was choosing to limit himself to in bringing salvation to the world. And I was able to understand how and why Nathaniel respected the monocultural majority as easily as he did.

In the morning, after a night's dream-thought about metaculture, monoculture, and catholicity, I punched his bunk and said, "Hey, Nathaniel! How many metaculturals does it take to screw in a light bulb?"

He said, "I don't know, Sean. How many?"

I said, "It takes fifteen:

- One to evaluate the meaning of the custom of replacing burnt out light bulbs and think of possible alternatives,
- one to drive off to a store to buy a fluorescent replacement to an incandescent heat bulb, judging the higher price worth the lessened environmental degradation and longer time to replace the bulb with one like it,
- one to read McLuhan and light a small votive candle, preferring the meaning of a candle to that of a light bulb,
- one to go outside under God's light and God's ceiling to see as men have seen for the other two million, four hundred ninety-nine thousand, and nine hundred years of human existence,
- one child to pull up a ladder, unscrew the bulb, and then dissect it to see how it works and whether he can get it working again,
- one tinkerer to assemble a portable light center with ten 120-watt bulbs, wired in parallel, powered by an uninterruptable power supply and a backup generator,
- five Society-for-Creative-Anachronism style re-enactor-ish metaculturals to try to use the occasion to grasp problem solving as understood by the monocultural mindset -- one of them holding the bulb, and the other four turning the ladder,
- one critic to point out that, of the last two segments, one wastes an excessive amount of money that could be put to better use, and the other is elitist and demeaning, monoculturalism being a legitimate and God-given form of human existence that has merits metaculturals cannot share in,
- one to observe the variety of facets of the process of changing a bulb into a list, to become an immortal e-mail forward among metaculturals,
- one to say, 'This joke is taking *way* too long and is *far* too complex,' and change the light bulb, and
- one to stick her tongue out at him and say, 'Spoilsport!'"

Without missing a beat, Nathaniel asked, "How many monoculturals does it take to screw in a light bulb?"

I thought for several minutes, trying to think of a good answer, and said, "I give up. How many?"

"One. You're making things far too complex and missing what's in front of your nose."

The problem with people like Nathaniel is that they're just too smart.

We went to breakfast in the dining hall, and after breakfast Nathaniel went up to speak. He cleared his throat and said, "Good morning. Do we have any feminists here? Good. In what I have to say, I'm going to draw heavily on a concept feminism has articulated, namely that rape happens and it should be worked against.

"The human psyche exists in such a way that rape is a devastating psychological wound. It's not just like the sting of a scorpion, where you have a terrible pain for part of a day and then life goes on as it was before; it is a crushing blow after which things are not the same. Perhaps with counseling there can be healing, but it's not something that gets all better just because time passes. Rape is worse than any physical pain; it is a different and fundamentally deeper, more traumatic kind of pain, a pain of a different order.

"I don't know of anyone, feminist or not, who believes in rape because he wants to, because he hopes to live in a world where such things exist. Everyone I've talked with would much rather believe that there is nothing so dark. But it does exist, and disbelief won't make it go away. That is why feminists are going to heroic efforts to promote awareness of rape, to tell people to be careful so that at least some rapes can be prevented.

"I am here tonight to warn you about a place, which I will call Rape because I know of no more potent image to name it. In fact, it is worse than rape, beyond even how rape is worse than a sting. I have given up much, more than you can imagine, to come here, and I will endure much, more than you can imagine, to finish my work, for one reason: to save you all from Rape. If you believed as I believe, you would crawl across America on broken glass to save people.

"You were created spotless, without flaw, and then you wounded yourselves and began to die. It is a fatal wound, one that causes your bodies to lose their animation after seventy years or so, and one that has far worse effects than the destruction of your bodies. Your consciousness will not end when you die; it will rot in a fashion that is beyond death, beyond rape, and it will rot forever. You are all headed for Rape, every one of you, unless you believe in me.

"There is much more I have to tell you, much more that I would like to tell you, grander things about a place of light and love. But that comes only after passing through this doorway. There is a place called Rape, and it is real, and it is more wretched than any vision of torment you can imagine, and I have come to save you from it. Follow me if you want to live."

There was a fairly long and stunned silence after that point; all of the feminists were enraged that a man would take the concept of rape which belonged to feminism and trivialize it like that. All but one. Cassandra neither regarded the concept of rape as belonging to feminism in the sense of an exclusively owned property that others dare not tread on, nor regarded Nathaniel's speech as trivializing rape. At all. This earned censure from the other feminists. She began to follow Nathaniel after that point; she didn't quite believe his conclusions yet, but she had real insight into what would prompt a man to dare to say something like that.

As I reflect back, I can see how someone like Cassandra could live a very lonely life.

That night, Cassandra asked Nathaniel, "What is your favorite movie?"

Nathaniel thought for a second and said, "I don't really have a favorite movie, but I was just thinking for a second about a movie idea that nobody has produced."

Cassandra asked, "What's that?"

Nathaniel said, "Opening scene, there is a prisoner shackled inside a dungeon cell, with armed guards posted around. Then it shows the hero and his assistants, armed with M-16 assault rifles and one silenced sniper rifle. They sneak up to the complex, the sniper neutralizing three watchmen along the way. One of the men knocks over a glass bottle, and chaos breaks loose when someone hears them and sounds the alarm. There is a big firefight, villainous henchmen dropping like flies. The hero releases the prisoner, and radios for a helicopter to come and pick them up.

"As the last of the hero's friends jump on board the helicopter, one last henchman comes running out, firing a shotgun at the helicopter. The hero takes a .45 caliber handgun, and blasts away his knee.

"The rest of the movie slows down from the action-adventure pace so far, and follows the henchman. For the remaining hour and a half, the movie explores exactly what that one gunshot means to him for the remaining forty years of his life."

Cassandra stood silent for a moment. I could see in her eyes that she was seeing the movie. Nobody said anything for a while; then Nathaniel said, "I want to talk with you more. I need some time by myself now, and then we can really talk."

Nathaniel would depart from us, heading off where nobody could find him, to pray and be with God. This time it was over a month before he returned, and when he did, he looked like a skeleton with skin on -- but he had this glow. He was very quiet, and it was a few days before he talked with us about what had happened.

He walked into the wilderness, until he came to a place under some evergreens, by a lake, and by a large stone. He slept on the stone at night, sitting and standing and wandering around in the forest during the day, and praying all the while. He had a sense that something was going to happen -- something big, something that would take all of his strengths.

At the end of that time, he was starving, and (on a fifty degree day) hypothermic. He sat there, hungry, shivering, when the Slanderer appeared before him and said, "If you are God and not just a man, strengthen your body so that it will never be touched by hunger or cold, and then you will be freed from physical distractions to pursue your ministry."

Nathaniel said, "I have come as a real man, with real flesh that feels real pain. My ministry is not furthered by selling it out. I would rather die as a real man than have a long ministry by having an inconsistent make-believe body that only affects me so far as is convenient."

The Slanderer said, "You know, that movie idea of yours was something deep. How would you like to be able to make as many movies as you want, to have whatever influence over television and radio, newspapers, magazines, books and internet you care to have? How would you like -- no strings attached -- to have as much media influence as you want?"

Nathaniel said, "If my mission could have been accomplished by blasting pictures on the sky, I would have done that. That isn't the type of influence I want. I want a real, personal influence where I teach people face to face and touch them. I want to give my friends hugs and kisses. I want something your media can never give."

The Slanderer said, "My, you are picky about my gifts. Here's a suggestion that should interest you. You are coming to offer a salvation, but a salvation that people can only have if they choose it -- else they will suffer a torment beyond rape. Why not make everybody accept your gift?"

Nathaniel glared at the Slanderer and said, "Never! I have come to call brothers and sisters, not make computers. My world can be broken as it is only because my Father and I would rather see it broken than break our creatures' free will. The metaphor of Rape is inaccurate in this, that it describes coercion from outside. The Place of Torment is self-chosen, and its doors are bolted and barred from the inside. Rape stands as the final testament to human free will, that my Father would rather see his creatures in everlasting torment than force them into Paradise. Get away from me!"

When Nathaniel said this, the Slanderer left him and angels attended him.

The next few days on the road were interesting. Several of the students at the camp went and followed us. We were on the road to a campustown, and I was beginning to perceive something different about him, something different in his awareness. He was putting weight back on, and there was something new in his eyes.

We arrived at a college campus; we were walking across the quad, and a young woman came up to us and said, "Help me! I am terribly sick, and neither the doctors nor Wicca have been able to make me better. I don't know how much longer --"

There are times when you want to be someplace else, anywhere but where you are now. This was one of those times. The woman became very pale, and lost consciousness; Nathaniel caught her and lay her down on the ground. Then her body became stiff, and from her still, unmoving lips came an ugly, raspy, man's voice, cursing and blaspheming God. Nathaniel alone was not afraid, but his face bore infinite gravity. He looked, and said, "What is your name?"

The demon said, "Our name in English is Existential Angst. Our name in our own language is --"

"Stop!" Nathaniel said. "I know that name, and I know that language, and you are not to utter either of them here."

"Our name is Existential Angst," the demon continued, "and she is ours, all ours, and so is this age."

"She is not yours any more, nor is this age. I have come to set the captives free. Come out of her!"

The voice said nothing more, but there was an unholy presence so powerful it could be felt, and a stench like the stench of rotten eggs, and then they left.

The woman opened her eyes, slowly, as if awakening for the first time, and then looked at Nathaniel. She didn't say anything, just looked, her eyes searching, filled with wonder. Finally, when she had seen what she was looking for, she said, "Thank you." Nathaniel didn't reply. He didn't need to.

By this time, a crowd had gathered, and Nathaniel told

Duncan to get a blanket from the van and buy her some bread and some Sprite. Then he looked around -- the crowd was very quiet, with everybody looking at him -- and Nathaniel stood up, and said, "You can plainly see that I have given something to this woman. What is no less true is that I have something to give each one of you, and you need it.

"Techies sometimes talk about a group of people they call 12:00 flashers. They call them 12:00 flashers, because their houses are filled with appliances with a flashing 12:00. What they mean by the term '12:00 flasher' is something deeper than just 'someone whose appliance clocks happen not to be set'.

"What they mean by '12:00 flasher' is someone who wants the benefits of technology, but is not willing to try to understand how technology works or how to use it. Their appliances flash 12:00 because they will not in a million years spend five minutes experimenting with the buttons or read the manual to see how to set a clock. This mindset affects every bit of technology they own, and invariably something will break -- quite possibly because it was misused -- and then they will invariably wait until the last minute, when there is an emergency, and ask a techie to "just tell me how to fix it." The 12:00 flasher is involved in a desparate attempt to cut a steak with a screwdriver, and when a techie begins to try to explain why he needs to set down the screwdriver and get a knife, the 12:00 flasher tensely replies, 'I don't have time to put down this screwdriver and go get a knife! I just need you to tell me how to cut this steak!'

"Friends, I am here to tell you that the 12:00 flasher phenomenon doesn't just exist in technology. It exists in human relationships. And it exists in spirituality.

"It's possible to get by as a 12:00 flasher. Nobody died because his living room was perpetually dark because he wouldn't sit down and figure out how to unscrew the top of his lamp and replace the bulb. And, when technological disasters become unlivable, it's usually possible to grab a techie, to the rescue. Never mind what it does to their blood pressure, techies usually can reduce an unlivable disaster to a tolerable disaster. But that isn't how we were meant to live, especially not in relationship with God.

"What is a spiritual 12:00 flasher like? Well, they take many forms, but one thing they all have in common is that, consciously or unconsciously, the question they ask of religion is 'What is the least I can do and still get by?' That question is the wrong question. It's like asking what the least a person can eat and still not starve. Never mind the fact that the experiment is quite dangerous; God did not make or want us to live just barely eating enough not to starve. He made us for rich, abundant live, far from starvation.

"Don't be a 12:00 flasher. Don't ask, 'What is the least I can do and still get by?' Don't run to God in times of crisis, and then when the crisis is over, forget him and go back to life without him. If you have a crisis, by all means, run to God for help. He welcomes that, and sometimes he uses crises to draw people to him as never before. But don't wait for a crisis to seek him out. Seek him out, prepare your spirit, work at a state of right relations with other people, while the going is easy. Don't wait until you're on a sinking boat to learn how to swim. Learn how to swim when you have free time and a swimming instructor.

"I was at the deathbed of an old man, a quiet member of the community who knew everybody by name, who always had time to listen to little children's tales and who would tell his own stories to anybody who wanted to hear. When he was on his deathbed, someone asked him if he would like to hear some Bible verses. He smiled, and to everyone's surprise, said, 'No.' Someone asked him, 'Why not?' He smiled again and said, 'I thatched my hut when the weather was warm.'

"Dear friends, thatch your hut when the weather is warm. You might not be able when there is storm or cold. What is there to do? I wish to mention two things; they are a lifetime's learning, and have been for me. Those two things are love and prayer.

"God loves you, and you are to love him with your whole being. You are to love *every*body. Even your enemies? Especially your enemies.

"Physicists are in search of a grand unified theory, where all of the laws covering all physical phenomena boil down to a few equations that can be written on one side of a sheet of paper. In spirituality, religion, and morality, love *is* that grand unified theory. There are great teachings -- of Creation, of repentance, of worship, of Heaven, of grace, of moral law -- and for each of them, if you cut into them, cut below the surface, the lifeblood that they bleed, the hidden lifeblood that keeps them alive, is love.

"One of the most important expressions of love, one of the most important incubators for love to grow in, is prayer. The Slanderer laughs at our plans, and scoffs at our power, but trembles at our prayers. Wrap yourselves in a cloak of prayer; pray for other people even as you look at them in passing; pray continually. Prayer is a place where God transforms us, and where God and we working together transform the world. It is a time to step out of time and into eternity, and it refreshes and renews us. Pray incessantly, until you have callouses on your knees from unanswered prayers. You cannot change the world, at least not for the better, on your own power. Prayer is how God makes you into his children and prepares you for results, and then (on his own time -- not yours) makes a lasting mark.

"Follow me, each of you, and I will draw you into love and prayer, into wisdom and truth, into live everlasting."

The people were impressed with his teaching. He spoke as if he knew the truth, not as if he were just sharing his own perspective, his own personal opinion.

It was perhaps because of this that, when we sat down at dinner, a young man approached him and said, "You spoke unlike anyone else I've heard. Do you claim to know absolute truth?"

Nathaniel said, "Yes."

The man said, "But we cannot know absolute truth, only relative perspectives. The quest for absolute truth has failed; all of the major thinkers of our era have renounced it. Who do you think you are to know absolute truth, God? Don't try the old 'You cannot make absolute statements against absolute truth' card; we have perspectives we expect to be binding without being absolute."

Nathaniel said, "As it turns out, I *am* God, but that is rather beside the point at the moment. You say that we cannot know absolute truth. I respond with a dilemma: are you making that claim as absolutely true, or as your own personal opinion? If you are making that claim as absolute truth, then it is self-contradictory, and therefore false, and therefore something I do not need to subscribe to; if you are making that claim as a mere statement of personal opinion, like your preference in ice cream flavors, it is therefore something I do not need to subscribe to. Before you respond, let me add nuance to this dilemma. I know that you would not say that your claim is absolutely true or a personal attribute, but somewhere in between. This dilemma gives you the freedom to choose a position somewhere between the two poles of absolute truth and personal opinion. Most dilemmas have a forced choice, one or the other. Not this one. On this dilemma, you may fall at a mixture of the two horns, that is, you are making a statement that is held to be 80% absolutely true, and 20% your own personal perspective. In which case, it is 80% incoherent, and 20% a personal attribute I can safely ignore. Or is it 30% absolutely true, and 70% your own personal perspective? Then it is only 30% incoherent, but it is 70% a personal attribute I can safely ignore. This dilemma offers you infinite flexibility in choosing how it affects you; the end result, however, is that your perspective is 100% a perspective I am free to ignore."

The young man had nothing to say to this.

There were a number of people who were beginning to follow him at that point, and I began to see a strand running through his teaching. Perhaps the best way to begin with it is by voicing the intuitions it runs counter to.

An obvious reading of what he says is that mankind has earned everlasting torment in Rape, and he comes through and offers a way of escape -- believing in him, and accepting a sacrifice that I didn't understand at the time -- and it is worth any amount of earthly effort and sacrifice to save one soul from Rape. So there are these people who have the good fortune to know about the escape, and they should devote their lives to making a difference, to saving as many people as they can.

That is true, and it is deeply true, and there is an opposite insight that is a deeper truth, one that is everlasting.

That insight says that the Father is omnipotent and is drawing people to himself, drawing people to share in the glory that God had before the worlds began, not only in a Paradise after death but here and now, in this world. In following Nathaniel, the escape from Rape is almost incidental in importance to communion with God, and our time on earth is as (Nathaniel was very emphatic about this) apprentice gods, whose time on earth is a time of preparation for the time when we will reign in Paradise.

The primacy of the second, mystical interpretation over the first, pragmatic interpretation is something Nathaniel was very emphatic about, and that has changed my whole way of viewing things. I didn't understand it fully until a moment came when I slapped my head: "How could I not have seen this before?" I had been listening to the stories of a number of incredibly devout and incredibly dedicated people who were operating in the first mode, who were trying to make the biggest difference, and fell flat on their faces hitting futile barrier after futile barrier. It made no sense. Then I heard stories of people -- Wesley, for one -- who were like this, and fell on their knees and cried, feeling like utter failures, and in a beggarly, ragged, ragamuffin way, became mystics, sought communion with God. And God gave them that mysticism. Then, sometimes, if he chose, on his time, in his ways, he took some of them and gave them power within the context of that mysticism, and those people shook the world with a force unlike anything they could have ever imagined.

What I came to realize through this is that God wants communion with us, and he wants it so badly that he would rather see a devout, dedicated son working in utter futility, with no results for his toils and watching souls perish, than let some of his children act as mere tools without being drawn first and foremost into communion with him. Drawing people into his presence, not just in the future but here and now, is *that* important to him. God does not want tools. All the angels in a thousand galaxies are his, and if he needed help, he would not tell us. He wants sons and daughters, and he will have us be that and nothing less. My head still spins a little when I think of this.

This account is written so that you may know Nathaniel and the abundant life that he brings, that you may be drawn into communion with God, not just in the world to come but in this world. Therefore I ask you, when you reach the end of this paragraph, to close your eyes, thank God for ten things you're thankful for, and spend five minutes contemplating God's glory. Do it now.

Did you do it? If you did, wasn't that wonderful? Wasn't that the best part of the text? Didn't you want to linger? If you didn't -- you're not going to get to Paradise if you won't let Paradise interrupt your reading of a text. This text exists to draw you into communion with God, and if you put the flow of reading ahead of that communion, you still have something to learn.

I've been thinking about how to explain what I want to say next, particularly to most Americans... perhaps the best way is to say that, to the American mind, 'nice' and 'good' mean almost exactly the same thing, and this is a perspective which Nathaniel did not share. Nor do I. 'Nice' is what is left of 'good' after 'good' has been flattened by a steamroller.

Nathaniel was, at times, very nice. He was someone who would look you in the eye and ask, "How are you?" -- slowly, because he wanted to hear the answer. He wouldn't just do this with close friends -- he was just as ready with strangers whom he could see needed it. But there was something about him that most definitely would not be cut down to fit into being nice. He met with members of the religious community, but his interactions could rarely be described as diplomatic. He lambasted Evangelicals and Catholics on equal terms. He didn't attack mainline Protestants, though. Never. Most of the time, when I mentioned them, he just shook his head and wept.

I'm not going to give a full list of the groups that Saint Nasty offended, primarily because my hard drive only has about nine gigabytes of free space. I do wish, however, to give an illustrative list. There are many more.

- *The gay community.* After a thousand voices had droned on about how AIDS patients are the outcast lepers of our society, Nathaniel said, "The status of AIDS patients in our society is not that of pariahs, but that of sacred cows." He challenged head-on the status of people who die from sexually transmitted diseases as martyrs, and furthermore laid bare how the movement lumps together acceptance and care of homosexuals, acceptance of them as humans, with a political agenda and lifestyle which kept them dead and miserable in their sins. "Come to me," he said, "and I will give you freedom and vitality such as your movement would never dream and offer." He loved gays too much not to strike down a whitewashed wall.
- *Business.* Nathaniel asked, "Was economic wealth created for man, or man for economic wealth?" He called advertising a modern fusion of manipulation, propaganda, and pornography, and took it to be the emblem of a mindset in which a business exists, not to serve customers, but to manipulate them into whatever will bring the most money into corporate coffers.
- *Consumers.* He accused them of entering into a sorceror's bargain to have wealth in our technology, being concerned with little as long as they had personal peace and affluence, and misusing wealth. He developed an argument, which I am not going to reproduce here, that both individual citizens and communities should take a good look at the Amish, not because they have a perfect solution, but because they are the one major group in America that does not automatically use every technology and service that comes out and that they can afford.
- *The tobacco industry.* To quote him: "You do something that kills people, for the mere purpose of obtaining profit. You are the largest assassins' guild in history."

- *Feminists.* His interactions with feminists were a little more complex than with some other groups, perhaps because of how deeply feminism has impacted not just a self-identified minority but the whole fabric of American culture, and because of how deeply he shared the concern of womens' status. Some of his remarks were flat-out incendiary. He said that, if feminism has to identify an enemy, a feminism that identified men as the enemy could be tolerable, but a feminism that identified non-feminist women as the enemy was inexcusable. "*Any* feminism worthy of the name," Nathaniel said, "*must* make the sisterhood of all women a central thesis." I think I saw him weeping over feminism more than any other group: when we talked, I began to see them through his eyes: not Rush Limbaugh-style feminazis, but lost sheep without a shepherd, women struggling to work against a curse and doomed to futility and backfire from the start, because they did not understand the nature of the curse, and so were like a doctor, giving higher and higher doses of medicine for the wrong condition, and wondering why the patient looked worse and worse. He tried to explain the remedy to that curse, and tried to explain it to a great many feminists -- a few of them believed him, but the vast majority were offended.
- *Academia.* The most striking comment I remember him making was, "Hitler now stands as our culture's single most essential symbol of evil, not because he slaughtered six million Jews, but because he does not have any advocates left in academia. There is another ideology more vile than National Socialism, an ideology that exceeds the Nazi body count by a factor of ten and has made blood flow like a river in every single country where it has come into power. Its name is Marxism, and it is considered perfectly acceptable to be a Marxist in academia, a breeding ground of every heresy and intellectual filth our society has to offer."

- *Environmentalists.* To them, he said, "You have defiled a concern for God's earth not only with nature worship but also with racist, eugenic Malthusianism."
- *Media, especially television.* Most of what he said there were footnotes to Postman, Mander, and Muggeridge, and the rest wasn't that important.
- *Sensitivity police.* Nathaniel criticized them for "using gasoline to extinguish a fire."
- *The pro-choice forces.* Nathaniel criticized them for making a convenient redefinition of the boundaries of humanity and taking an attitude of "it's not really there if you can close your eyes to it." He said that on any biological perspective even, what grows inside a woman's womb is an organism of the species *homo sapiens*, and that the question of whether a fetus is human or unwanted tissue is a philosophical question only in the sense that whether a woman is human or just a convenient rape object is a philosophical question -- that is, if you deliberately set out to make yourself stupider than you are and tarnish the name of philosophy by making it a smokescreen to hide what is obvious to common sense, then and only then can you satisfy yourself by saying "that is a philosophical question to which my answer is unwanted tissue." Nathaniel had other criticisms -- one of them beginning by saying, "A real pro-choice scenario would be an undoubted improvement on the status quo," -- but I do not wish to repeat them here.
- *The pro-life movement.* Nathaniel criticized them "for defending the sanctity of life from conception to natural birth."

Anyone who has not been offended by Nathaniel has failed to understand him.

There are many events which happened which I will not attempt to narrate. Nathaniel was healing people of all kinds of brokenness -- physical, mental, emotional, spiritual. He had begun to teach us that he was giving us his authority -- even over demons. He was explaining that he would need to die and rise from the dead, although none of us understood -- or wanted to understand -- what he was saying. And, through all of that, there were moments, precious, timeless moments, when we could have glimpses of who he was.

To begin explaining one of those moments, let me say that I am not affected by stage magic. It isn't just that I can (sometimes) see how a trick works; the actual illusion is only a tiny part of illusionism. It's indispensable, but it is unbelievably tiny -- I know, because I was once an amateur magician, and I disappointed my audiences by performing an uninterrupted display of clever tricks that were nothing more. The real life's blood of a magic show is showmanship, something that is normally invisible: one of the marks of good showmanship is that the audience is oblivious to showmanship and instead wonders how on earth the magician did it. (It is incidentally true that, however much a good magic show makes audiences wonder "How did he do that?", a good magician *never* tells his audience how it happened. It's not protection of an initiate brotherhood's closely kept secrets -- all such "secrets" are perfectly accessible to someone with a library card and a little spare time, just as the substitution-cipher-weak verification algorithm used for credit card numbers is available to anyone who can go to a search engine and type "mod10" in the query box -- but basic entertainment principle: people who find out how magic tricks work are invariably disappointed. That is why I never tell other people how tricks at a magic show work, even when I do know; figuring out one or two minor tricks makes someone feel smug and clever, but knowing how the big trick worked simply ruins it.)

I have spoken as if showmanship's illusion is one-sided, as if it's all up to the magician. And it is, in a sense. But in another sense, it isn't. If I had been better as a stage magician and gotten farther, I would have experienced firsthand the difference between an audience that is excited, eager to see what is going on, or in high spirits, and one that is hostile, cranky with low blood sugar, or doesn't really want to be there. The illusion is not one-sided; it is the creation of both parties, performer and audience, the result of their cooperation -- only the performer's cooperation is conscious and intentional, and the audience's cooperation is unconscious and unwitting.

There is something that happened with me, something that has broken the illusion by breaking my end of the creation -- conscious uncooperation instead of unconscious cooperation -- something that was closely related to my learning what is actually going on in television, and why I don't watch it. Now magic shows don't work on me. It's not that the illusion is broken because I can see how tricks work; rather, I see how tricks work because the illusion is broken. In Madeleine l'Engle's *A Wrinkle in Time*, on the nightmarish planet Camazotz, the man with red eyes gives Meg, Calvin, and Charles Wallace food. To Meg and Calvin it tastes like a wonderful turkey dinner. To Charles Wallace it tastes like wet sand. The man with red eyes can get into the chinks of Meg's mind, and Calvin's, enough to make an illusion mask how ghastly the food is. With Charles Wallace it doesn't work; the illusion doesn't work for him. I have been told I am very like Charles Wallace. I count it worthwhile that I am no longer automatically pulled by showmanship, particularly in an age where showmanship has taken a bloated role far beyond what any sane society would allow it. I count it my loss that I cannot now cooperate with the illusion even if I want to. (Nathaniel understands me on this score, and indeed has experienced the same awakening, but he can cooperate with the illusion. He also watches television for a couple of hours a month, only some of the time as a sociologist would.)

For these reasons, I was less than enthusiastic when Nathaniel showed me a flyer announcing a magic show for "children of all ages" in the bandstand at the park. I told him, "You go; I'll stay home and pray." He said, "Trust me."

We went about half an hour early. Parents were sitting in the bleachers, and kids were running about on the stage. We sat and talked for a few minutes, and then Nathaniel poked a little girl who was running by. She giggled, and he chased her on to the stage, and then started playing with another child, and another. He began to tell stories, ask questions, talk with them, hold them.

It seemed only a moment that the sky turned lavender and fireflies danced, and I looked down at my watch and realized that over an hour had passed. The magician never showed up, but not one of the children went home disappointed.

Whatever Nathaniel had, it was better than showmanship, better than illusion. He had a pull, a charisma, that drew people to him -- something that arose out of the love that flowed in his heart. I am no longer drawn by television because television is fake, because television does a spectacular job of covering how empty its center was. Nathaniel wasn't like that. His charisma was an overflow of how full his center was. The meaning of this moment grew on me when I understood what moment it was, what time it was, that he had chosen to spend simply playing with children.

As the sky began to grow dark and mothers called their children home, I could begin to see -- why hadn't I noticed it before? Nathaniel was afraid, and emotions of -- what? expectation? imminence? trepidation? -- were emotions that I could begin to feel as well. There was a sense that something important would happen. He purchased a loaf of bread and a bottle of wine, and called all of us to come into a deserted loft. We talked -- really talked, about love, about too many things to mention, and then as there was a height of tension, he took the bread, and said, "Take this, and eat it. This is my body, which is broken for you. Do this in memory of me." Then he took the cup of wine, and said, "Take this, all of you, and drink. This is the new accord in my blood, poured out for the forgiveness of sins." Then he passed them around.

I talked with the others, years later; I was the only one who realized the significance of what was going on. There are still many people who have difficulty believing it, which is fine; there are a lot of things about Nathaniel that take a lot of believing. When I ate his body, I was taking, was drawn into, his community; when I drank his blood, I drank the divine life. The latter especially was precious to me in a way I cannot describe; I am a mystic, and there is something about the blood, hidden in the flesh, that... it is best not to talk too much about these things. I think some of them are things that it takes a child's heart to understand.

He asked us to be with him, not exactly to pray with him (although I am sure he also wanted that), but just to have the human presence of someone who loved him, perhaps just to have any human presence -- and all I know I could think about was how long a day it had been, and how much I needed to get to sleep. We were awoken by a knock on the door, and Nathaniel looked at me -- ooh! That look broke my heart. He did not say anything. He did not need to.

Nathaniel was shaking when he walked out in front of a veritable mob, and asked, "Who do you want?" Someone in the crowd said, "Nathaniel." He said, "I am the person you want. Get away from the building; you want me, not the others."

I was watching from the window, and I watched in stunned disbelief what the mob began doing to him. Then I climbed down, and ran as if there was no tomorrow. I had no shoes on, only socks, and when I collapsed, in exhaustion, my feet were bleeding.

Somehow (providence?) the others managed to find me, and we were huddling in a room, the doors locked, bolted, and barred with furniture, all shades drawn, glued to the TV, demoralized, defeated, in abject bewilderment. I had thrown up all I could, and felt sometimes dizzy, sometimes hot, sometimes nauseated, sometimes all three. I was leaning against the window, desparately praying that my head would stop spinning, and that if there were any way possible for Nathaniel to have survived that assault --

Someone knocked twice on the window, right next to my head, and my head cleared.

I was struck with terror, pulled back from the window, and prayed aloud that whoever it is would go away.

I heard Cassandra's voice loudly outside, saying, "It's me, Cassandra! I've seen Nathaniel! He's alive!"

I knew her voice, and my terror turned to rage, turned to what the damned call 'righteous indignation'. I said, "Of all the sick jokes, of all the unholy blows that the lowest schoolyard bully would not dream of stooping to," and poured out a stream of invective unlike any I have uttered before or since. I did not stop, did not even falter, when I heard her crying, nor when her tears turned to wailing. At the climax I said, "Unless Nathaniel stands before me, unless I feel the bones that have been crushed, I will never believe your sick joke."

I felt a tap on my shoulder, and when I turned around, Nathaniel looked into my eyes, gazing with both love and sorrow, and said, "Sean. I am here before you. Touch every one of my wounds." Then he touched me, and healed me of the sickness I had been feeling.

What could I do? I fell to the ground, and wept, and when I could stand I immediately left to go out and beg Cassandra's forgiveness. She forgave me -- instantly. She gave me a hug, and said, "I had difficulty believing it, too. You are forgiven." I can not tell the depths of love that are in that woman's heart. Then I returned, with Cassandra, and Nathaniel looked at me and said, "Sean, you are a metacultural, but you are also an American. What is real to you is largely what you have seen and what *The Skeptical Enquirer* says is real. You believe after having seen. God's blessing is on those who can rise above your culture's sin and believe these miracles without seeing."

Nathaniel said and did many other things, far too numerous for me to write down. I have not attempted a complete account, nor a representative account, nor even to cover all the bases. (Other writers have already done the last of those three.) Rather, I have written to show you the fresh power of Nathaniel's story, a story that is and will always be *here* and *now.* Do you understand him better?

The Grinch Who Stole Christmas

My dear Wormwood;

I still do not have your report on the status of the yearly festivals. As you have not informed me of the circumstances for several years, I may unfortunately be forced to demonstrate drastic consequences in the case that you fail again to even tell what is happening.

Your affectionate uncle,
Screwtape

Dear uncle Screwtape;

It is about as well as could be expected. This is a time of festivities which we have very little difficulty turning the people away from; it is, also, one of the ones where there is joy and exuberance such that it is very difficult to introduce even a dead and ritualistic approach to ceremony. We have succeeded at least in enticing a handful of people to drunkenness and adultery on one hand, and on the others have slowly been building an interest in sorcery. I am currently contemplating the introduction of a number of grimoires to heighten the interest in spellcraft;

unfortunately, this is the rare exception rather than the rule, and we can make very little progress with the great many. I suppose that we should expect greater success at other times of year.

Your nephew,
Wormwood.

My dead Wormwood;

YOU IDIOT!

You speak of getting a handful of people interested in spellcraft as a great achievement. Were you here, you would see that your letter caused me to engage in something not unlike men's prestidigitation; I immediately raised my arm and extended my middle finger.

So, you have enticed a tiny handful. Whoop-de-doo. Nobody minds that you've chopped down a tree or two, but we are here to burn a forest.

It is evident that your abysmal lack of understanding of temptation has produced the silliest possible results. If you are going to tempt a man, TEMPT him. A large shipment of spellbooks to devout people is not productive. Have you no idea why you are trained to masquerade as an angel of light?

Use the right tool for the right job.

I want a full analysis of the situation, and a preview of any ideas, just to ensure that you do not do anything dumber.

Your affectionate uncle,
Screwtape

Dear uncle Screwtape;

It is the season when they celebrate the greatest gift they have ever received; namely, when the Enemy became one of them and died to create a way of escape from our trap of sin.

There are two basic intertwined ways in which they celebrate, and we have been able to do very little to stop either.

The first is by thanksgiving and enjoying what they have been given. They come to friends and family; they pray, sing songs, eat, drink, and be merry. A few we've managed to get drunk on the wassail or abstain from it as if it were an evil thing, but that is a chink here and there; we have had trouble making it larger. There is a wholehearted attitude of thanksgiving and worship at all the gifts which they've received; the time when we've set famine to take away some of their food only seems to make them all the more grateful and all the more prayerful.

The second is by giving each other gifts. Whether the gifts are simple or costly, they are heartfelt; they celebrate the gift given them by giving gifts to each other. Even in the lands where an evil duke has imposed harsh taxes on the peasant, so that they have little to give, their little gifts are taken as seriously as more lavish gifts from people who do have enough to live on.

I have been trying to deter them from the celebration and the gift giving, but results have been frustrating to the extreme.

Your nephew,
Wormwood

My dear Wormwood;

Having taken some time to think, I should like to temper some of my previous remarks. Nor that your bungling incompetence does not warrant them, but I should like you to be better informed.

There is both an individual and a corporate side to sin. The individual side is of extreme importance. Our father below personally tempted Job, and it is not an understatement to say that every last person should be tempted as far as possible. By chipping at one tree at a time, it is possible to clear cut a forest. (The importance of the individual is so great that it may be an interesting temptation to make people appear to be nothing but individuals). When the temptations facing a society do not affect a person, it is perfectly acceptable to give some variation. Once in a while, even that can be worked into a good plan for even greater corporate sin. It is spectacular to have a few become prostitutes and a great many become Pharisees; a few become witches, and a great many become witch hunters.

As important as individual sin is, it is now your responsibility to see to corporate sin, and tempt the society as a whole.

There is something I should like to remind you about the nature of sin.

Man is created to embrace what is good. Even in his fallen state, even with the power that we hold over them, that man still somehow desires to embrace the good is so true that it dictates the nature of temptation. When we tempt, it is necessary to give a candy coating to that sin with what is good. Sexual sin is only possible when we twist the tremendous goodness of human sexuality; idolatry can not exist except as an exploitation of the need of man to worship the Enemy.

There is a time and a place to use intimidation, terror, and force, but your attempts here to either tempt solid believers with sorcery, or make their celebrations impossible by physical hardship, are clumsy and inappropriate. Gold which is passed through fire only grows purer; that is why you see their devotion flowering. Instead, why don't you appear as an angel of light and lull them to sleep?

There is a note about patience... Though occasionally we manage the sudden and sharp, it is much better in most cases (including this one) to work ever so slowly. So slowly that there doesn't seem to be any real progress; so slowly that everything appears to them to be as they want it. If you suddenly hold a candle by a frog, it will jump away. If, instead, the frog is placed in a pot of cool water and the candle beneath the pot, it will never notice; nothing constrains it from jumping out, and yet you need only wait for the ever so slowly growing heat to destroy it. Be patient; wait for decades or centuries if need be.

Now stop wasting your energy on stupid spellbooks, droughts, and taxes. Take away these hardships; for now, I want you to only make things easier. Help their economic systems be productive; don't take away from the laughter at the feasts. If you find an opportunity to get someone drunk at a festival, then by all means take it, but don't worry about having things now. Just do as I have said, and wait.

Your affectionate uncle,
Screwtape

Dear uncle Screwtape;

It is ten years now, and I have done as you have said. I do not understand why; they enjoy the festivities as much as ever, giving and receiving gifts in a manner that enjoys each other; enjoying each other in a manner that loves and worships the Enemy. By all counts, things have only gotten worse. Am I to continue to wait?

Your nephew,
Wormwood

My dear Wormwood;

Patience, my dear. Patience. If you continue, you are making more progress than you think. Now, I still don't want you to do anything spectacular. Only give an idea to an inventor here, an economist there. Don't introduce anything nasty; just make the economic system more productive, and do nothing to impede their thoughts of giving generous gifts at this season.

Your affectionate uncle,
Screwtape

Dear uncle Screwtape;

It is twenty years since I last wrote you, and I still do not see the point. People have more money; they are giving it generously. The hungry are fed; the naked are clothed. The season is one of great festivity, and, as ever, they give generous gifts. Am I to continue?

Your nephew,
Wormwood

My dear Wormwood;

Still, you need patience. Now, I want you to do two things:

First of all, continue to increase the productivity of their economic system.

Second of all, without actively disparaging love for God or their neighbors, I want you to use the season to cause them to think about how good their material possessions are, and look forward to it.

Give it ten more years, and write back.

Your affectionate uncle,
Screwtape

Dear uncle Screwtape;

I have succeeded in making them think about the goodness of their material possessions (which I still do not fully understand; most of the time, you have had me delude people into thinking that the material is evil and an obstruction to spiritual growth; I am now emphasizing that truth in the matter as you say, and I don't see any real progress). It is ten years; what should I do now?

Your nephew,
Wormwood

My dear Wormwood;

Now, slowly, slightly, introduce seeds of greed. Not too much; just a little. And give them more money.

It is the time to twist, and everything you twist should be done, at least at first, in a slow and slight, imperceptible manner. Twist the good of the celebration and the presents just a little; that's all that it takes, for the moment. Just make the goodness of God and the gift the season celebrates seem less of an easy thing to think about than the goodness of all the material gifts.

Give it ten years or so, and write me back again.

Your affectionate uncle,
Screwtape

Dear uncle Screwtape;

Wow. Though it's been slow, this work has been beginning to show some real results. Though every gift given by one person is a gift received by another, people are thinking of this much less as a time to give gifts, and much more as a time to receive them. I've now made it a major part of their economy; people are beginning to look forward very much to all of the Christmas gifts they can receive.

Should I continue as I have been?

Your nephew,
Wormwood

My dear Wormwood;

There is something to be said about greed. Like most other sins, it produces satiety for the moment, but over time it yields only insatiety. Those who have enough and are content with what they have remain content; those who have much with greed grow more wealthy and less satisfied. More than that, many of those who have the most material possessions enjoy them the least; time to acquire possessions, and worry for them, becomes a consuming desire. A powerful chief executive officer who can buy anything he wants, will enjoy much less the leather seats of his Porsche, the view from his yacht, the beauty of his art collection, than many children of more modest means enjoy a chain of dandelions and a grape flavored lollipop.

Just continue, and put some serious thought into the trash that you teach them to prize. I could give more detail, but I think you're beginning to understand. Write me back in a few more years; tell me what happens.

Your affectionate uncle,
Screwtape

Dear uncle Screwtape;

Things have really been taking off.

The holiday celebration has become a tremendous commercial extravaganza, the best time of year when people look forward to getting glowing plastic dolls and combination pizza oven/clothes dryers. I have gone wild with the items which are produced. I've made one device so that much of the time people spend "together" is distant and mechanical, with no eye contact and no touch. They now have, and look forward to ever more advanced entertainment devices with blinking lights and spectacular sound effects, bright and shiny enough to distract people the emptiness within, and ever becoming more effective. (You might also be pleased to learn of the content; although the type of devices would facilitate excellent strategy games, I've made graphic violence seem more and more attractive; a wonderful entertainment. Now I don't even have to be slow and patient in making a more realistic sadism; all that needs to be done is put somewhere in the storyline that you're the hero and morally justified in wading through blood. (I'm working on taking that away as well)) I'm making sure that the games are solitary by nature; you can't really play these games with your friends the way you can play cards, having a friendly chat as well as thinking about what to do as the next move. On a scale of glitz and convenience, they seem far more attractive than reading a book, holding a friend's hand, going for a walk, or having a relaxed meal together. I've been working on a faster, exciting, frantic pace for the entertainment, and people are "learning" that having fun means moving at a breakneck speed; leisure is beginning to be considered boring. There is a great air of celebration and festivity, and an air of gifts; the facade is tremendous.

I think that the festival is mostly under control. Should we make a shift in strategy?

Your nephew,
Wormwood

My dear Wormwood;

Congratulations! You have passed this portion of your training with flying colors. Although I have more experience in this matter and have enjoyed many times sitting back and watching the flames as a society crumbles under the weight of its own sin, you have celebrated trivia to an extent that even I find astounding. My hat is off to you.

For now, your responsibilities (which you have made much easier) have been shifted; as you have so masterfully learned your lessons in corporate sin, it is now time for you to learn the next lesson. Your next area of training will be in the area of heresy, a battleground to which we are shifting focus.

I look forward to seeing what will come of your apprenticeship there.

Your affectionate uncle,
Screwtape

A Dream of Light

You pull your arms to your side and glide through the water. On your left is a fountain of bubbles, upside down, beneath a waterfall; the bubbles shoot down and then cascade out and to the surface. To your right swims a school of colorful fish, red and blue with thin black stripes. The water is cool, and you can feel the currents gently pushing and pulling on your body. Ahead of you, seaweed above and long, bright green leaves below wave back and forth, flowing and bending. You pull your arms, again, with a powerful stroke which shoots you forward under the seaweed; your back feels cool in the shade. You kick, and you feel the warmth of the sun again, soaking in and through your skin and muscles. Bands of light dance on the sand beneath you, as the light is bent and turned by the waves.

There is a time of rest and stillness; all is at a deep and serene peace. The slow motion of the waves, the dancing lights below and above, the supple bending of the plants, all form part of a stillness. It is soothing, like the soft, smooth notes of a lullaby.

Your eyes slowly close, and you feel even more the warm sunlight, and the gentle caresses of the sea. And, in your rest, you become more aware of a silent presence. You were not unaware of it before, but you are more aware of it now. It is there:

Being.

Love.

Life.

Healing.

Calm.

Rest.

Reality.

Like a tree with water slowly flowing in, through roots hidden deep within the earth, and filling it from the inside out, you abide in the presence. It is a moment spent, not in time, but in eternity.

You look out of the eternity; your eyes are now open because you have eternity in your heart and your heart in eternity. In the distance, you see dolphins; one of them turns to you, and begins to swim. The others are not far off.

It lets you pet its nose, and nestles against you. You grab onto its dorsal fin, and go speeding off together. The water rushes by at an exhilarating speed; the dolphin jumps out of the water, so that you see waves and sky for a brief moment before splashing through the surface.

The dolphins chase each other, and swim hither and thither, in and out from the shore. After they all seem exhausted, they swim more slowly, until at last you come to a lagoon.

In the center, you see a large mass; swimming closer, you see that it is a sunken ship. You find an opening; inside, all is dark, but you find a passageway.

After some turns, you come up in a different place. You come up through a fountain in a public garden; the bushes and ivy are a deep, rich shade of green, and sheets of water cascade down the yellowed marble of the fountain. It is ornately and intricately sculpted, with bas-relief scenes of a voyage.

As you study the pictures, day turns to night, and all that you see is bathed in moonlight. You are looking upon a statue: a delicate, slender, elfin nude, whose long hair cascades over her shoulders and about her body. She is reaching up to the sky, as if to touch the moon and stars. She is carved out of white marble, which looks pale blue, almost luminous, in the moonlight. It looks as if she was taken from the moon, and is rising up to touch it again.

The statue is on a tall pedestal of black marble. In the moonlight, the forest has a very deep color, a green that is almost blue or purple; the dark beauty of the night makes the statue seem almost radiant. Off in the distance, you hear a high, melancholy, lilting song; it is played on a harp and sung by a voice of silver. There is something haunting and yet elusive about the melody; it subtly tells of something wanted and searched for, yet not quite reached. And it is beautiful.

You sit, looking at the statue and listening to the song, for a time. They seem to suggest a riddle, a secret - but you know not what.

You walk along; fireflies begin to appear, and you can hear the sound of crickets chirping. There is a gentle breeze. The sky stands above like a high and faroff crystalline dome; the trees and grass below surround you, like little children who see a beloved elder coming, and run clamoring for a kiss. The grass is smooth and cool beneath your feet. There is a sweet, faint fragrance in the air, as of lilacs.

A round little girl, wandering through the forest, sees you and comes running. She is dark, with olive skin, and her black hair flares out behind her. She is wearing a dark green robe, the color of the forest, and her step is almost that of a dance - as if she is from a people where moving and dancing are not two different things. She is holding, in her hand, a simple bouquet of dandelions. "Look, look!" she says, "I have flowers!"

She jumps into your arms, welcoming you. Her touch is soft, and gentle. It is not near the softness of a grown woman; it has rather a ... simplicity. It is hard to find the right word. Then you recognize what it is. It has something of the carefree play of a child, but there is more than even abandon. She is holding you with complete trust. You do not doubt that she could fall asleep in your arms.

She begins to talk to you about many things. She talks about the forest, about people, about the stars, about God. After a time, you realize that she is not merely talking, but singing, as if the first words she heard were the words of a song. After another time, you realize that you have lost her words completely, and are entranced by the song. Presently she stops, and says, "Spin me! Spin me!"

Little children everywhere like to be held by the arms and swung around; this one is no exception. After you are both very dizzy, she takes you by the hand and begins, leading you along a path, to show you little details of the forest that you had never noticed before. Apart from the little details, there is something else which you begin to slowly see in the forest. The song by which she speaks, the dance by which she moves - and not just her, you do not doubt, but her people - seem to be echoed in the forest... and then you realize that rather they are echoes of the forest. Hearing, seeing, feeling that beauty from another person - you still do not doubt that they come from her, but they also help you to see what was always there but you had not noticed. As you walk along, you are lost in thoughts about the genius of all great artists... and begin to think about visiting an art gallery, not so that you can see what is in the gallery, but so that you can see what is not in the gallery.

The path widens out, around a shimmering pool. The golden flames of torches around the pool glimmer when reflected in the pool. There is singing - singing like that of the little girl, but the sound of a whole orchestra as next to the sound of a beginning flute. Men and women together pour fourth a rich harmony. The air is sweet with a delicate fragrance of incense; one of them brings you a cool wooden cup. Inside is a strawberry wine. It is sweet, and sour; the taste brings back memories of earliest childhood.

A circle forms among the people, then another, then another. Soon all of the people are spinning and weaving in a joyful dance. After a time, you realize that you are at the center; they are softly singing, "Welcome, Somebody," and listening intently. Arms and hands reach out, and sweep you into the dance. The dance is ordered, but also free; it draws you in, and, as you move, you feel that you can do no wrong.

How long the dance lasts, you do not know; still filled with its bliss, you find yourself sitting and talking with the people. One of them finds a soft seat of moss for you to sit on; another brings you a plum. Its taste is tart, and it has the texture that only a plum has -- and, when you bite into it, you know that it was still on the tree when it was chosen.

The night winds on, and, after a time, you are led into a building woven out of living trees, with a bed of loam. Into it you sink; it is soft and deep...

You find yourself standing at the edge of a forest and a grassy plain. The mouth of a cave descends into the earth, and just before this is an old man sitting on a three-legged wooden stool. He is wearing a coarse grey-green robe, and has a long, flowing white beard. He is staring intently into the forest, with a concentration you have never seen before. It is like a gaze into a lover's eyes -- nay, even deeper, a probe into the soul.

He shifts positions a few times, in his sitting, and at last stands up, takes the stool, and begins to walk towards the cavern. When he was looking into the forest, you were absorbed in watching him; now, you notice another man, a young one, approach the former.

"Is it Senex?"

"I am he."

"Senex, the great teacher?"

You see the old man's hand move to cover his mouth, but not quite quickly enough to conceal the faintest crack of a smile. The young man stands attentively, waiting for words to come.

The old man's frame shakes once. A second passes, and then it shakes again and again. Then sounds the laughter that he had been attempting to conceal. Soon, the old man is convulsed with mirth, and making no attempt to conceal it.

After a while, almost doubled over with laughter, he begins to pull himself up. You can see his face from a different angle, and you see a merry twinkle in his eye. He places his arm over the young man's shoulder.

"Forgive me, brother, but it has been ages since anyone has addressed me as 'teacher' or 'great'. You cannot imagine how funny it sounds to me."

"Are you not Senex, who has traveled the seven seas, who has seen visions and been visited by angels, who has written treatises and instructed many?"

The man chuckles, and says, "Yes, I am all that, and much more. I am the image, likeness, and glory of God. I pray, and in my prayers I touch the stars and shake the foundations of the kingdom of Hell. I am a king and priest. I am a son of God. My name is written in the book of life. I am a god."

"Then why do you find it funny that I address you as 'great', or 'teacher'?"

"Because I am more than a great teacher, as are the children who dance through this field, as are you." Here the old man smiles at the young. "Come, now. Do you doubt that you are God's own son? What teaching, or miracles, or visions, or conquests, or exploits compare with that?"

"But if you are so great, why should you object to being called a great teacher? Surely the title is not false."

"My dear god - and now I am not addressing the Creator, but you yourself - what is wrong with the title is not that it says that I am a great teacher. I am. What is wrong is that the title implies that there are others who are not so great," and here the old man gave a great belly laugh, "when the truth of the matter is that the other people are so much more than a great teacher. I will not mind being called 'teacher' by you, if you agree to address everyone else as 'god' and 'goddess'. But if you will not call them 'god' and 'goddess', then simply call everyone 'brother' or 'sister'."

The young man stands in silent reflection for a time. "I came in search of a man who could share with me profound wisdom; I see now that I have found him. So now I ask you: Give me a profound insight, that I may contemplate it for the rest of my life, and grow wise."

"Do you not know that God is love, that God loves mankind, that we have the new commandment to 'Love one another'?"

"All of this I have believed since I was a little boy."

"Then I give you one more lesson, to contemplate and learn for the rest of your life."

The young man listens, eager with expectation.

The old man bends down, plucks a blade of grass, and holds it in his outstretched hand.

The young man takes it, and waits for an explanation. When, after a time, the old man says nothing, he says, "This blade of grass is like the blade of a sword. Have you given this to me as a sign that I should contemplate spiritual warfare, and be ready with the sword of the Spirit?"

The old man says, "You should, but that is not why."

The young man thinks for a time, then says, "This grass is nourished by the sun, and so tells of it. Grass and sun exist as God's creation, and tell of him. Is this why you have given me the blade of grass?"

The old man says, "What you said is very true, but that is not why, either."

The young man says, "When Christ lived on earth, he lived as a carpenter, and observed and was surrounded by the birds of the air, the grass of the field, the lilies, and ten thousand other things. Have you given me this blade of grass to remind me of Christ's time on earth, or of his humanity, or that this is a place he passed by?"

The old man says, "You are still right, and you are still wrong."

The young man says, "Then what profound truth can you be teaching me? What secret key escapes my grass? I asked if you had given it to me as a symbol of a profound spiritual truth, and you said, 'no'. Then I asked you if you had given it to me that I might deduce by logic what it tells about God, and you still said, 'no'. Then, after that, I asked you if you had given it to me as a historical reminder of what has happened about blades of grass, and your answer is still the everchanging 'no'. What can I possibly be missing? What am I leaving out?"

The old man turns to face the young, and looks deep into his eyes. "This blade of grass I have given you," he said, "because it is a blade of grass."

There is a look of puzzlement on the young man's face, which slowly melts into dawning comprehension. He steps forward and kisses the old man, with a long, full kiss on the lips, and then steps back and bows deeply - and the old man bows to him - and says, "Thank you." When the old man has responded, "You are very much welcome, brother," the young turns, clutching the blade of grass as if it were a diamond - no, more than that, as if it were a blade of grass - and walks back into the forest. There is a smile on his face.

You walk off in the field, and lie down on the grass. The day is growing warm and sultry; a faint breeze blows.

The breeze carries with it a small, white feather of the softest down. It gently falls on the sole of your foot. The breeze blows this way and that; the feather catches here, rolls there on your foot, brushing ever so lightly, up and down, up and down.

You feel a finger, cool as marble, just barely touching the back of your neck. It tingles; you can feel the sensation radiating up and down your spine. The feather brushes against your foot, and the finger just barely touches the back of your neck. It is a slow, lingering, tingling sensation; as time passes, the sensation becomes more and more real, and just won't go away. It tickles so.

A time passes, and you find yourself walking along a beach. It is almost dusk, and the rainbow colors of sunset are beginning to spill across the sky. It is autumn, and the many-hued leaves of the trees fall about, twirling this way and that in the wind. There is a smell of mist and brine in the air; the waves run and twirl about your toes.

A bird flies off to the right; its flight is light and agile. It flies to and fro, this way and that, until it disappears into the sunset.

There is a feeling of wistfulness, of a presence departed. To the left, you see a grayed swing, rocking back and forth in the wind; its rusty chain squeaks. It is in the yard of a boarded up house, with a garden long overgrown in weeds.

On a whim, you slowly walk up the path into the yard, and

sit down on the swing. You rock back and forth; there is a feeling of emptiness. Images form and swirl in your mind.

A tree is felled; from its trunk are taken the staves of a barrel. Fresh and white, the staves are slowly covered with dust; each time the dust is disturbed or brushed off, the wood underneath is darker, grayer, rougher.

People are born, walk hither and thither, grow old, and die. Generations come and pass, and the earth grows older. People learn how to live - and then die. Vanity of vanities.

Everything is dreary, desolate, fleeting. The walls of your vision grow narrow and dark; your mind and imagination seem to protest the motion. It grows darker and darker.

After a time, you see a light - a little light. As everything around grows darker and more drab, the light does not grow brighter, but neither does it grow dimmer.

A voice sounds in the shadows - you do not doubt that is the voice of the light - says, "Come closer."

You come closer, and you see that she is a flame. A little flame.

A thousand questions form in your mind. They pour forth from you - Why is it all so meaningless? Why do things wither and decay? Why does evil run rampant?

The flame listens patiently, and then speaks. "Look into me."

You look into the flame, and you see everything you saw before, but it looks different. The boards of the cask are no less grey. But you see that inside the cask is wine - wine which grows rich and well-aged. The people still die - and now you see an even darker death for some. But you also see past the death, past the mourning and grieving, to a birth into life - a richness and a fullness that could not be imagined from before.

"Flame, can I step into you, so that I may be delivered from the unpleasant things?"

"No, dear one. That is not the way of things."

"Then what can you give me?"

"I give you this: that you may always look into me, and that

I will never be quenched."

"Flame, what is your name?"

"My name is Hope."

You look into the flame, and again see the outside world. There is still the sadness, but there is an incredible beauty. An ant crawls across your finger; you sit entranced at the wonder as its little body moves. Then you look at a rose bush, quivering in the wind - it is covered with thorns, but at the top of each stem is a flower that is still God's autograph.

You get up and walk further.

You see a little girl on her knees, and standing against her, a man holding an immense sword. The man raises his sword over his head, and brings it down.

Then you see the sword stop in the middle of the air. There is a clanging sound; the man's powerful muscles ripple in his exertion, but the sword does not move an inch further.

Then you slowly see a shimmer in the air, and there is another sword - a sword that seems to be forged of solid light. A sword that is blocking the first. As you watch, you see an angel beginning to become visible. It is powerful, majestic, and terrifying. The man drops his sword, and runs in blind terror.

You can see the angel's sword here, a hand there, the hem of his luminous robe. But what you see is fleeting, and you cannot see the whole angel.

"Why cannot I see you? I can see the grass, and see the girl. Are you not as real as they?"

You see a little boy, walking on the beach, picking up a pebble here, a shell there, a piece of driftwood every now and then, and putting them into a sack.

Then he comes upon a fallen log. And he grabs one protrusion, and then another, trying to lift it. But it will not budge.

"Some day, you will be able to see God himself. But now, you can not see things that are too real for you to see."

You see a diamond, slowly rotating, in light. One facet after another seems to sparkle.

As you watch, not just what appear to be the facets, but

what appears to be the diamond, seems to change form, shift, and sparkle in different ways. The light itself seems to shift color, direction, focus.

Then speaks an almost silent voice: "You are looking upon the one thing which never changes, in a light that has been the same since before the creation of time."

There is a moment of silence, and you feel a surge of power rush about you, and tear through your very being. It is like a blast of wind, throwing you off your feet so violently that wind itself is knocked out of you. It is like the liquid fire that explodes out of a volcano. It is like a flash of light beyond intense, light that is so much light that you cannot see. It bears like an immeasurable weight and presence on your mind and spirit; its might and force fills you with awe - no, more than awe, fear - no, more than fear: terror. It is a reality which lies beyond imagination.

A booming, thunderous voice commands, "Fear not!" Then a hand reaches out and touches you, and you are filled with strength. It holds and stills you; you dimly realize that you have been quivering as a leaf. You somehow find the strength to stand, and if anything see a greater glory and majestic power than before. This being before you is like a storm in solid form. His feet press into the earth with the weight of a mountain, and shine like the sun in full glory. He wears a robe woven of solid light, and at his side hangs a sword sheathed in fire and lightning. His hands radiate power; they seem by their energy as if they are about to tear apart the fabric of space. You dare not look upon his face. Suddenly, you find yourself falling at his feet.

Again booms the voice: "Do not worship me! I am not God!"

A hand lifts you up, and sets you on your feet. His touch is more intense even than his appearance - you are sure that it will destroy you - yet somehow it makes you more solid.

It is all you can do not to fall down again. Somehow the words come, "Who are you?"

"I am a spirit, formed before the foundation of the world. I am a star, who sang for joy as the world was created. I am a messenger, who stands in the presence of God himself and then flies out of the heavens to wage war against the darkness. I am your servant. I am an angel."

Suddenly, images flash through your mind, images to which it would be merciful to call surreal and bizarre. You see chubby little boys fluttering about on birds' wings. You see voluptuous women, suspended in mid-air, whose clothing is perennially falling off. It is as if you have all your life seen pictures of Don Quixote wearing a wash-basin as a helmet, holding a dull sword and sitting astride poor, plodding Rozinante - and then, suddenly and out of nowhere, find yourself staring the paladin Roland, with his sword Durendal drawn and the rippling muscles that have torn trees out of the ground, face to face. You find yourself babbling and attempting to explain what you remember, and suddenly see the angel shaking with a booming, resounding laughter.

"What, my dear child, you would wish me tame and safe, like a little pet?"

It would be much easier to face a creature which was safe, which one could predict. It would be a great deal less disquieting, and a great deal less disturbing. Yet, somehow, you feel a feeling deep within you that it would be an immeasurable loss.

He stretches out his hand. "Come, take my hand. I have something to show you."

You extend your hand, and find it engulfed in a force that is like electricity. Yet somehow, you feel something else as well - a touch. The angel spreads out great, glorious, golden, many-hued wings, and with a mighty jump launches into the air.

You speed along, both of you. Colors and forms speed by. Then, suddenly, you are at a place that is absolutely still, absolutely silent, and pitch black. "Where are we?"

"That is not a question that I can answer in terms that you will understand. Only watch."

You begin to see a pair of hands, They are together, and facing outward. Then they slowly move outward - and behind the hands is left a rainbow, in all its colors. The hands turn, move along, complete a perfect circle. It is the most perfect rainbow you have ever seen.

Then the left hand strikes the rainbow, and it shatters into innumerable miniscule fragments. The right hand takes the shards, and with a single motion scatters them across the blackness. Each piece of the rainbow glows with light, a little reflection of the whole, and then you see a faint, pale, crystalline blue glow. The pieces are scattered irregularly, and one looks almost like - here an insight comes like a flash - a constellation.

There is no horizon, no landscape, no other light. There are stars in every direction and from every view. The view is the most breathtaking view of the sky that you have ever seen.

Then the angel takes your hand again, and says, "Do you understand what you saw?"

"I think I do."

"Good. Then let me show it to you again."

Forms shift and move, and you see a faint, nebulous sea of matter spread about in every direction. It is not still - no, it is moving. You look deeper, and you can see that it is dancing.

Then you see a circle forming, and spinning. And another around it, and another. Soon many circles shift and melt together. The ones on the inside seem to move with more speed, vibrancy, energy. Then you can see a kind of a ball forming.

The swirling matter around it spins inward, more and more tightly, until a fire seems to light inside - and fills the new-formed sphere with radiance. Flashes of light, bursts of glowing forms, like water on a pot boiling, seethe and foment. In your silence and stillness watching it, you begin to realize that spheres are forming, coming to light, becoming stars, all around - and, just as the stars formed out of forms dancing, the stars themselves are forms dancing, in a great, glorious, majestic dance.

The strains of a Christmas carol ring in your ears: "Fall on your knees. O hear the angel voices!" Suddenly you realize that you and your host are not still at all, but swept into the great dance - and, about you, you can see shimmers of... you know not what.

After a long, glorious, blissful time, the angel again takes your hand, and again you find yourself swept away. When you find yourself at rest, you are again in pitch black.

"And why am I here?"

"To see what you have seen, for the third time."

You wait with eager expectation, to see what could be next. Inside you, the images foam and mix. The rainbow, containing each piece and found in each piece, the colors, the moving dance, the energy... You try to push it aside, so that you may attentively perceive whatever changes may be happening...

Time passes, with still the forms fermenting in your mind. You feel serene and at rest; the place is a place of profound peace. After a time the images begin to fade, leaving behind a feeling, a wholeness, a satiety. It is like, after a vivacious dance has ended, sitting down, cooling off - and, then, at rest, finding the joy and the intoxication of the dance still in your heart, and your head floating in the air. It is like, after finishing a meal, sitting with its feeling of fullness.

After a time, you break the silence. "Why has nothing happened here? Why have I seen nothing, heard nothing, felt nothing? Am I here to wait?"

"Has nothing really happened here?"

"Nothing that I can perceive. I haven't seen, or heard, or felt anything."

"Really? You have perceived nothing?"

"Perhaps I have perceived something so subtle and ethereal that I can not notice it. I do not doubt that this place holds something wonderful. But I have not noticed anything."

"Really?"

"Why do you answer my questions with other questions, with riddles, instead of telling me anything?"

"Do I?"

After a time, pondering what this could mean, you ask, "Am I here to wait, for something that will happen? If I am, can you tell me when it will happen? Or at least tell me if you can tell me?"

The angel is silent for a moment, and then says, "When you

have seen one of these things, you have seen more than one thing. You have seen the shattering of the rainbow; one of its fragments is the one near your home that shines light on your fields and mountains. But the rainbow is also the one, beautiful, perfect language that was before man took upon himself a second time the quest to become gods."

"But did not the sage say that we are gods?"

"Yes, you are gods, and more than gods, and will become more than you even are now. But the man who would exalt himself to godhood, blasphemes. Would that men could learn to be men, without trying to ascend to godhood or even be heroes."

"Should I not learn to be godlike?"

"Learn to be a god, not in the way of the man who wills to be the highest of gods, but in the way of the God who was willing to be the lowest of men."

After a time, the angel continues on.

"In a way, each shattered piece of the rainbow - including the language that you now speak - contains the pattern and image of the whole. But in another way, it has lost some of the colors. There are things that were in the whole rainbow, that are not in the piece.

"So I will answer your question, about waiting, with a word from another language. The word is not a word which answers the question, but rather which un-asks it. So I answer you with this word: Mu."

"But why do you un-ask the question, instead of simply answering it?"

"That I will tell you, if you first tell me, to use an expression from the child's' words of your land, if the elephant in your refrigerator is eating peanut butter. Is the elephant in your refrigerator eating peanut butter? Yes, or no?"

Your mind is quite full; it is slow work, pondering and absorbing all that you have seen and heard. Finally you ask, "Before anything happens, may I wait here and ponder, and digest things?"

The angel says, "Yes indeed; that is why you were brought

here."

A time passes in the silence, the stillness, the darkness. It is the beginning of the slow growth that makes a newborn experience into a full-grown memory, and brings it into who you are. It is the rest which makes every work perfect.

This lasts you know not how long. After a time, you realize that you are in a different place. You are with a man of sorts - if 'man' is the correct word to use. 'Man' is not a wrong word, but there are many others. He seems to be of no particular age. He is fully what every simple child is; he is fully what every ancient sage is.

After a time, you begin to wonder what his age is, and how long you have been there. You see him smile, and then burst out laughing. "Come," he says, "Let me show you what I see." He places his hand on your head, and suddenly you see an image - of a little child, in a magnificent and wondrous cavern full of rubies, and emeralds, and sapphires, and diamonds. He is off in a corner, picking up lumps of coal.

"This place is full of diamonds; come, enjoy, take and carry off as much as you are ready to carry."

Then you begin to look around, and see that you are indeed in a cavern of sorts. It is filled with a brilliant, powerful light; the walls and ceiling, full of irregular bulges and niches, seem to be gilded and encrusted with glowing gems. The space is full of forms magnificent and wonderful - fountains, statues, pedestals, crystalline spheres, animals. Everything in the room seems to have the breath of life.

You begin to gather gems; each one, luminous, seems to have its own particular feel, its own particular energy - you can almost hear a music when you touch them. Their cool, crystalline forms seem to be of congealed light.

After you have gathered a great many, you notice a peculiar phenomenon: the more you carry, the easier it seems to be to pick up even more. The gems embrace each other, and begin to form a vast interlocking structure about you. It forms a great, shining suit of armor - a scintillating armor of adornment, a living form that is as light as thought. As even more time passes, the gems begin to melt into you. As each flows into your body, you feel its energy and light, and soon, a high, subtle, ethereal music courses through your veins.

At last you stand, armored with an armor that is flawless. It gives, you do not doubt, a protection against blows that a man of iron would envy. Yet the armor is not dark and cumbersome; it is light and energizing. Your skin is as soft and sensitive as ever, and you feel the unfettered lightness of nudity, free as Adam - no, you realize, a greater lightness, for a nude person is only not fettered by clothing, but this armor fills you with the freedom of which fetters are but a crude attempt to oppose. Carrying this armor leaves you more free to move and dance, and fills you with a positive energy.

You revel in the fullness, the intoxicating lightness. After a time, you realize that the man is looking upon you. He is smiling.

You begin to ask how much you owe for this wonderful treasure, and he breaks forth in peals of merry laughter. "These treasures are not for sale. They are a free gift. Come and fill yourself to overflowing with these treasures as often as you wish."

"Then they cost nothing?"

"No, they are very costly. They are more costly than you can ever imagine. But they are given freely, like water and light and breath, and a thousand thousand other treasures that no money can possibly buy."

"Then why are they given freely? Surely such things are worth a price!"

The man laughs again. "You are beginning to grow alive - just beginning. When you are truly alive, you will dance so freely that you will need no one to tell you these things, because the answers will be in you."

After a while, he hands you a chalice. "Here, drink this, that you may remain dreaming." You drink it, and have a flash of insight that waking is not the only aroused state. In a moment, you reach out and touch a star.

You find yourself inside a castle of ice. It is cold, elegant, pure. It is night-time, and the deep blue of the starry sky provides the light. You walk about in a magnificent structure, through halls and archways, around pillars and doorways, all the time in a great silence. The place is majestic and massive.

The coldness of the ice fills the palace with a deep peace. There is a rest here. You cannot see, nor feel the presence of, yet you somehow sense a kinship to the resting dead, sleeping, awaiting the dawn when sleepers shall rise.

As you step, as you breathe, you hear your echoes, and then the echoes of your echoes. The silence has a presence.

It is a timeless place. There is no hurry, no rush, no clutter. The sparseness of the architecture is matched only by the stillness of the air. You stand and walk, footfall after footfall penetrating the vastness. For it is vast and large; it is ordered, and yet unknown.

Through the glassy ceiling above you see the stars, and as you look at them, you can begin to hear the faintest tinklings of ethereal music. Your ears listen with a new keenness, flowing from the crystalline armor, and you can hear, not a music breaking the silence, but a music in the silence. It is, like the palace, sparse, and simple. It has an order and structure, and yet not time; it is a music which sounds as if it has always been there.

After a time, you realize that you are singing a song - sparse, simple, crystalline, and beautiful. It would not be quite right to say that you started a song: rather, that you have joined a song - a song that always has been, and always will be - a song which is sung not by you alone, but by angels and archangels, by the living and the dead, by the rocks and stars and trees themselves. And for the tiniest fraction of an instant, you can almost see the song rising, as incense, in the presence of He Who Is.

As you walk through a corridor, a transformation begins. Tendrils of mist curl about your feet as a shroud slowly rises from the ground. The walls become the walls of tall, narrow buildings lining the sides of the road. They are like ancient, cracked vellum, and ivylike bushes of yellow roses climb the sides.

All is still as you walk the streets; the only motion you can see is that of the mist dancing about you. Every now and then, you catch, out of the corner of your eye, what seems to be the form of a person just disappearing around a corner - but you are never sure.

After a time, you come upon a massive, dark Gothic cathedral. It is carved out of black marble. As you pass through the doors, the air becomes very dry; there is a feeling of imminence.

As you step into the sanctuary, the building itself is rocked by a blast of sound. Your body vibrates as you hear the deep, rich sounds of an organ resound all about you. The song is a fugue, turgid and complex. You hear three parts playing, then four, then six - interwoven, turning about, speaking to each other. It is in the key of E minor.

The song continues for almost an hour, woven with a deep sense of mystery. Like the building, like the city, it is filled with a dark majesty. There is a strain you are listening to hear - and you seem almost to have caught it, now here, now there, but then it vanishes. The song comes to a climax, and then a thunderous resolution. Then the sanctuary becomes as silent as before.

A shaft of light falls, and you see a man walking towards you. He is tall and lean, and wearing a black robe with golden edges. He has black hair, and a thin, close beard. His step is stately and regal, but does not make a single sound. He reaches you, and, bowing deeply, says, "Greetings."

His eyes meet yours, and you see that he has a piercing, probing gaze. It is intense, looking deep into your eyes - no, more, deep into your soul. And there is something else - you can not tell what. You begin to gaze back, and you realize what it is. His gaze is gentle.

He reads the questions on your face, and after a time says, "I cannot tell you everything that you wonder now. If I were to say the answers, answers that I am only beginning to understand, they would sound like trivia, or sound meaningless. And if I could make you understand them all, I would do you a great disservice."

"Why?"

"Because the questions you ask are the right questions, but they are also the wrong questions."

After a time, he begins again.

"But there is something which I can do. I can lead you to the library."

He leads you through a twisted passageway, then down a stairwell. The stairwell alights in a room with shelves upon shelves upon shelves of dust-covered tomes.

"And," the man says, "I can give you this."

He reaches into the folds of his robe, and gives you a black rose.

It is a queer feeling to be alone with that many books. You reach on one of the shelves and pull one out. It is an illuminated manuscript. It tells a story deep, and detailed, and rich, and subtle. What you can read of it is like barely seeing the ripples on the surface of a lake, while untold forms move about below in the depths.

You replace it and look at another. It is a manual of philosophy and theology. It tells something about God - but it is also too subtle and complex to understand. And there is something else... It is like reading a book about arrangements and variations of color - to a man who has been blind from birth.

Then another... You can tell from its form that it has a sort of reason, or structure to it, but you cannot tell what. At first, you find what seem to be logical errors - and it does contradict itself, sharply and in many ways... and yet... you have the feeling that you are like a man, versed in logic and philosophy but devoid of emotion, poring over a joke, trying to understand it as an argument - and having no idea why others read it and then do something called laughing.

Another book, and another. Each time it seems like you understand something, you find yourself more confused than before. After a time, it becomes words upon words - and the more words are added, the less meaning there seems to be.

You sit down, exhausted and bewildered. After a time, you realize that a woman is standing some distance off. She is wearing a robe that is purple and black, with long sleeves and a long, flowing skirt. Her long hair, which falls behind her to a length you cannot tell, is jet black, and yet her skin is almost luminous.

She steps forward, and, embracing you, gives you three kisses on alternate cheeks. "Have you learned anything yet?"

"Nothing. I can't understand anything in the books."

"Have you thought to see what you can learn?"

"I have thought, and I do not doubt that there is a lesson, but it is seven times over too subtle and too complex for me."

"There is a lesson that you are missing, but not because it is too subtle and too complex. You are missing it because it is too simple and too obvious."

"I have read from two and ninety books, and cannot share with you the least shred of wisdom that is found in them. I do not understand. So in what wise am I to claim that I have learned?"

"Is there not even one thing you can claim to have learned?"

It is with frustration that you say, "Only the littlest thing - that I do not understand."

"That is not so little as you think."

She looks at you for a second, and now you can see, as well as a probing gaze, a hint of a smile. "Come; you are fatigued. Let me take you so that you can eat and rest." She places an arm around you - her touch is soft and responsive - and leads you through other passageways into a room with a table.

The table is set with plates of clear glass; the table is set with bread, fish, and white cheeses, and there are two glasses of white wine. She leads you to a chair, which offers a welcome rest, and then sits down opposite you.

After you have eaten a couple of pieces of bread, you see her again gently looking upon you. "I can see the question in your eyes. You are wondering, are you not, why you were not simply told that you do not understand."

"Yes."

"Would you have understood that you do not understand?

As you do now?" She pauses, and takes a sip of the wine. "A mouse can only drink its fill from a river, and no man can learn what he is not ready to understand."

The rest of the meal is eaten in silence. It is a calm, peaceful, prayerful silence. The bread is flavorful and dense; the cheese is mild; the wine is dry and cool.

After the meal, you both sit in more silence. It is a time of rest... and also of community. There are no words and there is no touch, and yet you can sense a kind of attention, a welcome, from the lady.

When you feel refreshed, she leads you through another passageway, and out to a door to the street. She gently embraces you, and says, "It is time for you to go, and begin to taste some of the other secrets of this city. I do not know if we shall meet again, but I suspect that it will come to pass. Fare Thee well."

The street is different from the one you first saw - it also is enshrouded by a cloak of mist, but it is wider, and there are people passing by. Their clothing varies some, but much of it is variation on a dark grey theme, almost seeming to be mist in solid form. A young woman passes by on the other side of the street; a cascade of ebon hair hides part of her face - yet you can still see, in one corner of her mouth, a hint of a smile.

You come across an open square, with an intricate pattern of stone tiles in the center. Two opposite corners have trees - gnarled, angular, and leafless. One of the corners has a fountain; cascading sheets of water fall between many-leveled pools, in which silvery and golden fish swim about. The opposite corner has a statue.

The statue is on a large pedestal of dark grey marble; the statue itself is of blackened bronze. It is of a man, gaunt and haggard, and clad in rags. His arms are raised up to Heaven, as is also his head, and yet his face bears a look of despair. The pedestal bears the inscription, "I am thirsty. Who will give me something to drink?"

You find a jug, and, filling it at the fountain, climb up the statue and pour water into the statue's mouth. You hear sounds of water flowing, and then there is a click. It is followed by a whirr of moving clockwork, and, getting down, you see that one of the sides of the pedestal has turned inwards, revealing a shaft descending into the earth.

A lantern is at your feet; you light it, and begin to climb down the ladder at one side. It descends into a passageway; taking one direction, you come to a four way intersection. The left path turns into a circular room, with a domed roof, and a pool in the center. You test its depths - and find it descends below the floor.

Inside, you find an underwater passageway. You swim through it, and surface in a room with rough walls. Climbing upwards, you find the room to narrow into a shaft, which turns into a low passageway, and then opens into another room.

This room is lit by the glow of torches; it is large and rectangular. At the center is a thick, low stone column, about three feet tall, with some protrusions bulging from the top. When you come closer, you see that it is an intricate clockwork device; working with it, you find a pattern in its motions, and work with it until there is a click, and a segment of the far wall slides into the ground.

The passageway is dark, as was the room and passageway which you traversed without your lantern, and it opens shortly into another room. At first you cannot see; then, as you step in, your eyes slowly adjust to the darkness. Inside this room, you see another statue.

This statue is a male nude. It is an iron statue; it is immense, and the figure is powerfully built. It is in the middle of a stride - a long, powerful stride, one which seems almost to shake the ground. His eyes bear an intense gaze, one which seems to almost flash lightning, and one arm is raised, and hand outstretched, in a gesture of authority. The surface of the statue is rough and unfinished. There is something in this statue that seems to almost radiate power and energy and weight and light.

And yet, when you look closer, you notice something different. The eyes seem sad. And then, looking closer, you suddenly realize that the statue is bound by shackles. The shackles are a monstrosity, a violation; they threaten to wear down his energy and burden his strength. You grab at the shackles to see if you can pull them free, and feel a chill and drain run through the body. You drop them in shock.

As you stand in the room, you seem to even more be able to see - not only the forms, but the absurdity and injustice. The man's great strength - it is straining against the binding chains. Your eyes trace the shackles to where they are engulfed by the floor.

Then you realize that there is another set of shackles, empty, open. You shudder to look at them; the touch of one of the chains sapped your soul; breathing felt as if you had been forcefully struck on the chest. You begin to back out of the room... and you see the statue's eyes.

He is not pleading; he is not begging. If anything, his eyes say "Go far away; that these chains imprison me is bad enough, without one more." You do not see pride, of someone unwilling to receive help, or the cowardice of one who dare not ask. It is rather the compassion, of someone who would not wish his worst enemy to feel the misery he feels. You feel a stirring inside your heart. What the man does not ask, conscience and every noble instinct demand. And you walk in.

A chill sweeps through you as you cross the threshold. You can almost see a presence that is unholy. At each step you are jolted. And yet... you have the strength to follow.

You fasten one of the open shackles about your feet; it stings like the sting of a scorpion. The other, and you feel as if you are sinking into the ground. A shackle is fastened around one hand, and it is all you can do not to fall down. You place your other hand in the last, and begin to close it...

The shackles fall from the man's feet, and you see a surge of power ripple through his muscles. He crouches down, and then jumps up with a force that shakes the earth. He raises his hands upward, and there is a blinding flash of light.

Your sight slowly returns, and you find yourself on a grassy knoll bordering a field. A small grove of saplings is to the left, and a field of dandelions is to the right. From somewhere near come the sounds of birds chirping, and a babbling brook.

You see the man who was shackled, standing nearby. He is looking upon you, and smiling. He picks you up and gives you a hug - a crushing, invigorating bear hug that makes you feel very much alive - and a big kiss. Then he sets you down and opens a large leather pouch. He fills two large stone bowls with stew, and draws two draughts of cider from a small barrel. The stew is a piping hot, well-spiced, and hearty beef stew, but the cider is cold and mild - you could drink quite a lot without getting drunk.

He tells you of how he came to be imprisoned - he let a love of probing mysteries become a love of secrecy, and a love of the beauty in natural darkness become a love of evil, so that what was wholesome and free became perverted and enslaved - and then asks of your story, how you came to rescue him. He listens eagerly and intently.

After a time, he says, "There are many people who knew of my disappearance and do not know that I am free; it is time for me to go and tell them that I am free, and how you rescued me. But before I go, I give you this." He raises one hand to Heaven and places the other on your head, and speaks a blessing. You cannot understand the blessing, but there is something about it that strikes you... and then you see, in an instant, not just one little fragment in the blackness, but the whole radiant rainbow. He is speaking the first language, before it was broken, and - though you cannot understand it - you are moved by its power, its love, its light.

He presses slightly harder on your head, and your spirit surges with joy. Then he runs off into the distance, bounding like a stag.

After a time, you begin to walk along, into the forest. It grows thicker, and the colors richer and deeper. You can feel warmth, and humidity, and wind.

As you walk along, the forest opens into a wide, grassy clearing, with thick, long bluegrass. A few small raindrops sprinkle on your face; thunder rumbles, and soon there is a heavy and torrential rainstorm. The rain is warm, and in it you begin to run and play.

A woman, short and with a full and rounded figure, begins to dance with you, and soon you are swinging around, and dancing in the rain. Sheets and columns of rain fall, and in the lightning flashes you can see the trees, the leaves - the whole forest - dancing and spinning in the wind.

The woman is laughing; you can hear the laughter in her voice and see the laughter in her eyes. On a whim, you reach and pinch her side; she laughs and squirms. She jumps and tackles you - it is half a tackle and half a hug - and knocks you over.

After wrestling around for a few minutes, she turns and walks towards a large, ancient, gnarled oak tree, and sits on a large bulge a little distance above the ground. As she sits, you vaguely realize that the tree's form has almost the shape to welcome a human - your eyes did not pick it out, but she seemed to have walked to it as naturally as if she were breathing. She is leaning a little to her left; a ledge of wood forms almost a cushion for her to lean on - one might say that her body is curled into the wood.

You begin to look on her, and see how beautiful she really is. Her skin glistens with little drops of water. She is dark, with olive skin and large, soft, welcoming eyes that seem to enfold you, taking you in as the waters of a lagoon take in a swimmer. There is something that draws you about your hands.

Her hands are small, and seem to contain the beauty of her whole body in miniature. They are rounded, curved, and Rubenesque. You can see soft skin gently enfolding the inside of her hands; it has a looseness and ampleness so that you do not see vein and bone, only the rich color of skin. Her fingers are tiny and thin, with very mignonne nails and fingertips. The texture of her hands is subtle, yet gives her hands reality; you can see the strata and shapes in the tiny wrinkles on the back of her hand,the dark, faint hairs, and the many sheets of lines that twist and turn over the inside of her hand. Through her fingernails, you can see a glimpse of white, pink color which contrasts brightly with the rest of her hand.

And yet the shape is only half of the beauty that is in her hands, for they are not still, but in motion. It is a slow, still, lyrical motion, an adagio dance. It does not overpower the senses or make a clamoring demand for your attention, but it is yet deeply moving. Her fingers, palm, and thumb slowly move, in a rich harmony. You can see waves in her fingers as they wend back and forth. The motion is extremely simple, and has a periodicity that comes back to a single thing, yet somehow you do not wish it to be more complex, or do something new - at the moment, you would have difficulty understanding why anybody watching this slow undulation would want to see anyone else. It seems that she is speaking in a language with her hands, and you long to understand what her hands are saying, to put it into words. Then you look deeper, and you realize that you do understand what her hands are saying, and you cannot put it into words because it is a truth different from what words express. You rather feel and sense... peace... rest... stillness... the motion of breath... the beating of a heart... the music that lies in and beyond silence... the ebb and flow of water... day and night and the four seasons turning in cycle... the rhythm of a song that does not pulse, and yet has order... tufts of long, dry grass, resting in a field... the tops of trees, blowing in a wind... a rock, buried deep in the earth, remaining a rock, in the process of not-changing... the light at dusk, and yet not the light of dusk for the sunlight at dusk fades, and this, even in its softness, would not rightly be said to fade.

She begins to walk along a path, leading you, and takes you to a small hovel. You step inside, and as your eyes adjust to the light, you see a very old woman. She is emaciated, and in her face are etched lines of pain. She begins to try to get up, and say something, but the sounds are hardly understandable as words, and the young woman gently places her hand over the old woman's mouth and leads her to lie down. Reaching up to the wall, she brings a flask of wine to the old woman's lips, and helps her drink a little. After that, she goes to a chair, and picks up a wooden recorder, and plays it. It is the same song as her hands danced: soft, still, and beautiful. It has a very soft, woody sound, and the notes themselves are... like the color grey, like a gentle light, like a friend's voice. You are lost in the music, carried away by its beauty. Slowly, the song tapers into silence, into a rest allowing the music heard to sink in. You look at the old woman, and see that she is still, absolutely still. Her eyes vacuously point into space.

The young woman gets up, with infinite gentleness, and with her hand slowly closes the old woman's eyes. She turns to you, and, speaking so softly that you can barely hear her, says the first words you have heard from her: "She was my grandmother." You can see the tears forming in her eyes.

It is dusk, and the last rays of the sun ebb into darkness, into a dark and moonless night.

The next day, you begin to build a pyre in the middle of the field. Some people come by from the wood and help; they are bearing little gifts, and each embrace her. There is not what you would understand to be a ceremony; they each come and go. After a time, you realize that the animals also come, and pay their respects in their own ways. Dusk comes again, and she takes a lantern and sets it at the bottom of the fire. Flames begin to lick upwards, and then touch the grandmother's body. Then the young woman screams, a piercing, dissonant, discordant scream of which you would not have thought her capable. She begins to sob uncontrollably, and weeps the whole night long.

The woman stands up to greet the coming of the dawn, the tears still streaming down her face. The first rays begin to break over her face, and then you notice something... different. Something that you had not noticed before.

You see pain in her face; it is of no effort to see that a great hole has been torn in her soul. And yet there is something else. She is beaten, but not crushed; wounded, but not destroyed. If she is bleeding, it is because there is living blood coursing through her veins. It would not be quite right to say that she is not too badly hurt because she is a deep person; rather, she is very badly hurt because she is a deep person. And yet... you cannot quite tell what it is.

She turns to you, and sees the puzzlement in your face. She reaches, and with one hand touches your eyes; her lips move in silent prayer. Then she takes her hand back, and you slowly see something else. You see angels all around, and feel the Spirit of God. One of the angels - great, mighty, magnificent - has wrapped his arms around her. The angels are still, and... intent. It would be a gross distortion to say that one of them waves a magic wand and makes the pain go away, and yet...

You cannot quite see, and yet in your spirit you sense, prayers, around and under and in her. You cannot understand all of what is going on. The pain is not taken away, and you share the pain as well. And yet... Though you cannot say what, you can sense someone, and something happening, which is infinitely greater than the pain. And you, again, hear singing.

> Sister, let me be your servant. Let me be as Christ to you. I will laugh when you are laughing. When you weep, I'll weep with you. Pray that I might have the grace to Let you be my servant, too.
>
> When you feel so weak and burdened, When the world is harsh to you, Know that Christ has gone before you, Felt the pain and shed the tears. As Christ has so giv'n to others, So he will also give to you.
>
> And e'en with Christ you're not alone, For we are Christ's body, too. We are all brother and sister. Your burden is our burden, too. As you have so giv'n to others, So we all shall give to you.

A little boy runs up with something clutched in his hand, and kisses her. He says, "I love you. Sorry you hurt bad. Havva big gift. Look!" He opens his hand.

Inside is a blade of grass.

Espiritichthus: Cultures of a Fantasy World not Touched by Evil

Nor'krin

The Nor'krin are tall and strong, with thick, sandy blonde hair, deep blue eyes, and white skin that turns reddish when they go south from their frost-kissed land; the Janra affectionately refer to them as the Northern giants. They love to run across the snowy plains and up to the peaks, to feel the crispness of the air, and to drink the cold and crystalline waters of the flowing streams.

There are not very many of them; they live nomadic lives, spread out across the snowy North, carrying with them only their clothing, their hunting weapons (a large bow and quiver of arrows, an axe, and a knife), a canteen, and a handful of tools and other miscellanea.

Theirs is a culture of oral tradition and folklore, filled with a richness of symbolic thought. Their thought is expressed by storytelling. Some tell of people and actions full of goodness, love, and wisdom; some are allegories packed with symbolic detail; some are both. The evenings -- from the meal onward -- are times when the clans gather together, and the oldest member tells tales until long into the night, when the fire has died down to embers and the icy mountain peaks glisten in crystalline blue starlight.

(The language is one which revolves around the oral tradition; its grammar is fairly simple, sufficient for basic expression, but there is an extensive vocabulary fitted to epic poems, great tales, and the transmission of a symbol-filled body of lore)

Their experience of sense is primarily aural, centering around the communication and preservation of their tradition. The other senses all play a part in their knowing about the world around them and its enjoyment, of course, but the ears dominate.

Coming of age is very significant in Nor'krin culture. It is the event upon which a child becomes a full member of Nor'krin community, and appreciates it fully, for it is accomplished in solitude. It is the same for male and female, big and small.

Denuded of all possessions save a hunting knife and the clothing on his back, the child begins a solitary trek, south through the land of the Urvanovestilli and Yedidia, penetrating deep into the thick forests inhabited by the Tuz, until he enters a village, and, coming inside a shop, says, "Blacksmith, blacksmith, find me a task, give me a quest."

There are as many quests as there are questions. Some are easy, some are hard; some are simple, some are complex. Whatever the quest be -- be it finding an amethyst in the caves, climbing an immense mountain, answering a riddle, memorizing a book -- he leaves the blacksmith shop and does not return until the quest is completed. (It must be said that, though some quests have taken years to complete, recorded history has yet to see a Nor'krin fail. A child leaves the immediate presence of his family, but remains in their prayers; they have great faith, and it is in this faith that they tread securely into the unknown.

Upon the return, the blacksmith begins to ask questions: "What is your name? What is your family? Who are you? What is your story?" -- and begins to fashion an iron cross. This cross is at once a cross as any other, and a unique reflection of the person who wears it; no two are alike.

It is with this cross worn about the neck that he returns to his clan, come of age.

Nor'krin greet each other by standing opposite the other, placing the left hand on the other's right shoulder, and lowering the head slightly; the gesture is a sign of respect.

The emotional side of their culture is not as intense or spectacular as many others, but is present and offers an important reflection of what they value. They know a deep sense of respect and appreciation; when they think of others, the first thought is, "This person is an image of God," and there is a feeling of respect. The mountains, the trees, and the streams all bear a magnificence which they appreciate. Nor'krin worship services are filled with awe at the One whose glory is declared by tales, by lives, and by the created order. They are traditional liturgical services, where the place of the homily is taken by long tales and stories, conducted by the eldest members of the clan.

The Nor'krin homeland is named 'Cryona'.

Tuz

Many wayfarers go south, early in life, to buy equipment; they need only wait, and a blacksmith will forge a pair of iron boots which will last for life.

The people are dark and strong; their eyes shine with power and lightning. The average Tuz male is short, stout, very broad-shouldered, and built like a brick wall; a thick, straight, jet black moustache and a thick, curly beard push out of leathery skin. Women are equally short and stout, but do not have such broad shoulders, being (relatively) more plump and less muscled, and do not have the moustache and beard (usually).

Their buildings are hewn of solid granite, with iron doors. The villages are small and scattered, joined by worn paths passing through the rich, deep green of the forest. It is this forest, fertile and full of beasts, from which the heart of their meal comes. They are more than fond of spicy meat stews and bear jerky. Their beer is dark, thick, and strong, and every house has at least a little bit of khoor, a spiced rum which is occasionally used by the other peoples as a pepper sauce.

The Tuz work hard and play hard. They are often hired for heavy work in the construction of Urvanovestilli palaces, and their work rarely receives complaint. After work is over, they tend towards wrestling and general rowdiness; if they are present, Janra children (and occasionally adults) are tossed about.

For all of their rowdiness, the Tuz do possess a great deal of restraint; even after a couple of beers, they seldom give each other injuries beyond occasional bruises and abrasions, and Janra children do not receive even a scratch. (Most of them rather enjoy being tossed about).

The usual greeting is a crushing bear hug, often accompanied/followed by a punch in the stomach, some wrestling or tossing around, etc; it is generally toned down a bit for children and visitors from afar, but there is always at least a spark of rowdy play.

As much as the Nor'krin are at home in the cold, loving everything that is crisp and chilly, the Tuz love heat. Their land is by far the hottest, but that doesn't stop them from munching on peppers and wrestling around. Blacksmiths' shops and fire and sun-hot iron -- these are a few of their favorite things.

The Tuz also build obstacle courses of stone and iron and rope, which the Janra have no end of finding new and inventive ways to use; a slack rope which Tuz climb along the underside of will be walked -- or occasionally run -- atop by the Janra; jumping shortcuts, backwards or inverted travel, and acrobatic ways of avoiding raw strength moves are common. Tuz, by contrast, have very slow and methodical paths.

They are, indeed, probably the most constant and unchanging of peoples; the process of maturing is a process of becoming more who they are. Their sense of order is also great; they value greatly the gift of being well ruled.

A child, at the age of ten, is presented to the village elders and the various guildmasters. They spend a day talking with the child and his parents, in order to determine his talents, interests, and personality; then they spend another day talking and discussing amongst themselves; then, on the third day, his profession is announced, along with the master to whom he will be apprenticed. The results are sometimes surprising, but always embody a great deal of wisdom, and the selection of a vocation is a gift for which the child is grateful.

Children learn a way of life filled with discipline, tradition, and respect for elders. It is quite simple, not at all ornate when compared to some other philosophies, but it has a power, a solidity to it, and love, faith, honor, friendship, and hospitality are things that they truly live by. Their families and communities are very close, and their friendships are loyal until death. They do not pay as much emphasis on verbal articulation of teaching as a way of life. There is thought, but in its expression, words take a second place to actions. That a life of faith involves discipline is declared very loudly by Tuz hands.

The are very aware of the value of solitude and prayer; it is a common practice to simply leave, taking nothing save clothing and a hunting knife or axe, and go up into the mountains for a few days of solitude, allowing time to pray and to be refocused.

Their language has, in speech, a very heavy, thick, consonantal feel, full of grated 'h's (which is often present in 'k's, 'r's, 'g's, and 'b's). The speech is terse and concrete.

Their experience of sense is also very concrete, centered somewhere between visual and aural. Sight tells what is around and where, and what is happening and where. Hearing tells what is happening, and where, and what is being said.

The emotional side of their culture knows such things as accomplishment, tradition, exertion, and discipline. There is an emotion that comes from a job well done and a challenge mastered; they value it. To have a heritage and respect elders as well as enjoy children brings a feeling of right order. To wrestle around, run, or laugh heartily has a pleasure. To control oneself has a joy. Things such as these are what they feel.

Tuz worship services are be short and sweet, with worship

embodying a great deal of fervor.

The Tuz homeland is named 'Rhog'.

Urvanovestilli

The first thing to strike a visitor is the devices. In every house and many shops there is a tinkering room; a large workbench is covered with every imaginable sort of gear, spring, hinge, lever, chain, and shaft; the clock is only the beginning of clockwork. Two nearby cabinets -- one filled with tools, one filled with parts and working materials -- stand neatly closed; at the touch of a button, a drawer springs out, and shelves slowly slide up.

The craftsmanship of clockwork devices is, along with the study of diverse subjects -- theology and philosophy, history and literature, science and mathematics -- a hobby that symbolizes the culture. Each piece is created not only for utility, but also for artistic effect. Cuckoo clocks and spring loaded umbrellas, Swiss Army Knives and mechanical pencils, player pianos and collapsible telescopes: mechanical objects such as these fill the land.

The ornate complexity of the devices reflects the ornate complexity of thought. The language, quite possibly the most difficult to learn, allows a speaker to express detailed and nuanced thought in exacting specificity. There are twenty four verb tenses, so that there is (for example) a different past tense for a brief, well demarcated action, and one which occurred over a period of time; there are twenty four other verb forms, which are like verb tenses as to conjugation and construction, but express the verb in an atemporal manner. Their language has much room built in for conjunction and logical connectives, nesting and predicates, as well as subtlety, implication, and allusion.

They have a complex and formal system of etiquette, although it must be said to their credit that they take no offense at a wayfarer who is warm and friendly but does not know their rules; they understand how simple the heart of politeness is.

Their speech is clever and witty, and they are fond of abstract strategy games. They enjoy ornate and complex polyphony, and will spend hours exploring theology and philosophy (two disciplines which they have the wisdom not to separate).

Urvanovestilli culture places a very heavy emphasis on a facet of virtue which they call contrainte. Contrainte is a kind of inner constraint, where order is approached by adjusting conditions inside before conditions outside, and not letting oneself be wrongly controlled by external circumstance. A similar concept is embodied in the words 'moderation' and 'self-control.'

Contrainte enables a man to be free and use that freedom responsibly; it enables a man to have access to drink without getting drunk; it enables him to think constantly without becoming rationalistic. The Urvanovestilli homeland has the richest natural resources in the world, and (with centuries of first rate craftsmanship and efficient work) they are by a wide margin the richest nation in the world. Despite this, they keep a very cautious eye on wealth, so as not to be enslaved by it. Theirs is not a culture of consumption; though some of their interests -- art, sculpture, board oriented strategy games, tinkering -- generally are pursued in a manner that involves wealth, the bulk -- discussions, prayer, dance, imagination, thought -- do not. Consumption as a status symbol and waste are both seen as vulgar.

In contrainte is also balance and complement. There is time in solitude and time in community, freedom and responsibility, private and public property, work and rest.

It is in contrainte that an ornate system of etiquette does not obscure love, and elaborate ceremonies do not obscure worship. Just as they do not have their sights set on wealth -- they do not look to it for happiness, security, and other things that it can not provide -- and are therefore able to enjoy it (among other and greater blessings) without being harmed, so also they set their sights on love and worship, and therefore do not permit rules of etiquette or liturgical forms to make themselves the focus and cause hearts to become cold and dusty.

Contrainte likewise allows them to act efficiently without becoming efficient. Off of work, life takes a calm and leisurely pace; nobody fidgets. It allows them to be very judicious in their use of money, and at the same time very generous; their hospitality is lavish, and it is unheard of for anyone -- friend or stranger, native or foreigner -- to go hungry in their land.

The single greatest mark of contrainte lies in that, with all of their achievements, they remain open to the gifts of God. Contrainte itself -- though they work very hard to cultivate it -- is not something that they try to achieve on their own power, but ask for in prayer, expecting to receive as a gift from God. Nor is it set up as the supreme context, the Supra-God to which God must bow down; they know nothing of religion within the bounds of contrainte. Contrainte does not "point to" itself as an object of worship, but rather God; it brings, in worship of God, a desire to grow in faith, hope, and love. It is like being reasonable enough not to be rationalistic.

On the surface, the Urvanovestilli culture appears to be the antithesis of that of the Shal. One is complex, and the other simple; one is rich, and the other poor; in one, people sit and talk for hours; in the other, people sit in silence for hours.

At the very heard, though, they are very much the same; Urvanovestilli, when traveling and visiting the Shal, feel that they are at home; the Shal find the Urvanovestilli to be brothers. They see beyond, rest in God's love, and love their neighbors.

The Urvanovestilli are quiet, patient, temperate, and refined. They are classically educated and cultured; their country is a federation of republics, each one ruled by a senate in a tradition that has remained unchanged for centuries. Tradition is strong, and families remain together; come evening, three or four, sometimes even five generations sit down at one table, eating and drinking, talking and listening, long into the night. There is a great respect for age, but a respect that in no way despises youth; the oldest spend a great deal of time caring for the youngest.

Indeed, one of the first sights to greet a visitor who steps inside an Urvanovestilli mansion is often a grandfather or great-grandfather, with a long, flowing white beard, sitting with a child on his knee.

Urvanovestilli names are long and ornate. The full name is rarely spoken outside of formal ceremonies; even Urvanovestilli do not often pronounce thirty syllables to refer to one entity; all the same, each one is considered important. The names are:

Family name: This is the first and foremost of names, and the most cherished; it is the most commonly used.

Maiden name: Among married women, this follows.

Birth name: This is the name given at birth, and is often used within families and when there are several people of the same family present.

Reserve name: This is a very intimate name, which is not always known outside of family and close friends; it is spoken with a great deal of affection and familiarity.

Baptismal name: This name is chosen at baptism by people who know the person well, and given a great deal of prayer; it is used especially in religious contexts.

Regional name: This tells of the city or village a person comes from, carrying with it connotations of regional flavor and culture. It is used primarily in reference to travelers or (occasionally) people far away.

Friend names: These names (some do not have any; a few have ten or eleven; the average is two or three) come according to friends; a friend can bestow a name, and it becomes thereafter formally a part of an Urvanovestilli full name. When such a name is bestowed, it will become the name used primarily by the person who chose it.

The phrases of politeness -- those which would correspond to hello, goodbye, please, thank you, you're welcome -- are all benedictions; they take innumerable forms and beauties according to the people and situation. Blessing is something which they value; they often speak of good things -- friends, virtue, art and music, food and drink -- as so many blessings from the heart of the Father.

The traditional greeting is a hand raised, open save that the ring finger bends down to meet the thumb, or (when greeting a child) placed atop the head; the gesture is a symbol of benediction. It is followed by three kisses on alternate cheeks.

In youth, Urvanovestilli are filled with a wanderlust. They voyage to many different places, seeing different nations and lands -- as well as the variety of their own cities -- and enjoy experiences which provide a lifetime's worth of memories. The wayfaring is never really complete, though, until it becomes the voyage home: the Time sometimes comes after two years of travel and sometimes after ten, but the Spirit always makes it clear. When that Time comes, each Urvanovestilli spends a little longer -- perhaps a month -- with the people he is visiting, and then leaves, with a very passionate and tearful goodbye.

It is Time to return home, to put down roots, to deepen, to mature; Time to wholly enter into the homeland. From this point on, the Urvanovestilli is no longer a wayfarer. The memories of his travels are cherished and very dear, a set of riches that he will always carry with him, and he will still send blessings, gifts, letters, and occasionally visits to friends in far away lands, but it is no longer time to go here and there; it is Time to grow into family, friends, and city.

Urvanovestilli writings and teaching, the means by which theology and philosophy are transmitted, take many forms -- poems, riddles, parables and allegories, personal conversations, to name a few -- but the predominant form is a systematic and structured logical argument: point one, point two, point three, subpoint three b, conclusion one... The structure carries allusion, nuance, and beauty; it leaves room for the speaker to make a very beautiful craft of words.

They enjoy being absorbed in thought; it is how they spend a good time of each day. They do not look down on sensation -- indeed, they have a great appreciation for what is a very highly developed art, music, and cuisine -- but it does not fill their world as it does that of many others. Abstraction and complexities of thought are fundamental to their experience of the world: sensation leads into perception, perception leads into concrete thought, and concrete thought leads into abstract thought. Moments of immersion in the senses are rare, Sensation, being the outermost layer, is governed and enjoyed from within. Its form is generally of aural and visual character; the aural side is shaped by words, and then accommodates the other plethora of sounds, and the visual side is shaped by the forms, the spaces, and the interactions of their devices, and sees something of springs and gears in the world around.

Their faces appear at first glance to be almost expressionless -- a faint hint of a smile, perhaps -- until you look at their eyes, the first window to the fire and intensity within. Urvanovestilli eyes -- whether brown, amber, hazel, grey, or blue -- bear an intense, probing gaze; in Urvanovestilli culture, eye contact is almost continual, and reflects a fire, an intensity, a passion, that fills their way of life. It does not take long to be reminded that eye contact is a form of touch; their eyes seem to be looking into your spirit. The gaze, in its intensity, is never cold and calculating, never the chilling, devouring stare of a steel face beyond which lies a heart of ice; at its most intense and most probing, it is the most filled with love, and most easily shows the intense fire within. They can rest -- and they know calm and tranquility -- but there is a great energy within, an energy that shows itself in their artwork and writings. Those who read their theologians certainly do not fail to notice the depths of wisdom and insight, but what is most striking is their love for God. The passion -- of their love for God, for spouse, for family, for their neighbor; of desire to grow in virtue and knowledge, for their work -- burns, and their experience of emotion -- of discovery, of awe, of appreciation of beauty -- is long and intense, complex and multifaceted. This emotion is the other side of contrainte; it is the same virtue that enables them to enjoy wine in temperance, and to be moved to tears by music and theater. It is not a "virtue" of stifling -- that would be far too easy, but of control and proper enjoyment. Just as they find abstinence from drink to be too easy, a way of dodging the lesson of moderation, stifling emotion and crushing it would be, to them, a way of dodging the lesson of passions rightly oriented in accordance with holiness and love -- not to mention an unconscionable destruction of an integral facet of being human.

Those Urvanovestilli who are the most virtuous, the most filled with contrainte, are nearly always the most passionate.

Urvanovestilli are usually short, but look like very tall in miniature, with clear white skin and jet black hair. The men have a thin and wiry frame, with sharp and angular features. They have flaring eyebrows coming out of a prominent brow, a thin, hooked nose, and tufts of fine hair flaring away from their ears. Skin holds tightly to bones, muscles, and veins, and arms end in long, thin hands with nimble fingers. Their voices are a very soft, almost silent tenor.

The women are somewhat slender, but a slenderness which is graceful and rounded. Their features, as well as their build, bear this slender, graceful, rounded character, and their movements are light and flowing. (If the men know more of passion, the women know more of calm). Their voices are high and clear, with a sound that is like silver, like cold and crystalline water, like clear, light, dry Alsace blanc.

Urvanovestilli worship services are long and complex, with ornate liturgy and ritual. The language is florid and ornate (like that of the liturgy stemming from St. John Chrysostom) and every sentence of the liturgy would embody theological truth. The homilies (although not the only part of the service which varies (much of the liturgy itself changing according to a traditional pattern dictated by a complex algorithm) from week to week) are themselves not that long. They are of moderate length, and differ from the liturgy -- which presented different doctrines sentence by sentence -- in being a full and well-developed presentation of one single idea, expressed in unequaled detail and eloquence.

The Urvanovestilli homeland is named 'Flaristimmo'.

Urvanovestilli city -- Capitello

Capitello is the capital of the Urvanovestilli land, and the classical Urvanovestilli city.

At the very heart lies a cruciform cathedral. It is an immense domed building, the outside in white marble, covered with statues and spires. Inside, all is dark -- or so it seems to a person who first steps in.

Someone who steps in first stands in place, seeing nothing really, perhaps a few points of light in the darkness... and then, very slowly, begins to adjust. It is cool inside, and very still. The silence is a silence that can be heard, a very real and present stillness. As he begins to step into the coolness and the silence, he begins to see light -- light that had gone unnoticed at first, but as he steps into it, becomes more and more visible. The light is shining through a thousand candles, each one bringing a little bit of light, a little bit of warmth, to what is around it. Then, after the candles become visible, it is seen what they illuminate -- mosaics, worked with colored dyes and gold leaf... and faces.

Outside of the cathedral lies an open garden with fountains and statues. Around the garden lies a circle of seven great halls. In clockwise order, beginning south of the cathedral, they are:

Library: This collection, the largest in the world, has at least one copy of all known writings, and a scriptorium in which they are copied and transmitted.

Device museum: This is a clockwork building filled with exemplary devices (and copies in various states of disassembly).

Senate: This building is decorated with arts and crafts from the cities throughout the land; it is a place where senators (two from each city and one from each village) meet to govern the nation.

Mayorship: This is the local senate, the seat from which public affairs are run; the majority of political power is on a local level (the senate being the head of a confederation), vested in the town elders.

Forum: This is an immense amphitheater which hosts a variety of speakers, panels, and open talks. Lecture is the predominant medium and presentation, but poetry and storytelling occur not infrequently. The forum, along with the evening worship services in the cathedral, walking in the garden, attending a concert, or looking through the art museum, is appreciated as an enjoyable way to spend a night out.

Music hall/theater: This hosts concerts and recitals, theatrical performances, operas, dances, pyrotechnic displays, occasional Janra acrobatic performances, dramatic readings, puppet shows...

Art museum: Half of the space is devoted to permanent exhibits, and half to temporary displays. Most of the finest artwork ever produced by Urvanovestilli, and a good deal of the finest artwork from other cultures, may be seen here.

Outside of the seven halls lies what is called "the mélange"; outside of the mélange lie fields, pastures, and vineyards; outside of the farmland lies forest.

The mélange is a large annulus which contains mansions, shops, roads, paths, public squares, gardens, open lots, little forums and theaters, restaurants, and so on. It is where a great deal of life and culture transpires; in the little nooks and crannies, inside the parlors of the houses, a lot transpires.

The Urvanovestilli enjoy going out, but the enjoyment does not come from despising being at home. The parlors, which have the distinction of being within a person's home and hospitality, are lavishly furnished, with couches, chairs, lanterns, some instruments, a liquor machine, some sculpture or paintings, often a fountain or clock or... and people enjoy sitting around, talking, reading, performing music...

Urvanovestilli city: Éliré

Éliré is known among the Urvanovestilli as the city of seashells. While most Urvanovestilli cities are built out of white stone, in ornately embellished classical geometric forms, Éliré is built out of sandy yellow stone, in flowing curves; buildings seem like giant seashells. The artwork and jewelry are crafted from seashells and other treasures from the sea -- coral and pearls -- and the public squares are filled with fountains and pools, where colorful fish swim about.

The people enjoy swimming, and often meet the dolphin population; they enjoy each other.

Urvanovestilli city: Mistrelli

Mistrelli lies in the heart of the Fog Valley; a shroud of mist cloaks the ground, out of which rise trees and tall buildings with spires and towers. Inside the buildings are all manner of tunnels of tunnels, secret passages, and trapdoors; there are clockwork devices in each one. Throughout the city are spread a handful of entrances to a vast underground labyrinth, of which the better part is known; there are all manner of doors and puzzles inside.

The city is full of rose bushes, climbing up the sides of the buildings, over and around gates; most are yellow, but there are some of every color.

The people take a long time to get to know, and their personalities always have hidden gems. Their study of theology emphasizes mystery and the incomprehensible nature of God; Connaissance, a theologian from Mistrelli, began and ended his magnum opus with the words, "I do not know."

Urvanovestilli city: Fabriqué

Fabriqué is the biggest of Urvanovestilli port cities; it lies on the Tuz border, and is the site where ships -- full rigs with multiple masts, many sails, and innumerable ropes -- are built. They are polished and ornately carved, well suited for transport and trade as well as a work of art. The crews hired tend to be heavily Tuz -- strong and sturdy workers who have no problem tying a rope as thick as a wrist in waves and storm -- and set sail to other Urvanovestilli ports and ports around the world, transporting voyagers and cargo to destinations near and far.

Yedidia

The Yedidia culture is a culture of vibrant life. They live in buildings woven out of living trees and plants; the doorways are filled by hanging curtains of leafy vines which softly part as a person passes through.

Their manner of gardening spins out of a wonderful talent for drawing beauty out of the forest; many visitors come for the first time, do not even realize that they have stepped into a garden; they only notice that the forest's beauty is exceptional there.

The Yedidia are very sensitive to the rest of Creation; they speak in a melodic, lilting tongue of the purest song, but even that language is not the one that is closest to them. The first language of every child is that of rocks and trees and skies and seas. They know how tot call birds out of the forest to fly into their hands; they know how to make plants flourish.

They have ears to hear the crystalline song by which the Heavens declare the glory of their Maker. They appreciate the beauty of the created order as it tells of the Uncreate with a power that can not fully be translated into words -- and they use the language of Creation to speak of the mysteries of the Creator, whose fingerprints are everywhere in nature.

They look into the great and unfathomable vastness of space; it furnishes the language by which they tell of the great and unfathomable vastness of the Creator. They know the energy, the great fire out of which the sun pours out light and energy; it furnishes the language by which they tell of the energy and great fire in the heart of the Father, offering warmth and light freely and without cost. They dance in the rain, the life giving water poured out from above; it furnishes the language by which they speak of springs of living water come down from Heaven. They admire the beauty of the lilies of the field, which simply rest in the sunlight, rain, and dew showered on them; it furnishes the language by which they speak of resting in the love poured out. Their eyes are not closed when a grain of wheat falls to the earth and dies...

They are sensitive to the silent beauty that is sometimes unnoticed even by the Janra. They enjoy the brilliance of the sun, and the pale blue luminescence of the moon; the gentle warmth of a summer night, and the powerful motion of a pouring rainstorm (and there are few things many Yedidia enjoy more than being thoroughly drenched). They look at the veins of a leaf, the hairs of a caterpillar, the motion of a snail; they listen to the song of birds, the sound of wind whispering amidst the leaves, the splashes of water flowing over rocks; they taste the cold freshness of water, the tartness of lemons, the sweetness of strawberries; they smell the soft fragrance of jasmine, the spice of cinnamon, the freshness after a rain; they feel the velvety softness of a rabbit's fur, the raspiness of a rhubarb leaf, the roughness of bark, the smoothness of a worn stone, the gentle kiss of a summer breeze, the springiness of pete moss, the shimmering heat of fire long into the night, the light tickle of a crawling gecko, the fineness of a child's hair, and the warmth of a friend's face.

They are as intuitive as they are perceptive; the emotions of friends especially, but strangers as well, are quickly understood; be it singing together, a friendly joke, talking, listening, leaving alone, sitting together in silence, holding a hand, giving a hug -- they always seem to know.

The Yedidia make wines and incense which even the Urvanovestilli do not come close to. It is, though, the Urvanovestilli who make their garments. Some are short, some are tall; some are slender, some are rounded; they tends towards being fairly short and fairly round, but there is a lot of variety. All, though, have olive skin and dark, shiny black hair; the women wear a long, flowing robe of kelly green, over which cascades of hair fall and spin, sometimes reaching to the waist, sometimes almost touching the ground; the men wear cloaks and tunics of walnut brown. The clothing is soft and light as air; it streams out in the motion and jumps of dance -- like their music, smooth, soft, flowing, graceful.

"Dance, then, wherever you may be, for I am the Lord of the Dance, said he." Theirs is a culture full of joy and celebration; it is full of smiles, and always willing to welcome a visitor. Finding something good, they look for someone to share it with.

They are very sensitive to the cycles of nature, of the day, of the phases of the moon, of the seasons in turn. They shape the regular rhythm of their songs, and provide a sense of constancy and regularity, again, which furnishes the language by which they speak of the constancy and regularity of the Creator.

The traditional greeting is a soft and gentle hug, one which often lasts a while (or a butterfly kiss, or...). That touch, as their faces and voices as they speak, bears a great deal of expression: The phrase of greeting used means, literally, "Here is a person in whom I find joy." The words remain the same, but the music of the speech colors it to perfection.

Though each culture has its own drink -- even the icy cold water enjoyed by the Nor'krin is appreciated by visiting Janra, who recognize it as a gift given without sowing or reaping -- drinks are one of the first things that come to mind when most people hear the word 'Yedidia'.

First of all are their wines. Nearly all of the finest wines are made in their land. Red and white, and a little bit of rose and green, are stored away in caves to age for years, perhaps decades, before being opened to enjoy with friends and memories.

After the wines come cider; it is served hot and well spiced; the spicing is done in many different ways, and gives a wonderful variety to a very soothing drink to warm a cool evening.

There are fruit juices of every color of the rainbow; strawberry, pear, guava, banana, apple, peach, and fig are but the beginning of a very long and flavorful list. There is, though, one strong point of commonality: the fruit is always still attached to the plant a few minutes before it is served.

(the variety of fruit juices is fermented and aged as are grapes to make wine, but that variety of drinks is reserved for very special occasions)

They also enjoy teas and infusions; the trees and herbs provide another spectrum of tastes to sip with friends.

Roots of various plants are sometimes spiced to provide another drink.

Yedidia cuisine varies somewhat from region to region. In some places, it is based on fresh fruit, and in others, on breads, cereals, thick soups and vegetable stews; the latter is spiced, lightly salted, and often has some meat for added flavor. All forms of Yedidia cuisine begin with a small salad (either garden or fruit), have a main course of some form of the local specialties, are followed by a platter with an assortment of breads and fresh fruits, and end with a dessert of cheeses or cured fruit.

Life, to the Yedidia, is one big, long party, and, to the Yedidia, song is the symbol of celebration. They sing in the morning, and sing in the evening; they sing while working, and sing a prayer -- hands joined together -- before meals. Thought is expressed in song; the first place to look for an expression of their perspective on theology and philosophy is in the verses of their hymns. There are many cherished songs shared across the nation, but there is also much spontaneity and improvisation; their way of speaking/singing is in metered verse, and a wealth of their wisdom is embodied in the rhythm of hymns, regular and dependable as the cycles of nature. The day, the moon, the year -- these different cycles are echoed in the structure of verses.

> For the beauty of the earth, for the glory of the skies,
> For the love which from our birth over and around us
> lies: Lord of all, to Thee we raise this our hymn of
> grateful praise.
>
> For the beauty of each hour of the day and of the
> night, Hill and vale and tree and flower, sun and moon
> and stars of light: Lord of all, to Thee we raise this
> our hymn of grateful praise.
>
> For the joy of human love, brother, sister, parent,
> child, Friends on earth, and friends above; for all
> gentle thoughts and mild; Lord of all, to Thee we raise
> this our hymn of grateful praise.
>
> For Thy church, that evermore lifteth holy hands
> above, Offering up on every shore her pure sacrifice
> of love: Lord of all, to Thee we raise this our hymn of
> grateful praise.

> For Thyself, best Gift Divine! To our race so freely given; For that great, great love of Thine, peace on earth, and joy in Heaven: Lord of all, to Thee we raise this our hymn of grateful praise.

> This is my Father's world, and to my listening ears, All nature sings, and round me rings the music of the spheres. This is my Father's world: I rest me in the thought Of rocks and trees, of skies and seas; His hand the wonders wrought.

> This is my Father's world, the birds their carols raise, The morning light, the lily white, declare their Maker's praise. This is my Father's world: He shines in all that's fair; In the rustling grass I hear him pass, He speaks to me everywhere.

> This is my Father's world, O let me ne'er forget That though the wrong seems oft so strong, God is the Ruler yet. This is my Father's world: the battle is not done; Jesus who died shall be satisfied, and earth and Heaven be one.

The Yedidia are the most alive to sensation; each sense is valued, and each one provides something a little different.

Touch is pre-eminent; it is enjoyed immensely, and they consider it the most informative of senses. Touch tells them of texture and temperature, of moist and dry; by how things respond to pressure, they can feel what is present beneath the surface and what structure it forms; it tells much of emotion. When sensation yields perception, touch provides them with the greatest richness.

Smell is a sense of memories; to walk through an orchard is to remember seasons past. It no less bears a tale of what has happened; each person bears his own distinctive smell, and a place by its smell tells who has passed by. Many different things leave a mark on a placés scent, and to smell is to be told, as if in a far-off memory (indeed, like those that smell mysteriously triggers), what plants are present, what the weather is like and has been, who has passed by, what fruit was picked -- though not all of this is perceived all of the time, the fragrance of a place often tells bits and pieces.

Sight is a sense that works by light illuminating all that it shines on (and this is something from which they draw a lesson). It tells of the color, the form, and the beauty of what is around; what is moving and what is still; it tells of what is far away and can not yet be touched. It serves as a guide to what is around, as a guide by which to move and act in an unknown situation, and it bears its own beauty; all of this provides lessons about God and about faith.

The first sound in their mind, and the one they most love, is song. The song of a friend's voice, the song of a bird chirping, the song of a babbling brook, the silent song of silvery blue starlight -- all of these are listened to and enjoyed.

The taste of food tells of the time of year and of culture. Drink and food are a kind of art, and its taste tells both of the time of year and how it was prepared.

Yedidia emotions have a fluid character; they are a sensitive people who are easily moved and who show their emotions quickly. Their celebration is filled with smiles and mirth -- as is, indeed, much of life. Tears are held to be very precious -- in their language, the same word means 'tear' and 'diamond' -- and they know tears, not only of sorrow, but also of joy. Tears come to greet both memories and powerful music, and mark as both sign and symbol the most significant events in life -- farewell and death, yes, but also a loved one regained, and birth, and marriage. Memories and hopes, also, are precious. They know sorrow, but never bitterness; however deep and angst-ridden the sorrow may be, deeper and more healing is the joy. Farewell is always marked by the thought of, "I will be able to enjoy your presence again;" on many a deathbed has been spoken the words, "We will be brought back together again in the heart of the Father. It will not be long."

Yedidia worship services are filled with songs -- celebrations in which everybody participates.

The Yedidia homeland is named 'Syllii'.

Yedidia character: Sylla

Sylla is relatively short and rounded; she has dark, olive skin and soft, brown eyes. Her hair falls down to her waist, and she wears a long, flowing kelly green robe, as is traditional among Yedidia women; more often than not, a chain of flowers rests in her hair. She chooses to go barefoot, so that she can feel the grass, the moss, the earth, and the stones beneath her feet.

The only possession which she carries is a small harp; a slow strum accompanies a soft and gentle song. She also has with her a pet: a milshh: a small, eyeless animal, about two feet long, with brilliant golden fur that is long and soft, two large, pointed ears, eight short, flexible legs ending in large paws, and a shiny black nose which is always sniffing inquisitively. It is both shy and curious, and it is very warm and affectionate; it is usually very calm and sedate, but often becomes very excited when it smells someone familiar.

A quote:

> Fair is the sunlight;
> Fairer still the moonlight:
> Fairest of all, is the light of thy face.

Jec

The Jec life is filled with faith, humility, and simplicity. They live in small rural villages, where farmland -- pastures, fields, orchards and vineyards, the village commons -- outlies a few houses, some artisan's shops, and a simple church.

They are peasants very much like those chosen to be apostles, and the carpenter who chose them. Farmers, blacksmiths, cobblers -- clothed in rough, plainly colored robes, they are the sort of people one could easily overlook in the search for the spectacular. It is calloused hands and dirty fingernails that are lifted up to God in worship, and that continue to worship by placing a yoke on a pair of oxen, gathering firewood, peeling carrots and potatoes, or threshing wheat. There are many who are given great wisdom and knowledge, a faith to move mountains, or who speak in the tongues of men and angels, but they do not bear an otherworldly air or a strange electricity; they appear as men and women like any other, usually harvesting barley or carving wood.

Their thought is expressed in parables, little stories, and proverbs, the first and foremost of which are "Love Yahweh your God with all of your heart, and all of your soul, and all of your mind, and all of your might," and "Love your neighbor as yourself." There is a great sense of community and continuity, carrying the torch passed down by the saints who walked before.

They do not really travel; most are born, live, and die within a few miles of a single point. They do not look down on wayfarers who voyage far and wide to see the height of mountains and the vastness of seas, and enjoy the richness of the visible and invisible artifacts of the variety of cultures, but they pay a lot of attention to what is easy to pass by without noticing. They know their culture, their village, and its people very well.

Jec culture is a culture of the very small. They see the great in the small; in the Law of Love is seen all of virtue and right action; in a tiny shoot pushing out of the ground they see an immense oak whose branches will someday provide shade; in a simple gift, they see the love that gave it. They are fond of the words, "He who is faithful in little is also faithful in much." Piety is given expression in the tiny details of everyday life, to which careful attention is devoted. They search to love God by seeing to the needs of whoever they are with.

Gift giving occupies an important cultural position; each

gift serves as a little symbol, a little morsel, of love. The gifts are very simple -- poverty does not permit the spectacular -- but are given generously. A flower, an apple, a song, a blessing, a handshake, a prayer, a poem, a cup of cold water wood carved into a statue or a whistle, an oddly shaped pebble, a skin of wine, a walk, a story, a patterned candle -- all of these are given.

Sight, sound, touch, smell, taste -- there is nothing really special about their use of senses. They notice and enjoy little details; there is not much more to say.

The language has simple rules and few words; it is one of the easiest to learn, and bears well the load of talking about everyday matters, about personality and friendship, and about God.

When two Jec meet, one is usually coming to visit the other, and something of this notion of visit and welcome is embodied in the greeting. The visitor comes with one arm outstretched and hand open, saying, "I give you my love." The host clasps the outstretched hand, bowing slightly, and says, "And I return to you mine." These actions are accompanied by a gentle smile.

They are fairly short, with tan skin, brown eyes, and hair that is usually brown (and sometimes black or sandy blonde).

Their emotions are the emotions of being human, the common points of feeling shared across all culture. They know at least something of laughter and peace and passion and tears and awe; if there is one point that runs strong, it is a sense of tradition, community, continuity, and place; they have a sense of unique importance and a part in the great plan (two concepts which are not really separate in their thought).

Jec worship services are simple, without any real distinguishing remarks -- no bells and smells, just a week by week liturgical service presenting the Gospel message and embodying worship. The opening words of each service are, "Hear, O Israel, Yahweh your God is one. You shall love Yahweh your God with all of your heart, and with all of your soul, and with all of your mind, and with all of your might. You shall love your neighbor as yourself. Love one another."

The Jec homeland is named 'Tev'.

Shal

The language is soft, gentle, simple, and calm. It is spoken slowly, as if it were a lullaby; it has few words: simple, little words with rich and profound connotations; 'Way', 'Tao', and 'Word' are like the nouns which are used.

Even the verbs are rarely verbs which tell of action. Rather, they describe that which is; 'be', 'abide in' 'embody', 'love', 'nourish', 'support', 'is the friend of', 'know', 'receive', 'is from', 'resemble', 'live', are the essential words which a child would learn as one of our children would learn words such as 'walk', 'talk', 'eat'. Just as our language has different words -- 'walk', 'run', 'jog', 'sprint', 'mosey', 'trot', for example -- which tell of the action of moving by the us of legs, so their language has at least a few different words to tell of being, or understanding, or abiding, or loving. The way of speaking sometimes does not even need verbs; there are more adjectives than adverbs.

The genius of the language is embodied in a flowing prose which is the purest poetry; words with the simplicity of a child. It does not have abruptly ending sentences, but rather slides somewhat like Hebrew; one thought gives form to the next. It has something like the feel of the prologue to John's account of the Gospel, or his first letter; it has something like the feel of a Gregorian chant; there is nothing abrupt in their speech or music. They speak, but even more, they are silent; there is a communion.

The understanding is one which see beyond, which looks at the surface and sees into the depths. They stand dazzled by the glory of the starry vault, and worship the awesome Creator who called them into being; they look at a friend's face and see the person behind.

Their culture is a place of perfect order. It is ordered by things being placed rightly; by God worshiped by man, the spiritual ahead of the physical, being beyond doing.

It is of this that God is known in all of his majesty, that spirituality becomes rich and profound, that there is a right state of being. This brings the lesser things to flourish. Men shine as they reflect the glory of God. That which is physical is enjoyed immensely -- the warmth and softness of a friend's touch, the sweetness of a freshly picked orange, the fragrance of a garden of flowers, the sound of a bird's song, the colors of a sunset -- all of these things are received gratefully. Being, they do; they tend the garden, and create.

The order flows from resting in the Spirit and from love; there is no one who thinks of order. The truthfulness knows nothing of oaths; the order knows nothing of rules, nor even of honor and morality.

The culture is best understood, not by looking at men, but by looking at God. God gives generously, and they receive and rest in his love.

There are many people in modern society who, when waiting in an office or at a traffic light, become agitated and begin to fidget; they are hollowed out by an excess of doing. The Shal are innocent of such hurry. They act, but it is a doing which flows from being.

Food, wine, music, incense, touch, silence, storytelling, dance, drama, puppetry -- it is not often that they all get together to have a celebration (they prize greatly time spent alone with one person, and then extended families and tightly knit communities).

Shal culture does not exactly have greetings as such; their way of thought works differently.

To say 'hello' or 'goodbye' is an action of an instant, in two senses. In one sense, it lasts for an instant; no one says 'hello' twenty times or shakes hands for five minutes. In the other sense, it marks an instant, the instant where absence becomes presence or presence becomes absence.

The Shal do not really think in terms of instants; time is measured and perceived -- or, rather, not measured and not perceived -- by moments. A friend is present, and he is enjoyed, and then he is absent, and then there is solitude. In the place of a greeting, the Shal have a presence. With the Shal, you never get the feeling that you are alone and there is another person nearby who is also alone; you never get the feeling that there is a close group of friends nearby and they are inside and you are outside. If a Shal is nearby, he is present; indeed, the Shal have a very present touch.

Life, to the Shal, is full of moments. There is a meal with friends, and then there is reflection in solitude, and then there is a beautiful song, and then there is time with a friend, and then there is prayer, and then there is sleep, and then there is work tending to the trees... There is not interruption or haste; a moment lasts as long as it is appropriate for a moment to last.

Their moments of community are profound; their moments of solitude are even more profound. 'Withdrawing' is what they call it; it is a time of stillness, and an expression of a love so profound that all other loves appear to be hate. It is a time of finding a secret place, and then withdrawing -- from family, friends, and loved ones, from music and the beauty of nature, from cherished activities, from sensation -- into the heart of the Father. It is a time of -- it is hard to say what. Of being loved, and of loving. Of growing still, and becoming. Of being set in a right state, and realigned in accordance with the ultimate reality. Of purity from the Origin. Of being made who one is to be. Of communion and worship. Of imago dei filled with the light of Deus. Of being pulled out of time and knowing something of the Eternal.

This withdrawing fills them with an abundant love for other people, and gives them a renewed appreciation for nature and music; it fills them with silence, and fills their words and song.

Their perception of the world is quintessentially tactile. Sight, hearing, and smell all work at a distance; touch perceives what is immediately present. The eyes, ears, nose, and tongue are all organs of sense at one place on the body -- more sensitive in some places and less in others, to be sure -- and feels all of what is immediately present. Touch provides the physical side of the presence which is so greatly valued.

The emotional side of the culture is filled by peace, in which is embedded joy and contentment. It does not change very much or very quickly -- though it encompasses affection, or appreciation of beauty, or a special serenity, or absorption in thought.

Their appearances have the peculiar property of not seeming to be any particular age. If you look, age is not very difficult to judge, but somehow the thought doesn't come up. They have a rounded shape, soft eyes, and warm, soft skin.

Shal worship services are different from the others. They are characterized, not by the presence of words, but by the presence of a profound and penetrating silence where God is imminent. There are a few words, but they are not where the essence lies.

The Shal homeland is named 'Liss'.

Janra

The Janra, unlike any of the other cultures, have no homeland; they voyage among the other lands, where they are generally well-liked and warmly received. Their wayfaring is at once literal and symbolic: literal in the sense that they know that they are passing through this earthly country for a better one. They enjoy all of the lands that they visit -- they have an informal character, and always seem to be at home -- but they know that none of them is really home.

It must be said that they know how to move. They can walk, skip, and run, of course, but that is only the beginning. Trees, buildings, and cliffs are climbed like ladders. Come oceans, rivers, and lakes, they will happily swim. Be it lightly skipping atop a thin wall, or jumping out of a window to grab a tree branch and swing down, or running at top speed through the twisty passages of the Southern mines and caves, they make acrobatics seem another form of walking. Somehow, even flipping through a window or somersaulting under a table, they have an extraordinary knack for barely missing collisions with hard objects; the Urvanovestilli are still debating whether this is the result of skill or luck.

The dances of the Urvanovestilli have a marvelous complexity, and those of the Yedidia are known for their flowing grace, but there is still nothing like the spinning energy of the Janra. The Janra are very adaptible, pulling bits and pieces from other cultures and setting them together in vital new combinations. In some of the dances can be seen bits and pieces -- moves of strength that look like Tuz wrestling, or complexity from the Urvanovestilli -- and the result is nothing short of breathtaking.

In their adaptibility, they usually speak at least a few words of each language, and usually borrow whatever form of greeting is common in the land they are visiting. They are familiar with the household objects (often enough to use them in new ways). This, combined with a flair for practical jokes, is occasionally enough to annoy the town guards, but (more often than not) their antics leave people laughing, sometimes to the point of tears.

The Janra have a remarkable talent for not remaking God in their image. Their description of Jesus is anything but boring and respectable -- a firebrand with a phenomenal knack for offending religious leaders, in the habit of telling respectable pillars of society things such as, "The prostitutes and tax collectors are entering the Kingdom of Heaven ahead of you." -- and they are known for an honesty that can be singularly blunt. They know that he passed over scribes and lawyers to call, as disciples, a motley crew of fishermen, tax collectors, and other peasants -- one terrorist thrown in to make matters interesting. They are, however, just as cautious not to water him into only being a social reformer who had nothing to say about sexual purity.

For all of their sharpness, for all of their ability to bring forth the most embarrassing Scriptural teaching at the worst possible moment, it must also be said that the Janra have hearts of pure gold. Love and compassion are constantly in their thought and action; they are the first to share their food with a beggar, say hello to the person who is alone, or ask, "Are you hurting?" The accusations brought against them are accusations of having too many quirks, not of being unloving.

Their language is of a force that is not easily translated into writing; of course it has nouns, verbs, adjectives, adverbs, etc. and respects masculine and feminine, but intonation, speed, vocal tension, and other factors tell at least as much; they carry connotation and sentiment, express the level of clarity of understanding the speaker believes he has, and many more things. There are also a number of verbal tics, on the order of two or three dozen ('Eh?' is, however, not included, and apparently perceived to be a mark of general silliness); in a sense, they don't do anything, but in a sense, they add a very nice pepper to the speech.

Janra thought involves a kind of sideways logic, which is part of why their ways of speaking are difficult to describe. They take little bits and pieces from different places, and put them together in unexpected ways, making connections that can be very surprising. They are very good at reading between the lines, and sometimes perceive things which were not intentionally meant to be communicated. Sometimes they borrow manners of speech from other people -- conversation, structured argument, metered verse, stories, parables, and so on -- but their usual way of speaking has all sorts of sideways jumps and turns, with segues that can be rather odd, and often leaves gaps; these gaps are not a matter of sloppiness, but rather something like a joke or riddle where the hole is intentionally left to be filled in by the listener.

> "When it comes to games, never try to understand the Janra mind."
>
> -Oeildubeau, Urvanovestilli philosopher and anthropologist

It is known that Janra sports usually last for at least half an hour, involve a ball, two or more teams, running and acrobatics, and animated discussion. Beyond that, neither the Urvanovestilli's logic nor the Yedidia's intuition are able to make head or tail of them. In general, the teams appear to have unequal numbers of players; the players often switch teams in the course of play; teams are created and dissolved; the nature of the activities makes sudden and radical changes; there is no visible winning or losing. There are occasionally times in the course of play when some intelligible goal appears to be being approached... but then, all players seem to be approaching it in a rather erratic manner (when asked why he didn't do thus and such simple thing and achieve the approached goal by an inexperienced anthropologist, one of the Janra said, "Technically, that would work, but that would be a very boring way to do it," and then bolted back into play: the extent to which game play is comprehensible heightens its incomprehensibility). Late in life, Oeildubeau hinted at having suspicions that, if the Janra believe that they are being watched, they will spontaneously stop whatever sport they are playing, and instead begin a series of activities expressly designed to give any observer a headache.

Janra come in all shapes, sizes, and colors, showing bits and pieces of other races; they tend to be of moderate to tall height and a lithe build. Most are fairly light skinned (although a few are rather dark); a fair number of them have skin spotted with freckles. They have every imaginable color of hair (black, brown, blonde, grey, white, red, tweed, shaven head, etc). and eyes (brown, blue, hazel, grey, amber, purple, etc). They wear loose clothing in a variety of colors, usually quite vivid; red, purple, and green are the most common of solid colors, and patches or stripes of some pattern or the whole rainbow appear not infrequently. Therefore, Al is a pud.

Their sensation of the world is primarily visual, and in a way patterned after their thought; visualizing and visual problem solving comes very naturally to them. They see, as well as beauty, a world to interact with, and parts to rearrange and make something new. Sound and touch serve largely to complement and extend visual image; taste and smell are enjoyed, but do not play a terribly large role. The other side of the coin (to problem solving) is observing and enjoying, which is also very much a part of culture.

Their emotional life has several sides. They carry with them, in their emotions, a little bit of every place and people they visit -- the passion and control of the Urvanovestilli, the peace of the Shal, the festivities and music of the Yedidia, the respect of the Nor'krin, the enjoyment of exercise of the Tuz, the common factor of the Jec. Perhaps the most prominent side of all is laughter. Janra are immeasurably fond of banter and practical jokes, and have an uncanny knack for guessing who is ticklish. There is an element of what is carefree, spontaneous, and given to pure enjoyment of simple pleasures; there is also a large element of being immersed in sidethink, and they enjoy greatly the flash of insight when everything fits together. They are curious and enjoy discovery.

There is another side to this emotion which seems paradoxical, but fits perfectly. There is a difference between childlike and childish, and not a trace of childishness is to be found among them. They enter the Kingdom of Heaven as little children -- in particular, like one little boy who stood up before crowds of thousands and asked, "Why is the Emperor naked?" Of all the skills people learn as a part of growing up, they know perhaps least of all closing their eyes and using intelligence as a tool to make oneself stupid. They are moved by what goes unnoticed, smiling at the beauty in a single blade of grass, and weeping at the death of a beggar who, homeless, friendless, handicapped and burned, explained that he was unable to drop a knife taped to his defunct hand for self-defense, but was still shot and killed outside of the White House by men entrusted with the responsibility of protecting innocent life.

There are two things to said about Janra worship. The first is that they adapt and participate in whatever is the local manner of worship (as do traveling Urvanovestilli and other wayfarers) -- in that regard, they make no distinction between themselves and the peoples that they visit. The second -- and this does not stem from any perceived defect in the other forms of worship, but from who they are -- is that they hold their own worship services.

These services do not occur at a fixed time and place (though they occur more frequently when Janra are on the road between different locations), but at random intervals and locations, spontaneously. Anyone and everyone is welcome, and children and sometimes adults of other races are usually present.

They are a warm and informal occasions, where anyone can take the lead, and a great many activities are recognized as worship; the Janra have a particularly strong emphasis on the priesthood of the believer and the sacredness of everyday life. People sit in a big circle, and people or groups of people come to the center to present or lead as they wish.

There is no canonical list of activities that are performed at these services, but the following are common.

* Songs. The Janra sing their own songs (often improvised) or those of other peoples; those of the Yedidia are especially treasured. While singing, the people are sometimes still, sometimes swaying, sometimes clapping, and sometimes dancing with their arms.
* Prayer. One person will lead a prayer, or people will pray popcorn style, or...
* Sermons. A theologian or philosopher will preach a sermon.
* Sharing. Someone will share an insight or experience from personal life.
* Dance. The whole assembly will dance, sometimes in a long, snaking line.
* A joke is told. The Janra are fond of laughter.
* Drama. One of a few people will present a dramatic presentation, play, or skit.
* Group hug, usually in whatever is the common greeting of the land.
* Ticklefest. "Blessed are the ticklish, for the touch of a friend will fill them with laughter."
* Silence. This is treasured.

* Reading from the Scriptures.
* Reading or recitation of poetry.
* Storytelling.
* Juggling and similar activities.
* Acrobatics.
* Instrumental music.
* Non sequiturs.
* Miming.
* Mad libs.
* Impressions and impersonations of various and sundry people.
* Janra-ball. This occurs in a modified form such that members of other races, while still not understanding anything, are capable of participating. (Nobody gets a headache.)
* Eucharist. This is the most solemn and important moment, and occurs exactly once in a service -- at the end.
* None of the above. This category is especially appreciated.

Janra character: Nimbus

Nimbus is fairly short and wiry; he has light, almost white blonde hair, deep, intense blue eyes which sparkle and blaze, and a rich, laughing smile. He wears a loose, shimmering two-legged robe of midnight blue, from the folds of which he seems to be able to procure innumerable items of Urvanovestilli make (for example: goggles (waterproof), telescope, silk rope and grappling hook with spring-loaded launcher, climbing/rapelling harness and gear/self-contained, spring-loaded belay), lantern, tool kit (large blade, precision blade, compass, wire saw, corkscrew, ruler, reamer, chisel, pliers, scissors, needle, punch, protractor, file, and sharpening stone), paper pad, mechanical pencil, supply kit (string, pencil lead, chalk, flask of oil, wire, miscellaneous device components (gears, springs, shafts, etc.), cloth), meal kit, tinderbox, mechanical puzzle, mirror, whistle...).

During childhood, he spent a lot of time in the land of the Urvanovestilli, and began to take an interest in tinkering. He has very much his own way of tinkering, from an Urvanovestilli perspective; he is fond of all manner of kludges. The resulting devices have caused his Urvanovestilli mentors to conclude that he is mad (the truth of the matter being that he is not mad, but produces and modifies contraptions in such a manner as to drive any honest Urvanovestilli tinkerer mad). When the city unveiled a new fountain in the public square, he added a pyrotechnic spark; when, in a public ceremony, the mayor celebrated his wife's birthday by presenting a specially commissioned music box, the tune somehow changed from "Happy birthday to you" to "The old grey mare ain't what she used to be."

He does, however, possess a sense of what is and is not appropriate; his practical jokes never take on a mean or spiteful character, and he does possess a strong degree of contrainte. He does appreciate the variety of cultures he visits, and enjoys Urvanovestilli philosophical and theological discussions.

He is, in short, as Janra as any -- left-handed and colorful, warm and compassionate, and a heart of solid gold.

A quote: "What? You think *I* would do something like that? I'm hurt." (generally accompanied by a wide grin)

A Cord of Seven Strands

Chapter One

"Boo!" Sarah, who had been moving silently, pounced on Jaben, and wrapped her arms around him.

"Hi, Sarah. Just a second." He typed in a few more lines of code, saved his work, and ran *make*. As the computer began chugging away, Jaben reached down and pinched Sarah's knee. She jumped, and squeaked.

"Aren't you ever surprised?"

"By some things, yes. But I have a preconscious awareness of when you're trying to sneak up on me."

"Even when you're deep in concentration, programming your whatever-it-is on the computer?"

"Even when I'm deep in concentration, programming my whatever-it-is on the computer."

Sarah paused, and looked around. They were in the place where their circle of friends met -- a big, old house which an elderly couple in the church was allowing them to use. It had many niches and personal touches, nooks and crannies, and was home to a few mice, especially in the winter. (There was a general agreement not to get a cat or mousetraps, but simply to minimize the amount of food left about.) The house even had a not-so-secret secret passage, a perennial favorite of the children who came to visit. This room had deep blue, textured wallpaper, with a painting hanging on the wall: an earth tone watercolor of the sinful woman kissing Jesus's feet. There were bits and pieces of computers lying about, and a few computer books, some of which were falling apart. That room -- and the whole house -- was a place that bore someone's fingerprints, that said, "I have a story to tell."

"I was listening to the radio," Sarah said, "and the fire danger has gotten even worse. Things have gone from parched to beyond parched. It wouldn't take much to start a blaze."

"I know," Jaben said. "We can only be careful and pray."

Thaddeus drove up to the rifle range. He reached into the back seat, and pulled out a blue .22 competition rifle, a box of rounds, some nails, a small hammer, some targets... He sat down on a bench, and slowly cleaned his gun. There was a funny smell, he thought, but he did not pay it much attention.

He went over and nailed a target to a stump, then moved everything in front of him and to the left, lay prone, and slowly waited for target and sight to align, and fired. Nine points. Good, but he could do better. He reloaded, and this time went more slowly. He drew a deep breath, grew still, waited even more slowly for the sight and target to line up, and fired. Ten points, dead center. The same for the third round, and the fourth. "Good." Confident, Thaddeus fired a fifth shot, and frowned. He had only gotten seven points.

He started to go up to replace the target -- "This time if I slow down and really concentrate, I think I can get 50 points." -- and unwittingly kicked over a small plastic bottle. Then he turned around, and said to himself, "I think I'm going to try to shoot the nail." He lay down, loaded another round, and fired. Lead splattered at the top of the target face, and the target fell. He relaxed, and let his gun down.

"Boy, the sun is blistering hot today." Thaddeus blinked; the air seemed to shimmer as if it were a mirage. Then he looked around a bit. His eyes widened, and his jaw dropped.

There, in the dry grass before him, were dancing flames.

Thaddeus groaned; he immediately recognized the funny smell he'd ignored. He hadn't exactly grabbed the right fluid to clean his gun...

He threw his apple juice on the fire, which hissed and sizzled, but did not diminish much. Then he grabbed his gun and ran to his car.

As he drove away, Thaddeus heard the report as the unused rounds exploded.

Thaddeus ran through the living room, upsetting a game of Mao that was being played. He dialed 911. "There's a fire! Rifle range near this house." After a few questions, he called a phone tree and hurried those present into the cars. Sarah and Jaben joined Thad in his car -- a rusty, ten year old black Cadillac with the driver's side window broken and deep blue pictures painted on the side -- and the other four got into an equally rusty trade van, a nondescript brown with a ladder, some rope, some tools, several rolls of duct tape, some paint cans, some tents, inside. They locked up, and began to bounce up and down some primitive roads.

As they passed, the spreading wall of fire loomed ahead of them.

"What do we do now?" Sarah said.

"Floor it!" Thad said.

Jaben did. He jounced through the straight stretch of road by the rifle range, where everything on the ground was glowing ashes; the heat, coming through the broken window, was incredible, and singed Jaben's hair. "We're coming through the other side of the fire!" They did, and flew out. Behind them, they could see a falling sapling land on the van. A quarter of a second earlier, and it would have shattered their windshield.

Jaben breathed a little easier as cool air blew in through the window. "Woo-hoo!" shouted Thaddeus. They slowed down, and drove.

Chapter Two

They continued several miles, and then Jaben pulled into a gas station, low on fuel. As he fueled up, Amos stepped out of the van and walked over.

"What do we do now?"

"Well, I think we're far enough away, and we're near Frank's Inn. It might be nice to sit and collect our thoughts there."

"Jaben, I like a good drink as much as you do--"

"--Miller Genuine Draft does *not* constitute a good drink--"

"--but do you really want the smell of a smoky tavern?"

"That's actually why I thought of Frank's. The new proprietor is allergic to cigarette smoke, and thought it would be nice to have one place in this county where people can have a good drink with their friends without having to breathe that stuff. I like the atmosphere there. People predicted that it would die out, but it's flourished."

"Frank's it is."

There was a moment's silence, as Jaben waited for the tank to fill up. He started to turn away to put the pump up, and Amos said, "You look like you have something to say."

"I know, but I can't think of what." He put the pump up. "It's one of those annoying times when you can't put your finger on what you want to say. I'll think of it later, as soon as you're not accessible."

Amos laughed a deep laugh.

Jaben walked in, paid, and drove to Frank's Inn.

As they walked in the door, Désirée breathed a sigh of relief. A large "Out of order" sign was on the television. There was some rock music playing, but even with the music the din was not too bad. They sat down around a table, and Jaben waved to the bartender.

A bartender walked over, and said, "Hi, my name's John. Will you be wanting something to eat?"

"Please," seven voices said in unison.

"I'll be back with menus in just a second. What can I get

you to drink?"

"I'll have a cherry Coke," Thaddeus said.

"Sprite," Sarah said.

"A pint of Guinness," said Jaben, and winked at the bartender.

"MGD Lite," said Amos.

"I'm sorry," the bartender said, "We don't carry Miller. Can I get you something else?"

"Just give me the closest thing you have to a Miller."

"Ok."

"Strawberry daquiri," said Désirée.

"I'll have a glass of the house white," said Lilianne.

"A strawberry kir," said Ellamae.

"Oh, come, Belladonna, are you sure you wouldn't rather have a strawberry shake? It looks much more you," said Jaben.

Ellamae, who had somehow grown to womanhood without losing the beautiful visage of a little child, gave him a look you could have poured on a waffle.

"Could I see some ID, please?"

Ellamae, doing her best to keep a straight face, fished in her purse and procured a driver's license.

The bartender looked hard at the license, then at her, and said, "Thank you," returning the license, and walked off.

"Too bad he left," said Jaben. "He seemed to raise his eyebrows at hearing that name."

"Who asked you?" said Ellamae, trying to look cross while suppressing a laugh.

"Jaben, would you tell us--" said Amos.

"Shut up," laughed Ellamae.

Jaben continued. "Belladonna, n. In Italian, a beautiful lady. In English, a deadly poison. A striking example of the essential identity of the two tongues."

Ellamae, laughing, said, "Die, Jaben, die!"

Some more people walked in the door, and the bartender came back, set seven menus on the table, and began to distribute drinks. "A strawberry daquiri for you, a glass of the house white for you, a strawberry kir for you, a cherry Coke, a Sprite, a pint of Guinness, and -- aah, yes, the closest thing we have to a Miller." He set down a pint of ice-cold water.

Amos looked at his drink a second, and then burst into a deep laugh, shaking his head.

"Jaben, if you ever..." his voice trailed off.

The menus were passed around, and after a little discussion they decided to eat family style. They ordered a meat lover's pizza, a salad, and some French onion soup.

As the circle of friends sat and waited for the food, the song on the radio ended, and a news report came on. "The forest fire that we have all been worrying about is now burning. Starting somewhere near the campgrounds, it has been the subject of an evacuation effort. The rangers had a helicopter with a scoop at the lake for training exercises, and so the blaze should be put out speedily. Authorities are currently investigating the cause of the fire. Details coming up."

Thad sunk into his chair.

Lilianne caught his eyes. After looking for a second, she said, "Want to talk about it?"

"Not here."

"Want to take a walk outside, after dinner?"

Thaddeus nodded.

He really needs to talk -- thought Jaben -- but he's not in any hurry. Living in Malaysia for a couple of years has that effect. It changes your sense of time. It changes a lot of things.

Jaben longed to be back in France, longed for the wines, longed for the architecture, longed for the sophistication and the philosophical dinner discussions, longed for the language most of all.

"*Tu as amis içi*," Lilianne said in broken French. "You still have friends here."

Yes -- Jaben mused -- that was true. The friendships in this circle of friends are more friendships in French (or Malaysian) fashion than in the American sense, which is really closer to acquaintanceship than friendship. Here are friendships to grow deeper in, to last for lifetime instead of for a couple of years until someone moves. Here are kything friendships. That is something. And my friends know what is close to my heart, and give me things that mean a lot to me. Désirée, Lilianne, Ellamae, and Sarah each give me kisses when they see me, and Lilianne is taking the time to learn a little French. She doesn't believe me when I tell her, but she has the gift of languages. *J'ai encore des amis içi.* And God is the same God in France and America; from him come the best of both. Perhaps it would be fitting to give him thanks now.

Jaben brought his hands up to the table. "Shall we pray?"

The others joined hands. Amos said, "Lord, you are faithful, as you were faithful to Israel."

Désirée said, "Lord, you are vast enough to care for our smallest details."

Lilianne said, "Lord, you have the imagination to create all the wonders about us."

Ellamae said, "You are he who searches hearts and minds, and perceives our thoughts."

Thaddeus said, "You are the fount of all wisdom."

Sarah said, "You are the Artist."

Jaben said, "You are the worthy recipient of all our worship."

Then Amos said, "Lord, I confess to you that I have harbored wrath against my white brothers and sisters, and seen them first through the label of 'racist'."

There was a silence. Not a silence at Amos confessing a sin -- that was appropriate at that point of this form of prayer -- nor that he would be guilty of that particular sin. It was rather that he had the courage to admit it, even to himself. Ellamae was reminded of a time she had spoken with a Canadian and, after a long discussion, watched him finally admit that he was anti-American. Jaben squeezed Amos's hand, and said, "I love you, brother."

Finally Désirée said, "Lord, I have coveted the time of others."

Lilianne said, "Lord, I have been vain, and not always relied on your help."

Ellamae said, "Lord, I have held pride in my heart."

Thaddeus said, "Lord, I have ignored the prompting of your Spirit."

Sarah said, "I have been quick in temper, and impatient."

Jaben said, "I have also been proud, and been unwilling to embrace America as I have embraced France."

Amos said, "Thank you for the many friends and family" -- here he squeezed Désirée's hand -- " that I have."

Désirée said, "Thank you for the butterfly I saw today."

Lilianne said, "Thank you for washing us clean from sin."

Ellamae said, "Thank you for drawing us into the great Dance."

Thaddeus said, "Thank you for the helicopter."

Sarah said, "Thank you for letting me paint."

Jaben said, "Thank you for my time in France."

Amos said, "Please allow the fire to be extinguished quickly, and not to do damage to our meeting place."

Désirée said, "Please help me to know the hearts of my friends better."

Lilianne said, "Please draw my heart -- all our hearts -- ever closer to you."

Ellamae said, "Please bless my music."

Thaddeus said, "Hold me in your heart, and keep my steps safe."

Sarah said, "Bless my touch."

Jaben said, "Bless my wonderful friends."

There was a moment of silence, and then they raised their voices.

Praise God from whom all blessings flow.
Praise him all creatures here below.
Praise him above, ye heav'nly host.
Praise Father, Son, and Holy Ghost.
Amen.

The place grew a little more silent as their harmony filled the room. The stillness was finally broken by Amos saying, "I'm ready for some good food."

Sarah heard some noise behind her, and turned and looked -- there was a waiter bringing the food. As it was set on the table, she waited, and Thaddeus scooped some of the soup into her bowl. She took a sip, and said, "This is certainly turning out to be an interesting day."

Jaben reached his arm over her shoulders and gave her a squeeze. "I don't know if I'm going to sleep like a rock tonight, or not be able to sleep at all."

Ellamae said, "Whenever you say that, you sleep like a rock."

Jaben mumbled, "I suppose."

Lilianne took a hearty scoop of salad. "What were we talking about earlier?"

Ellamae said, "Moral theology. Good and evil. Except that I don't think Jaben really wanted to talk about good and evil. I think he wanted to talk about something different."

"But he still wanted to talk about moral theology, like the rest of us," Désirée said.

"How was that again?" said Amos.

Jaben said, "One way to put it would be like this: if goodness is likened to health, and evil to disease and death, then most of the discipline of moral theology may be likened to a debate about the boundary that separates health from disease, life from death. That is certainly a legitimate area of study, but I think it is overemphasized. I would like to see a moral theology that is concerned with the nature of life itself, abundant life. I would like a moral theology that studies people as they dance rather than debate over the boundary line between a dying man and a fresh corpse."

"Aah, yes," Amos said.

Thaddeus said, "Western culture has a very disease-centered view of medicine. The point of medicine is to keep a person out of disease."

"What else would medicine be about?" said Sarah.

"Instead of trying to keep a person out of disease, keeping a person in health. We have some elements of this concept. Preventative medicine kind of makes this step, and gradeschool schedules have physical education. It is picked up by," Thaddeus shrunk back into his chair slightly, and mumbled the words, "New Age--"

He turned to Jaben, waiting for a wisecrack. When none came, he cleared his throat and said, "New Age is half-baked and goofy, and if you talk with a New Ager about medicine, you'll get some garbled version of an Eastern religion's balancing energies or whatnot, but at the heart of that goofiness lies a real idea of cultivating health, a health that is a positive concept rather than a negative concept. That is worth paying attention to."

Désirée said, "That's deep."

Thaddeus paused a second, chasing after a thought. The others read the expression on his face, and patiently waited. Ellamae took a piece of pizza.

"In China, people do -- or at least did -- pay doctors, not when they got sick, but when they were well. If you think about it, that difference in custom reflects a profound difference in conceptions of medicine."

Lilianne turned to Amos. "Amos, can you think of a difference in black custom that reflects your ways of thinking?"

Amos paused, looked like he was about to speak, and said, "Could I have a minute to think about that?"

Lilianne nodded.

Sarah said, "Today I had the idea for the coolest painting, and I started sketching it. It's in my studio -- a big watercolor, with all of the colors of the rainbow swirling together. The real essence of the picture, though, will take a lot of looking to see. In the boundaries between color and color lie the outlines of figures -- horses, unicorns, men fighting with swords, radiant angels."

Jaben said, "Interesting. Where did you get the idea to do that?"

Sarah said, "I don't know where I get my ideas from. I like

color, moreso than shape even. I like Impressionist paintings. I guess I was just daydreaming, watching the colors swirl, and I had this idea." She smiled.

Thaddeus smiled, waited a moment, and then poked her in the side. Sarah squeaked loudly.

Jaben said, "Blessed are the ticklish--" and stopped, as Sarah's hands were covering his mouth.

"For the touch of a friend shall fill them with laughter," Amos said through a mouthful of pizza." Thaddeus poked Sarah again. She moved her hands to cover her side and her knee.

Jaben poked her in the other side. In her laughter, she began to turn slightly red.

"Ok, I thought of an answer to your question," Amos said to Lilianne. "Our family structures are different. Where you usually have a nuclear family living together and nobody else, we will often have not just a nuclear family but cousins, aunts, great-aunts, uncles... The extended family lives together, tightly knit. The difference has to do with how white culture is about individualism, and black culture is about community, in a sense. Three of the seven principles of Kwaanza -- Unity, Collective Work and Responsibility, and Cooperative Economics -- are explicitly community oriented, and all seven of them say 'we' and 'our' instead of 'I' and 'my'. We have all sorts of stories, but you'll have to look pretty hard to find a black Western."

"Was it hard way back when," Ellamae said, "hanging out with a group of otherwise white friends? Is it hard now?"

Amos said, "I'm not sure if you noticed then, but I didn't say 'Hi' to you when you walked by when I was with a group of black friends. It's just one of those things a black man doesn't do. It would be a lot harder if I didn't have some black friends and my family to be around. There are still some people who think I'm trying to act white by hanging around with you."

"And when you liked Country and Western," Désirée said.

"We all have our problems," muttered Thaddeus.

"And when I liked Country and Western, yeah. People say that if you don't like rap, you ain't black. Well, I like rap, but liking Country and Western is even worse in some folks' eyes than not liking rap."

Lilianne frowned. "Nobody thinks that a white man who listens to rap is trying to act black. I suppose that if I made heroic exertions to be like a member of some other race, people might think I was weird, but I can't imagine having to cut back on some part of being myself for fear of someone thinking I was trying to act Chinese."

Désirée nodded. "You got it, honey. It's hard for us."

Lilianne squeezed her hand.

Jaben turned to Amos and said, "There's something I've been meaning to ask you. Why did your parents name you 'Amos'? What with Amos and Andy and all, it seems a rather cruel name to give a little black boy."

Amos said, "I did get teased, and I ran home crying a couple of times. I asked them why. They explained to me what the name means -- 'strong', 'bearer of burdens', that it was the name of a prophet. Then, when I was older, they explained to me something else." Here his voice rose. "My parents were determined that Amos and Andy should *not* have the last word about what it means for a black man to be named Amos."

Ellamae nodded. "Your parents named you well. They are strong people. So are you."

"Thank you," Amos said.

"Who are Amos and Andy?" Sarah asked.

"Amos and Andy were a couple of black comedians who acted the perfect stereotype of black men before their audiences."

"Ok," Sarah said. "Kind of like Eddie Murphy?"

Désirée giggled.

"Uh..." Amos's voice trailed off. After a second, he said, "Jaben, help me out here."

"Eddie Murphy's humor is coarse, vulgar, and entirely without class. That stated, he invites his audience to laugh *with* him, and there is a glow of camaraderie about even *Raw*. Amos and Andy invited their audiences to laugh *at* them, to laugh at the stupid blacks. Eddie Murphy is the sort of comedian who would strengthen a racist impression of blacks, but the whole point of Amos and Andy is to pander to racism."

By this time, the food was mostly finished, and the bartender had brought the bill. They fished in their wallets for cash, paid the bill, bagged the remaining food (none of the pizza or soup was left, but there was still some salad), and got up and walked out. Ellamae caught Thad's eyes, and the two of them walked off.

Thad and Lilianne stepped out into the privacy of the street. A car passed by; it was twilight, hot but not humid.

"Riflery is one of the times I can most grow still," he said. "I never touched a gun in Malaysia -- was never interested in one, for that matter -- and the concentration of riflery is different from the laid-back attitude Malaysians hold. All the same, the slowing down of riflery is a special treat, the one thing you don't have to fight against hurry to do at its own, unhurried pace."

Lilianne walked in silence.

"I must have grabbed the wrong bottle. I remember something smelling funny. I ignored that funny smell, all through cleaning my gun, and with it ignored a gut feeling. I didn't want to know where that gut feeling led; I wanted to clean my gun, and then I wanted to shoot. I fired five rounds -- forty-six points -- and then shot the nail off the target. And when I looked, a fire had started."

Lilianne said, "You feel awfully guilty."

"Shouldn't I feel guilty? After starting a forest fire?"

"If I had done something like that, would you love me any less?"

They walked in silence past a couple on the street.

Lilianne wanted to speak, but knew the futility of winning an argument. "Amos loves you. Désirée loves you. Ellamae loves you. Jaben loves you. Sarah loves you. I love you."

The two walked on in silence, turned a corner.

"I'm also scared," Thaddeus said. "Will I get in trouble? Will I go to jail?"

"You are in God's hands," Lilianne said.

"I know, but it doesn't make me feel any better," Thad said.

Lilianne stopped walking, turned, and gave him a long, slow hug. "You are in God's hands," she said.

"Thanks, I needed that."

They turned, and walked back in silence. For Thad, it was a silence that was wounded, but also a healing silence, the silence of healing washing over a wound. For Lilianne, it was a praying silence, a listening silence, a present silence. They walked slowly, but the time passed quickly, and they were soon back at the cars, and met the others.

Chapter Three

Désirée stepped away from the tents and walked down the trail. It had been an exciting day, and she needed some time to quiet down.

She moved down the trail noiselessly. Up above was a starlit sky with a crescent moon, and around her were tall, dark pines. Below was a thick carpet of rusty pine needles. As she walked along, her heart grew still.

Thoughts moved through her mind, in images, sensations, and moments more than in words. She smiled as she recalled Sarah asking, "Kind of like Eddie Murphy?" She also cherished the expression on her husband's face, the look he had when a question arose, and he knew the answer perfectly, but didn't know where to begin to explaining. That look on his face bore the same beauty as it often did when she teased him.

She saw a glint out of the corner of her eye, and looked. For a second, Désirée couldn't make out what it was, and then she recognized it as a monarch butterfly, illuminated by a single shaft of moonlight. Désirée prayed, and slowly reached out her hand; the butterfly came to her finger, rested for just a second, and then flew off into the night.

Désirée sat down on a rock in silence. She heard the footfall of a small animal -- a rabbit, perhaps. The sounds of insects rang faintly about her; she slapped a mosquito. To her, it was music,

music and a kind of dance. She drank it in, praying as she breathed. Standing up, she walked further along the path, as it passed by the lapping shore of a lake. An abandoned canoe lay along the shore.

O-oh God,

she sang.

O-oh God,
Build up your house.
O-oh God,
Build up your house.
Your Kingdom in Heaven,
Your Kingdom on earth.

O-oh God,
O-o-o-o-oh.

A-a-a-a-men.

Stopping in the stillness, she heard a twig snap behind her, a heavier footfall than that of a small animal. Quickly but yet unhurriedly, she melted into the blackness. She looked out, and saw Lilianne's silhouette against the moonlit ripples dancing on the water.

"Désirée?"

Désirée stepped out of the shadows. "How are you, sister?"

"I wanted to talk."

"Something troubling you?"

"No, I just wanted to talk."

"Need to talk, or just be quiet together?"

They walked along the shore together. The path on the shore widened into a clearing filled with tall grass. Désirée took Lilianne's hand, and they spun around, dancing under the starlight.

After a time, they sat down, and Désirée said, "You know, I just realized something."

"What?"

"In parts of Africa, one of the biggest compliments paid for dancing is, 'You dance as if you have no bones.' Dancing is one of the things that couldn't be completely taken away in slavery, and... white folk in general would do better to learn to dance. I mean, really dance. There are so many good things about it, and the people who would benefit the most are the last people you'd find dancing. But what I realized is this, maybe something I saw but didn't believe: you dance as if you have bones, but your dance is no less beautiful for it. It is graceful, and has a different spirit."

Lilianne's blush was concealed by the moonlight and starlight.

"Ever sit and cloudwatch?" Désirée said.

"It's been a while," Lilianne said.

"What about with stars?"

Lilianne shook her head, her fair skin looking almost radiant in the moonlight.

Désirée and Lilianne lay down on their backs next to each other, looking up into the sky.

Lilianne said, "All I see are isolated stars. It's not like clouds, where there are clusters."

"Hush," Désirée said. "Look."

"That bright cluster over there looks like a blob, except a sparse and prickly blob."

"Just relax. Don't rush it."

Lilianne lay on her back. The stars just looked like stars. Then she saw how much brighter some were than others. Her mind began to enter a trance, and she almost thought she heard faint, crystalline singing. Then--

"There!" she pointed to the crescent moon. "There, a Phoenecian trading ship, laden with goods, with the moon as its sail."

Désirée blinked, and said, "That's it. The biggest jewel in the sky. I hadn't thought to look for a picture that would include the moon."

Lilianne sat for a few minutes, breathing in and out, and

said, "Let's not look for any more patterns tonight." Thoughts moved in her mind about moderation and enjoyment and "A person who is full doesn't ask for more." She didn't want to see any other patterns. She was content looking on that one.

They lay in stillness for -- how long? Neither one of them took any notice of time.

"When you were a little girl," Désirée said, "what did you most like to do?"

Lilianne paused, pondered the question for a few moments, and then said, "I liked to read, or have stories read to me, and imagine -- imagine being long ago, and far away. Maybe it would be imagine. I still daydream a lot."

"I'm not sure why I had such difficulty with the stars tonight -- or did I?" she continued. "My daydreaming is somewhere faroff, and seeing things in clouds at least requires that you be right there. Somehow I was able to look at the ship, though my mind wandered. Am I making sense?" She saw the two of them, as little girls, laughing and running, hand in hand, through a field in the summer's sun.

"Perfect sense, dear. Don't worry about making sense when you're telling the truth, my mother always says."

"What about you, Désirée? What did you like to do as a little girl?"

"Ask questions of the grown-ups, and listen. I would ask questions most of all of my elder relatives. I can still remember asking a question of my grandfather, in his old, careworn rocking chair, and listening to all the stories he'd tell. He'd sit there with his corncob pipe, smelling of smoke and the sweat of hard labor, and speak in this deep, deep bullfrog voice. Listening to him always made me feel like I was curled up in his arms and falling asleep. I liked the new stories he told, but the old ones best of all."

"What were some of the stories he told you?"

"Let me see... there's one... wait, I shouldn't tell you that one."

"Why not? You can tell me anything, Désirée."

"Um... You won't get mad at me if you don't like it?"

"Désirée, you know me."

"Ok. Once there was an unusually kind master, Jim, who would talk with his slaves, especially a witty one named Ike. He would tell him his dreams, except, well, they were made more to impress than dreams. And Ike would tell good dreams, too, but they weren't usually quite as good as Jim's.

"One morning, Jim said, 'I had this dream, that I went to Negro Heaven. In there, everything was broken; the houses had holes in the walls and broken windows, and there was refuse in the streets, and the place was full of dirty Negroes.'

"Then Ike said, 'Wow, master, I had the same dream as you. I dreamed that I went to White Heaven. There, everything was silver and gold; there were great, spotless marble mansion, and the streets sparkled. But there wasn't a soul in the place!'"

Lilianne laughed. "That's very funny. It reminds me of Jewish humor."

Désirée said, "I don't know much Jewish humor."

Lilianne said, "Too bad. I'll tell you a couple of their jokes if I can remember them. Jaben commented that Jewish humor is subtle, clever, and extremely funny." She cleared her throat, and said, "Tell me another story."

"Grandpa was always telling stories about the animals, stories that he learned sitting on his grandfather's knee. Let me see... Aah.

"Brer rabbit saw Sis Cow with an udder full of milk, and it was a hot day, and he hadn't had anything to drink for a long time. He knew it was useless to ask her for milk, because last year she refused him once, and when his wife was sick, at that.

"Brer Rabbit started to think very hard. Sis Cow was grazing under a persimmon tree, and the persimmons were turned yellow, but they weren't ripe enough to fall down yet.

"So Brer Rabbit said, 'Good morning, Sis Cow.'

"'Good morning, Brer Rabbit.'

"'How're you feeling this morning, Sis Cow?'

"'I ain't doing so well, Brer Rabbit.'

"Brer Rabbit expressed his sympathy and then he said, 'Sis

Cow, would you do me the favor of hitting this persimmon tree with your head and shake down a few persimmons?'

"Sis Cow said 'Sure' and hit the tree, but no persimmons came down. They weren't ripe enough yet.

"So then Sis Cow got mad, and went to the top of the hill, and she lifted her tail over her back and came running. She hit the tree so hard that her horns lodged in the wood.

"'Brer rabbit,' said Sis Cow, 'I implore you to help me get loose.' But Brer Rabbit said, 'No, Sis Cow, I can't get you loose. I'm a very weak man, Sis Cow. But I can assuage your bag, Sis Cow, and I'm going to do it for you.

"Then Brer Rabbit went home for his wife and children, and they went back to the persimmon tree and milked Sis Cow and had a big feast."

Désirée had been speaking with animation, and Lilianne said nothing for a while. Désirée broke the silence. "You don't like it?"

Lilianne paused, and said, "No, and I'm not sure why. Hmm... I've heard a few more of those stories, but I can't remember any off the top of my head. I have this impression of Brer Rabbit as the hero, a hero who is characterized by being--" here she paused, "'intelligent' is not exactly the right word, and 'clever' comes closer but isn't quite what I mean. 'Cunning'. Brer Rabbit manipulates and uses the cow, and it is cast in a good light. The cow is mean, so it's OK to do anything to her. Same logic as 'Take ten!'" Then she hastily added, "Same logic as a lot of things in white culture as well. Same logic as *Home Alone* -- the burglars are Bad Guys, therefore it's OK for Kevin to torture them."

She looked at Désirée, forgetting that the faint light would not permit her to read Désirée's expression. She paused, prayed a moment, and said, "Did you like that story?"

"My favorite."

Lilianne shuddered. "It's a terrible thing to bruise a childhood dream. I'm sorry."

They lay in silence for a minute.

Désirée said, "I was hurt, but I'm not sure you did anything wrong. When you're a child, you like things simply because they are, and because they're yours; everything lies under a cloak of wonder. Those stories were time with my grandpa, and they taught me that there is justice and injustice; they taught me that it is good to use my mind; they taught me that there is a time to trust and a time to be wary. Have you seen those *I Learned it All in Kindergarden* posters?"

"Yes."

"I learned it all from Brer Rabbit. I see the problem you point out, but those stories will always be to me the starting-place of wisdom, and a point where I can remember my grandfather's love."

Lilianne lay in silence, pondering what Désirée said. Then she slowly reached through the grass, fumbled, squeezed Désirée's hand, and said, "You ready to go back now?"

Désirée wiped a tear away. "Yes."

"Let's go."

Chapter Four

Jaben asked, "Could I have the canteen?" As Sarah handed it to him, he took a swig of stale water, and rubbed his eyes. The harsh sun blazed in his eyes. "Why don't we do Bible study now, and then worry about what else to do today? I'm sure we'll be able to find something," he said, then muttered under his breath, "though I'd much rather be programming," and continued, "and, with something to eat, we'll have the day before us."

The others yawned their assent, and went back to the tents to get their Bibles.

"Whose turn was it to read? Lilianne's?" said Sarah.

Lilianne said, "No, I think it was Amos's."

Amos said, "Yeah, that's it." He paused a moment, and said, "Shall we pray?"

They joined hands, and bowed their heads in prayer. Jaben squeezed Lilianne's hand.

Lilianne prayed, "Father, we come before you a little

excited, a little nervous. We don't know what the course of the fire will be, or how long it will burn, or why this is happening. We ask that you preserve our meeting place and the property around it, and most of all human life. We thank you that we were able to escape the fire, and we meet to give you glory. Amen."

They were sitting in a circle, on some logs, around a fire pit. Amos said, "I'll be reading from I Kings 18, verses 41-46. Elijah has been chastising king Ahab, there is a drought, and Elijah has at the end of chapter 17 been staying with the widow. Earlier in the chapter, he has his famous contest with the prophets of Baal, where he called fire from Heaven down on the bull." He cleared his throat.

"And Elijah said unto Ahab, 'Get thee up, eat and drink; for there is a sound of abundance of rain.' So Ahab went up to eat and to drink. And Elijah went up to the top of Carmel; and he cast himself down upon the earth, and put his face between his knees, and said to his servant, Go up now, look toward the sea. And he went up, and looked, and said, 'There is nothing.' And he said, 'Go again,' seven times.

"And it came to pass at the seventh time, that he said, 'Behold, there ariseth a little cloud out of the sea, like a man's hand.' And he said, 'Go up, say unto Ahab, "Prepare thy chariot, and get thee down, that the rain stop thee not."'

"And it came to pass in the mean while, that the heaven was black with clouds and wind, and there was a great rain. And Ahab rode, and went to Jezreel.

"And the hand of the LORD was on Elijah; and he girded up his loins, and ran before Ahab to the entrance of Jezreel."

Amos had been bending over the Bible, looking intently; now, he rested and sat up.

Jaben said, "Thoughts? Observations?"

Désirée said, "This story is one of my favorites, with the one before it. I like the Elijah stories."

A minute passed, in which they looked at each other. "Lilianne?" Jaben said.

Lilianne stared off in space.

"Lilianne?" he said a bit louder.

"Huh? Oh, I was having a daydream about three mermaids swimming in a moonlit pool, and chasing the fish around, and petting them..." She paused in thought a moment and said, "I think I got into that daydream by thinking about the water in the story."

"Sarah?"

"It's a good story."

Amos said, "What about you, Jaben? You've got to have something to say."

Jaben said, "I always have something to say when I've had my morning bowl of coffee. Ugh, not even an espresso machine. Let me get back to you."

Ellamae said, "Why don't we get some more sleep, then go into town and get something to eat, maybe some coffee, and then maybe, maybe, try this again."

The others nodded their groggy assent and padded off back to the three tents: one for the unmarried men, one for the unmarried women, and one for the married couple.

Jaben woke up, feeling delightfully refreshed. He felt sweaty, and the air was oppressively hot. The air felt slightly humid to him. He sat up, and looked around. Thaddeus was still sleeping, breathing deep breaths. Jaben slid out of his sleeping bag and stepped out of the tent.

The sun was high in the sky, and the sky was clear. He walked around on the pine needles, and lazily yawned. He walked over to a log, sat on a low part, and began to think.

That was a magnificent passage of Scripture, he thought, and the climax to a larger story. I've always taken away from it something about the wind of the Spirit. In a land dessicated by drought, the servant is told again and again to go back to look for signs of rain, going back even though he has seen nothing. On the seventh time, the servant sees a cloud the size of a man's hand. And then, "Gird up your loins and run, lest the rain overtake you!" That's how the wind of the Spirit blows -- nothing for the longest time, and then a faint, imperceptible breeze, and then a storm.

His knee felt funny, as if there were pressure inside.

Now feels like the eye of the storm. Before was the fire, and now a moment of calm, and then there will be cleaning up. But this is a different kind of storm. Or is it?

He felt a soft arm over his shoulders, and turned and looked. Sarah kissed his cheek, and sat next to him.

"Hi, Sarah," Jaben said, and gave her a hug and a kiss. "Are any of the other women up?"

"Yes, we've been up for about an hour. Talking."

"'Bout what?"

"Nothing."

"What kind of nothing?"

"Silly stuff. Girl stuff. You wouldn't be interested."

Jaben reached behind her, and touched the back of her neck very, very lightly with the tip of his finger. She curled up.

Jaben looked at Sarah, as she sat back and relaxed. She had straight red hair cascading over her shoulders, and a round, freckled, face, with fair skin and a ribbon of deep red lips. Her body was -- 'fat' would be the wrong word; 'plump', perhaps, or 'rounded'. *Gironde*. She was attractive. He looked at her, and felt glad that there are some women who do not feel the need to be twenty pounds underweight. Jaben smiled. Sarah plays the perfect ditz, he thought, and getting her into a deep conversation is usually impossible, but there's more to her than meets the eye.

"Did you go and see the lake?" Sarah said. "It's still, still, and every now and then a fish breaks the surface, and then ripples spread."

"I just got up. I paced around, and sat down, and thought. Then you came."

"Whatch'ya think about?"

"The Bible passage. I was thinking through. I feel that there's another thought coalescing, coming together, but I can't put my finger on it."

A faint rumbling came from faroff.

Sarah looked thoughtful for a moment, and said, "Think it'll rain?"

"I don't think so. It could, but... Looking for a prediction of the day's events in the Bible has the same aura as using it as a tool for divination. The fact that we read that passage today just means that this particular passage is what came up on the schedule."

"So you don't believe the Bible applies to our lives?"

"I do, it's just -- not that way. I wouldn't have been thinking about it if I didn't believe it applied."

The land around them darkened, and they looked up. A cloud was between them and the sun.

"Hi, guys. May I join the conversation?" Lilianne was behind them.

Jaben's hand shot out, and poked Sarah in the side.

"Eep!" Sarah jumped.

Sarah's face turned slightly red, and she turned to face Jaben. "Do you never tire of tickling me?"

Jaben grinned, and winked. "Never."

"Oh, well." Sarah said, in mock resignation. "I suppose it can't be helped." She looked at Lilianne. "Do you think it's time to wake everyone up?"

"Yes, let's go."

A few minutes later, they were all out sitting on the logs. Ellamae said, "I think we've all had some rest now; food wouldn't hurt, but it's nice to be here, and we should be able to pick up that Bible study. What do you think?" Désirée said, "Um..."

"Yes, Désirée?"

"Well," she said.

There was a rumble of rolling thunder.

"Never mind. Let's go on with the Bible study."

Amos opened the Bible. "I liked the part where Elijah said--"

Splat! A fat raindrop splattered across the page.

Amos's jaw dropped. He wiped the page off, closed the Bible, and looked up.

Another raindrop hit him in the eye.

Soon rain was falling all around them -- sprinkles at first, then rain in earnest, then torrents. It was a warm, wet, heavy rain, with the sky dark as midnight, and the scene suddenly illuminated by flashes of stark, blue lightning. The wind blew about them; trees swayed rhythmically back and forth in the rain. Everything about them was filled with dark, rich, full colors, and was covered with the lifegiving waters.

The seven friends joined hands and danced in the rain.

Chapter Five

"Well, look what the cat dragged in today!" said the waitress. The friends had burst in the door, laughing, and soaked to the skin. "I wish I had some towels to give you."

"That won't be necessary," Jaben said, looking around the diner. It was a small, cheery place, with a friendly noise about it. "Seven, nonsmoking."

The waitress counted out seven menus, and said, "Walk this way, please."

Sarah said, "Did you see the look on those people's faces when we walked in?"

Thaddeus said, "Yep."

They sat down around the table, and began to look through the menus. But not for long.

"Hey, Désirée. Tell us that joke you told me," said Lilianne.

"Ok," Désirée said. "There was once an unusually liberal and generous slave owner named Jim, who had a witty slave named Ike. Each morning they would tell each other their dreams (or so they said), and the one with the better dream won. Usually it was the master, Jim.

"One morning, Jim said, 'I dreamed that I went to Negro Heaven, and in there everything was broken and dirty. The houses had holes in the walls, the windows were broken, and there was mud in the streets, and there were dirty Negroes all over the place.'

"Ike said, 'Wow, master. We must have dreamed the same thing. I dreamed I went to White Heaven, and everything was spotless and immaculate -- gold and ivory -- and there were mansions and silver streets, but there wasn't a soul in the place!'"

Lilianne said, "I remembered the joke I mentioned to you last night, Désirée, but couldn't remember. There was a Jew named Jacob, who was financially in a bad way. He went to the synagogue, and prayed, 'God, my bank account is low, and business is bad. Please let me win the lottery.'

"Some time passed, and he didn't win the lottery. He ran out of money, and was in danger of being evicted. So Jacob went to the synagogue and prayed more fervently, 'God, I've worked for you so hard, and I ask for so little. Please let me, just this once, win the lottery.'

"More time passed, and Jacob lost his house, his car. His family was out on the street. He came to the synagogue, and prayed, 'Why, God, why? Why won't you let me win the lottery?'

"The voice of God boomed forth, and said, 'Jacob! Meet me half-way on this one. *Buy a stupid ticket!*'"

There was silence, and then one laugh, and then another. The waitress came back, and asked, "Are you ready to order yet?"

"Um, uh, order. We were telling jokes. Could you give us a few more minutes?" asked Thaddeus.

"Certainly," the waitress said, walking off.

This time, they made use of their menus, and thought of what to eat. The waitress came at the end, and they ordered -- a few sandwiches, some soups, some fish...

"What do you call someone who speaks three languages?" asked Jaben.

"Uh, trilingual?" said Désirée.

"Good. What do you call someone who speaks two languages?"

"Bilingual!" said Sarah, smiling.

"And what do you call someone who speaks only one language?"

There was silence.

"American," Jaben said.

Lilianne, smiling, said, "Here's one. An English politician was speaking in a town near the Scottish border. In his speech, he slowly and emphatically said, 'I was born an Englishman, I was raised an Englishman, and I will die an Englishman.'

"A Scottish voice from the back asked, 'Ach, man. Have you no ambition?'"

After the chuckles died down, Thad said to Ellamae, "You look like you have something to say."

Ellamae nodded, and said, "I do, but it's a story I'm thinking of, not a joke."

"Go ahead and tell it," Désirée said.

"My mother has a harelip, as you know; that is a bit difficult for her now, but it was devastating to her as a little girl. She was teased quite a bit, and she would tell people that she had cut her lip on a shard of glass -- somehow that was easier to admit than a physical deformity from birth. She was always unsure of herself, embarrassed, feeling less than her peers.

"One of the teachers was a kindly, plump little woman, Mrs. Codman, who had a sunny soul and was the delight of the children. Children would clamor about her, and her heart was big enough for all of them.

"The day came for the annual hearing test, when the children would cup their hands to their ears, and Mrs. Codman would whisper a sentence into their ears -- something like 'The moon is blue,' or 'I have new shoes,' and the children would say what they heard.

"My mother's turn came, and Mrs. Codman whispered into her ear," -- and then Ellamae spoke very slowly, and her voice dropped to a whisper -- "'I wish you were my little girl.'"

There was silence. Ellamae sat with a kind of quiet dignity; she glowed.

She continued. "Those seven words changed her life. She became able to trust people, to venture forth, to have courage and see her own beauty. I think those words have changed my life, too. Now that I think of it, the unspoken message she gave me throughout my childhood was, 'I'm glad you're my little girl.'"

She smiled, in a subtle, subdued manner, her elfin features bore a look that was regal, majestic, aristocratic.

"Wow," Thaddeus said. "I never knew that about you or your mother." He paused, closed his eyes in thought a moment, and said, "And I can see how it has shaped you."

Ellamae's eyes teared. "*Terima kasih.*"

Thaddeus's eyes lit up. "*Sama sama.*"

They sat in blissful silence, a silence that spoke more powerfully than words.

Words were not needed.

The food arrived, piping hot; they joined hands and sat together in silence, their wet clothes beginning to dry. Finally, Amos said, "Amen," and they began to eat without breaking the quiet.

Or at least they did not use their voices; I cannot tell you in full truth that they did not talk. They looked at each other, smiled, squeezed hands, let a tear slide, prayed. No words were exchanged, but a great deal was communicated.

When they finished, the waitress came with the check, and tarried a second.

"Ma'am?" Thaddeus said.

"Yes?" she said, slightly surprised.

"There is something you want to say to us, or ask us. What is it?"

She looked startled, and hesitated.

"You won't offend us. Promise," he said.

"Well, uh... You seem a little odd, not talking a whole meal long."

"That's not really what's on your mind."

"Ok, honey. Why are y'all telling racist jokes?"

Thaddeus said, "Thank you for being honest. To tell you the truth, we were a bit giddy. We probably shouldn't have told those jokes in a restaurant."

"No, I mean, why y'all telling racist jokes in the first place? You guys don't seem the type that needs to tell those jokes. You look me in the eye, for one thing. You confuse me."

"Do you ever tease your friends? Or do your friends ever tease you?"

"All the time."

"Do you ever insult your friends? Or do your friends ever insult you? A real insult, I mean?"

"Never."

"You see these jokes as being insults. Which racist humor may be. But this is not *racist* humor. It's *racial* humor. It's really much more like teasing."

"That joke about the Jew was just plain mean."

"That joke," Lilianne said, "is a Jewish joke, and was told to me by a Jewish friend. It is quite typical of Jewish humor."

The waitress hesitated. "But why do you need it in the first place? Don't race relations matter to you? I would hope so, seeing as how you have a group of friends with both black and white."

"They matter to us a great deal. What would your friendships be like if there was no room for teasing's rowdy energy, if you always had to always walk on eggshells? Wouldn't a friendship be better if it could absorb the energy of teasing and laugh a big belly laugh?"

"Could I have some time to think about it?"

"Take as much time as you want. We come by this town every now and then; we might stop in, and maybe we'll be able to see you. And at any rate, I think you grasp our point, whether or not you agree with it."

The waitress said, "Thank you." She turned, started to walk away, and said, "And thank you for explaining. By the way, I was listening to the radio, and the fire is put out. The helicopter plus that tremendous rainstorm did it, not to mention flooded a few basements."

"Woo-hoo!" shouted Sarah.

They paid the bill, leaving a generous tip, and headed out the door.

Chapter Six

The vehicles drove slowly along the winding roads, and as they came closer, each heart prayed that the meetingplace would be OK. As they cleared the last turn, they parked the car and the van, and got out in silence.

The meetingplace was reduced to cinders.

"My computer!" Jaben said.

"My paintings!" Sarah said.

As they stood, speechless, memories flashed through each

mind, of moments spent there, treasures that were no more.

"I heard a story," Sarah said through tears, "in which a man was fond of books, and had a massive library. One night, his angel appeared to him in a dream, and said, 'Your time is near. Do you have any questions about the next world?'

"'Will I have at least some of my books?'

"'Probably.'

"'Which ones? There are some that I really want to keep.'

"'The ones you gave away.'"

Jaben completed the thought. "And now the only paintings of yours that you can still see are the ones you gave away." He prayed a moment, and said, "You gave away some paintings that were very close to your heart. Now you can still see them."

"What shall we do? What shall we do?" said Désirée.

Silence.

Then Ellamae, in her high, pure, clear voice, sang the first notes of a song.

Silence.

She sang the notes again, and reached out her hands.

The friends formed a circle, and joined hands.

"Praise God from whom all blessings flow.
Praise him all creatures here below.
Praise him above ye heav'nly host.
Praise Father, Son, and Holy Ghost.
Amen.

Chapter Seven

"Well," Amos said, "we should probably go and talk with the Weatherbys about the house.

Sarah slumped. "I don't wanna talk to them about it."

Amos said, "Neither do I, but we still should, and they are kind people. This is the first time I've thought about visiting them and not wanted to do it."

"What'll we say?" said Sarah.

"I don't know," said Ellamae, "but that is not reason not to go."

"Let's go," said Jaben.

They slowly got into the van.

The drive to the Weatherbys' dilapidated mansion seemed unusually long and slow, and Jaben carefully parked the van in the driveway. The friends got up, and walked up the gnarled path to the front door. Ellamae rang the doorbell, and listened to its echo.

"Well, at least the fire didn't get their home."

"Some of the plants are starting to bloom. The water was invigorating to them."

Silence.

Ellamae rang the doorbell again.

Silence.

"Maybe they're not home," Sarah said.

"That may be," said Ellamae. "We should probably leave them a note, and stop back. She fished in her purse for a pen and a notepad.

They talked a bit about what to say, and then wrote down:

Dear Mr. and Mrs. Weatherby;

As you know, there has been a fire; it was started by a riflery accident with Thaddeus. None of us were hurt (we do not yet know if others were hurt), but the house you allowed us to use is in ashes.

We do not know what to say. We are very grateful to you for the use of that house, and we know it was a special place to others -- children most of all. It was a place of memories for us, and we are the richer for it. We regret both to inform you that that wonderful house of yours is gone, and that you were out when we came, and so have to leave a note.

Thank you for the use of your house. We hope

to be able to connect with you in person to speak about this.

The Kythers
Amos, Désirée, Jaben, Thaddeus, Sarah, Ellamae, Lilianne

The friends walked back, and got back into the van. "Where do we go now?" said Sarah.

"There's the cave where we used to meet before the Weatherbys let us use the house," said Lilianne. "Why don't we go over there?"

"I want to give a gift to the Weatherbys," Sarah said.

"What do you have in mind?" said Jaben.

"I don't know, something special. Maybe something we could make."

Jaben turned the keys, and they drove off.

The cavern was refreshingly cool, with air slowly passing through, sounding like a faint breathing. Amos's flashlight swept over a few small crates that served as chairs and larger ones that functioned as tables, candles, matches, some flashlights, papers, some blankets, some sweaters, a sleeping bag, a pillow, a few other odds and ends, and a toolbox. Jaben struck a match, and lit the three wicks of a large candle. Amos turned the flashlight off.

Sarah picked up a moist flashlight, and pressed the switch.

Nothing happened.

She opened it, and dumped out two corroded D cells.

"Why do we store all of our bad batteries in our flashlights?"

Ellamae, shivering slightly, put on a sweater. It was loose around her elfin frame.

Sarah snuggled up against Thaddeus, and put an arm over Lilianne's shoulder. "You know, it's been a long time since we've role played."

"Where were we?" Thaddeus said, interested.

"You were in the village, outside the castle. Looking for something -- I don't remember what."

"And something happened when we drank from the spring," said Lilianne. "It was a cold spring, like the one running through this cave."

Sarah said, "Remember the time we went deep into this cavern, and found that pool this stream empties into, and petted the blind, eyeless fish?"

Lilianne nodded. Sarah had enjoyed that a great deal, and would have waded in had the others not stopped her.

Jaben closed his eyes, and appeared to be concentrating. "You are under a tree outside a chicken coop in the Urvanovestilli city Candlomita. There are children running around. About a hundred feet away, you see a troupe of performing Janra. One is juggling daggers and singing, one is playing a flute, three are doing acrobatics, and two are talking."

Lilianne said, "'Janra always make a day more interesting. Let's go over.'"

Sarah said, "'Yes, let's.'"

Amos said, "'Janra always make a day a little *too* interesting, if you ask me.'"

Sarah said, "'Spoilsport!' I take Rhoz by the hand and start walking over."

Jaben said, "A little Janra girl comes running, with brightly colored ribbons streaming from her wrists and ankles, and says, 'Spin me! Spin me!'"

Sarah said, "I take her to a clear spot and spin her."

Jaben said, "The path is narrow, and there are people passing through. There aren't any good places to spin her."

Sarah said, "I pick her up, give her a hug and a kiss, and say, 'What's your name?'"

Jaben said, "She says, 'Ank. What's yours?' and, before giving you time to answer, grabs your nose and says, 'Honk!'"

Sarah said, "I'm going to set her down."

Jaben said, "She runs over to Rhoz and says, 'Hey, Mr. Tuzman! Throw me!'"

Amos said, "I'm going to pick her up and toss her about, while walking to the other Janra."

Jaben said, "A young Janra in a shimmering midnight blue robe approaches you, holding a small knife and a thick, sculpted white candle. He says, 'Greetings, fellow adventurers. May I introduce myself? My name is Nimbus, and I would like to offer you a greeting-gift. This is a candle which I carved. Perhaps, when you light it, it will remind you of the hour of our meeting."

Amos said, "I'm going to take it and look at it."

Jaben said, "Wrapped around the candle is a bas-relief sculpture of a maiden touching a unicorn, next to a pool and a forest grove. The detail is exquisite."

Amos said, "I'm going to hand it to Cilana for safe keeping and say, 'Thank you, Nimbus. I hope to be able to get to know you.

"'Do you know anything about the crystalline chalice?'"

Jaben said, "'The crystalline chalice? Yes, have heard of it. I used to own it, actually. The last I heard of it, were rumors that it was either in the towers of the castle, or possibly in the depths of Mistrelli's labyrinth. But those are only rumors, and they are old rumors at that.'"

Sarah said, "What time is it?"

Jaben looked at his watch, and said, "7:58."

Sarah gave him a dirty look, and said, "You know what I mean."

Jaben grinned and slowly said, "Oooh! In the game!"

Sarah continued to give him a dirty look, and said, "Yeeees."

Jaben said, "It is now dusk; you have been on your feet all day, and feel tired, dirty, hungry, and thirsty."

Sarah said, "'Nimbus, would you like to join us for dinner?'"

Jaben said, "'I would love to, but I told a group of friends that I'd meet them for some strategy games and discussion. If you're looking for a good bite to eat, I would recommend *The Boar's Head*;' and here he turns to Rhoz, 'it's the one place in this whole area where you can get a good beer. You know the saying, "Never drink Tuz wine or Urvanovestilli beer!" Well, they don't serve any Urvanovestilli beers. Plenty of Urvanovestilli wines --

they even have Mistrelli green."

Ellamae's eyes widened.

"'But for beers, they have a couple of Yedidia and Jec lagers, and then a Tuz stout, and then a Tuz extra stout, and then a Tuz smoked!'"

Amos looked up. "'Thank you, Nimbus.'"

Jaben said, "Nimbus bows deeply, and then walks away at a pace that manages to somehow be both slow and relaxed, and move faster than you could run. After he leaves, a small, multicolored ball rolls between your feet."

Amos, Désirée, Ellamae, Thaddeus, Sarah, and Lilianne said, in unison, "We run, *post haste*!"

Jaben said, "You move along, and manage to clear the game, although you hear its sounds behind you. When you slow down, you come to an intersection of three streets; there is a beggar here."

Ellamae said, "I'm going to give him a silver crown, and say, 'Hi, there! Could you tell us where *The Boar's Head* is?'"

Jaben said, "The beggar points along one of the streets, and says, 'Two streets down, on the corner.' You reach the inn without event, and a pretty waitress leads you to a table. She recommends boar in wine sauce, and the chicken broth soup."

Amos said, "'If there are no objections, I think we'll go with that. I'd like a double of the Tuz smoked.'"

Ellamae said, "I'm going to set the candle Nimbus gave us in the middle of the table, and light it."

Jaben said, "The wick does not burn like most wicks; it sparkles brightly."

Ellamae said, "Interesting. I'm going to watch it."

Jaben said, "The wick burns down to the bottom, and then appears to go out. A thin column of white smoke rises."

Ellamae said, "That's odd."

Thaddeus said, "'I'd like a glass of mild cider.'"

Jaben said, "She turns to you and nods, and then something odd happens. The candle begins to shoot brightly colored balls of fire. One of them lands in a nearby patron's drink, and another in some mashed potatoes. Most of them bounce down and roll around on the tablecloth, which catches fire. The waitress pours a pitcher of cider from a nearby table over the burning tablecloth, and turns to you, puts her hands on her hips, and says, 'Guests will kindly refrain from the use of pyrotechnic devices while inside the restaurant!'"

Amos buried his face in his hands, and then said, "'He gave us a Roman candle!'"

Jaben said, "'Well of course it's a Roman candle! What did you think it was?'"

Amos said, "'No, you don't understand. A Janra named Nimbus met us and gave us what looked like a perfectly ordinarily candle.'"

Jaben said, "She rolls her eyes, and says, 'Oooh, Nimbus! Please excuse me one moment.' She walks away, and in a moment returns with something in her hand. 'Please give this to Nimbus for me.' She heavily places a large lump of coal on the table."

Amos said, "I'm going to take it, and say, 'Thank you. And who should I say that this lump of coal is from?'"

Jaben said, "'Oh, he knows perfectly well who I am. We're good friends, even if he is always trying to tickle me.'"

Thaddeus and Lilianne both poked Sarah in the side.

Amos waited until the others had finished ordering, and said, "'Well, Nimbus was right about at least one thing.'"

"'Ooh?'" Lilianne said.

"'When we lit the candle, we remembered the hour of our meeting with him.'"

Chapter Eight

She stepped onto the construction site, and looked. The building's frame was almost complete, and workers were beginning to lay conduit and 4x8" sheets for the floors.

A young man -- short, pale, wiry, and with sweaty black hair showing from under his headgear -- walked over. "This site is dangerous. You need to wear a bump cap."

"A what?"

"A hard hat. Like I'm wearing. C'mon, I'll take you to get one."

They walked along in silence. "Penny for your thoughts," he said.

"Oh, I was just thinking about a book I'm reading."

"What's the title?"

"I'm not sure it's something a construction worker would recognize, let alone read," she said.

"Try me," he said.

"*Addicted to Mediocrity: 20th Century Christians and the Arts*, by Franky Schaeffer."

"Aah, yes. Like *Why Catholics Can't Sing*, only better. I liked, and wholly agree with, the part about the deleterious effects of pragmatism. Franky's father wrote some pretty good books as well; have you read *How Shall We Then Live: The Rise and Decline of Western Thought and Culture*? The history of art is summarily traced there. *Modern Art and the Death of a Culture* is another good title on that topic."

Her jaw dropped. "How long have you been a construction worker?"

"Only a few months. I've worked in a number of other professions -- truck driver, child care worker, and firefighter, to name a few, and enjoyed them all. Why do you ask?"

She did not answer the question, but said, "Forgive me for asking this, and I know I'm breaking all sorts of social rules, but why on earth are you working as a construction worker? Why aren't you working as a software engineer for instance?"

He smiled and said, "Well, I do program in my spare time; I've written a couple of applications in Java. But that's not answering your question."

He stopped walking and closed his eyes in thought for a moment, and then said, "I suppose there are a two reasons, a lesser and a greater. For the lesser -- have you read Miyamoto Musashi's *A Book of Five Rings*?"

"No; I don't think I've heard of it."

"*A Book of Five Rings* is considered by many to be *the* canonical book on martial arts strategy. It--"

"You're a martial artist, too?" she said, her jaw dropping further.

"No, but martial arts embody a way of thinking, and that way of thinking is beneficial to learn. *A Book of Five Rings* was written by Miyamoto Musashi, the greatest swordsman in Japanese history, perhaps the greatest swordsman in world history. The book itself is cryptic and deep, and is used as a guidebook by some businessmen and some computer techs, though I came to know about it by a different route. After a certain point, Musashi would enter duels armed with only wooden swords, and defeat master swordsmen armed with the Japanese longsword and shortsword.

"One of the pivotal statements is, '*You must study the ways of all professions.*' And Musashi did. In the book, he likened swordsmanship to building a house, and he was an accomplished artist; he left behind some of Japan's greatest swords, paintings, and calligraphy. Not to mention a lot of good stories. Anyway, his legendary stature as a swordsman came in large part through his extensive study of disciplines that are on the surface completely unrelated to swordplay.

"I had not encountered that book yet in college, but (though my degree is in physics) I studied in subjects all across the sciences and the humanities. And I learned more outside the classroom than inside."

The woman closed her mouth.

"Now I am, in a sense, moving to another phase of my education, learning things I couldn't learn in an academic context."

By this point, they had reached a van.

"And your other reason?" she said.

"My other reason? It's work. Honest, productive, valuable work. It may be less valued in terms of money, and I may eventually settle down as a software engineer -- I've gotten a few offers, by the way. But I am right now building a building that will house books, for people to read and children to dream by. It will give me pleasure to walk in these doors, check out a book, walk by a little girl, watch her smile at the pictures in a picture book, and know that I helped make it possible. Surely that smile is worth my time." He reached into the van, and pulled out a bump cap. "Here's how you adjust the strap to fit your head. The cap should rest above your head, like so, rather than being right on it. That gives the straps some room to absorb the shock if something falls on you from above."

The woman, looking slightly dazed, extended her hand and said, "We've talked, but I don't think I've introduced myself properly. My name is Deborah."

The man shook her hand. "Pleased to meet you, Deborah. My name is Jaben."

Chapter Nine

Ellamae heard a soft knocking on the door. "Come in, Sunny. I've been waiting for you."

A little girl with long blonde hair walked in, and held up her mouth for a kiss. Ellamae gave her a peck, and then helped her up on the piano bench. "What are you today?"

"I'm a flower. A daisy."

Ellamae thought for a second, and then said, "The petals on a daisy go around; if you move your finger along, you come back to the same one. With music, it's the same, but there's a twist. If you trace along the notes, you come back to the same one." She played a few notes, and then closed her eyes and said, "To you, are the notes a circle, like the petals of the daisy, or a line, like the piano keyboard is laid out?"

"A circle! A circle!" Sunny said enthusiastically.

"Ok. I want you to improvise something for me that sounds like a circle. It's interesting to me that you hear it that way."

"Why?" the little girl asked.

"Why do I want you to play a circle, or why is it interesting?"

"Why is it interesting?"

"Because you hear things in ways that I don't, and sometimes I learn something new from you."

"Even if I'm a little girl?"

"Especially if you are a little girl. To me, the notes sound like a line, and so I want to hear you play. I want to hear the circle through your ears. Besides, it will help me teach you."

"What keys can I use? The big ones, or the little ones, or both?"

"Right now I want you to stay with just the big keys, although you can feel the tips of the little keys to help you keep your place. And remember that, when you are not talking with me or your parents, you need to call them the white keys and the black keys."

"Why?"

Ellamae closed her eyes in thought. "A smooth surface and a rough surface feel different, right?"

"Yes."

"And loud and quiet sound different, right?"

"Yes."

"There is a difference between the white keys and the black keys that is like those differences to a sighted person."

"On some pianos, the big keys and the little keys feel different. The big keys feel smooth, like hard plastic or glass. The little keys felt smooth, but a different kind of smooth, like bare wood. And on Gramp-Grampa's piano, the big keys feel like that funny stone in Polly's cage. I don't like pianos where the big keys and the little keys feel the same. Is that what you mean?"

Ellamae played a few notes, a musical question. Sunny played a startlingly simple answer.

"You hear and you touch, but they are different, right?"

"Yes, they are different."

"Well, seeing is different from hearing and touch, in the same way. It's hard to describe. Describing seeing to you is kind of like describing music to a man who doesn't hear."

"But music is like dancing! And swimming! And skipping!"

"Well, ok, I guess you're right." Ellamae's eyes lit up. "Imagine that you took off your shirt, and wherever you went, everything became really small and pressed up against your chest and your tummy."

"That would be fun! And confusing."

"But do you see how that would help you know where things are around you?"

Sunny frowned for a second, and said, "I think so."

"That is what seeing is like."

"I wish I could see!"

"I do, too. But you know what? You see a lot of things that other people don't. Your sense of touch picks up on things that most people don't -- like one of my friends, Sarah."

"I want to meet her!"

"That can probably be arranged. Anyway, you hear things that other people don't hear. When we improvise together, you do things that I wouldn't imagine, and in a way I can hear them through your ears. When you play music, you let other people hear the things you imagine, and that is a great gift."

Ellamae placed the child's hands on the keyboard, her left pinky on middle C. "Now, I want you to play music in a circle."

Sunny struck middle C, then the C an octave above, then the C an octave below. She played these three notes, venturing an octave further. Then she added D, F, and G, almost never striking two consecutive notes in the same octave. Then she added E, first playing fragmented arpeggios, and then all five notes, and then the whole scale, ranging all across the keyboard -- quite a reach for her little body! Ellamae didn't like it at first; it sounded jumpy and disjointed. Then something clicked within her, and she no longer heard the octaves at all, but the notes, the pure colors of the notes, arranged in a circle. This must be what it is like to have perfect pitch, she thought. Sunny wound the music down.

"That's very good, Sunny. Sometimes I think I learn as much from you as you are learning from me. Did you practice 'By the Water' this week?"

The little girl placed her finger on her lip.

"Do you still remember how it goes?"

Smiling, the child started to plink the tune away, in a light, merry, happy-go-lucky way. Ellamae said, "That's how we play 'At the Circus.' 'By the Water' is slow and restful, like Mommy reading you a story at bedtime. Think about drinking hot cocoa when you are sleepy. Can you play it again?"

Sunny played the song again, but this time at a placid adagio place. Her touch was still light, but it was light in a soft way.

"That's good, Sunny. Now, would you scoot over a little, to the right? Let's play Question and Answer."

Sunny moved, and Ellamae sat down on the bench next to her. Ellamae played a phrase, and the little girl responded. Then she played something slightly different, and the child varied her response. Ellamae played a slightly longer question, and Sunny played a much longer, merrier, dancelike answer.

"That's good, Sunny. Keep your hands dancing on the keyboard."

Ellamae started to play a complex tune, and at the very climax stopped playing. Sunny, without missing a beat, picked it up and completed it. Then Ellamae joined in, and the two began to improvise a duet, a musical dialogue -- sometimes with two voices, sometimes with one, sometimes silent. Many threads developed, were integrated, and then wound down to a soft finish.

They sat in silence for a while, breathless, and then Ellamae reached atop the piano.

"I have something for you, Sunny."

"A CD!" the girl said, with excitement.

"Yes, this is a Bach CD. For practice this week, I want you to spend a half hour listening to the Little Fugue in G minor. Have the CD player repeat on track seven. Then I want you to spend half an hour improvising with the theme. Stay on the big keys; it'll sound a little different, but stick with it. Next time, I'll show you a way to use some of the big keys and some of the little keys."

"Cool!"

A knock sounded from the door. "Is Sunny ready to go yet?"

Sunny gave Ellamae a hug, and turned away. "Mommy! Mommy! Look what Teacher gave me!"

With that, she was off, leaving Ellamae in silent contemplation.

Chapter Ten

Thaddeus marched down the steps, into the unfinished basement. He ducked under low hanging pipes and air ducts, not bothering to turn on the lights because he knew its nooks and crannies so well. He stepped onto a screw, yelped, and then ducked into a place called "the corner."

There was an armchair among the various odds and ends -- old, tattered, and very comfortable. He wrapped a blanket around himself in the cool air, and sunk in.

He closed his eyes, and began to pray:

"Our Father,
who art in Heaven,
hallowed be thy name.
Thy kingdom come,
thy will be done,
on earth as it is in Heaven.
Give us this day our daily bread.
Forgive us our trespasses,
as we forgive those who have trespassed against us.
Lead us not into temptation,
but deliver us from evil.
For thine is the kingdom,
and the power,
and the glory forever.
Amen."

He began to grow still, grow still.

As he became quiet, he examined himself, confessed his sins. He began to sink deep into the heart of God, and there he rested and loved. Words were not needed.

Thaddeus held his spirit stiller than his body, in a listening silence.

"Yes, God?" he asked without words.

He sat, still, in wordless communion, feeling with his intuition, with the depths of his being. And waited.

Gradually, a message formed in his heart. A message of task, of needed and even urgent action, of responsibility.

What kind of assignment, what kind of need? he thought.

Silence. A dark cloud of unknowing. Darkness and obscurity.

What do I do? he wondered.

Wait, child. Wait.

Thaddeus had a timeless spirit; he knew not and cared not whether three minutes had passed, or three hours. He let himself feel the notes of the timeless hymn and Christmas carol, "Let all mortal flesh keep silence." If he rested in God, he could wait.

Thaddeus slowly returned to consciousness, and left, his heart both peaceful and troubled.

Chapter Eleven

RING! Sarah picked up the phone.

A businesslike and official voice said, "Hello. May I please speak with the Squeaky-Toy of the house?"

"Oh, hi, Jaben. What's up?"

"Amos said he was going to meet me for dinner to talk about some stuff, and he hasn't shown up. I called Désirée, and she said he's not in any of his usual haunts. It's not like him to break an appointment, and I was wondering if you would happen to know anything about it."

"Wow, no I don't. The last time I saw him was in the cave. By the way, do you know where my red bouncy ball is?"

"No idea."

Chapter Twelve

Six friends stood in the cave in the early, early morning; none of them had slept well, and Jaben hadn't bothered to have his morning bowl of coffee.

"I called the police," Désirée said, "and they said that he can't be officially treated as a missing person until he's been gone for twenty-four hours. They asked me a number of questions -- his height, weight, physical appearance, when he'd last been seen, and so on -- and then left."

"I was praying yesterday," Thaddeus said. "I was praying, and I had a feeling of -- urgency, but even more strongly of waiting. I'm confused. Usually, when God tells me to wait, it is for a long period of time. This was an eyeblink. Does this mean that the waiting is over, or that I -- we? -- should still wait?"

No one answered.

"What do we do now?" Sarah asked.

"We can sing," Ellamae said. "Sing and pray."

"Sing?" Désirée asked incredulously. "At a time like this?"

"How can you *not* sing at a time like this? If you can't sing at a time like this, when can you sing?" Ellamae replied.

Désirée nodded.

Ellamae's high, pure voice began, and was joined by other voices, deeper voices.

"O the deep, deep love of Jesus, vast, unmeasured, boundless, free!
Rolling as a mighty ocean in its fullness over me!
Underneath me, all about me, is the current of Thy love
Leading onward, leading homeward to Thy glorious rest above!

"O the deep, deep love of Jesus, spread His praise from shore to shore!
How he loveth, ever loveth, changeth never,

nevermore!
How he watches o'er his loved ones, died to call them all his own;
How for them he intercedeth, watcheth o'er them from the throne!

"O the deep, deep love of Jesus, love of every love the best!
'Tis an ocean vast of blessing, 'tis a haven sweet of rest!
O the deep, deep love of Jesus, 'tis a heaven of heavens to me;
And it lifts me up to glory, for it lifts me up to Thee!

Désirée's heart had calmed considerably during the singing. "Let's sing it again," she said. And they did. Then her voice led a song:

"My life flows on in endless song above earth's lamentation.
I hear the sweet though far-off hymn that hails a new creation:
Through all the tumult and the strife I hear the music ringing;
It finds an echo in my soul-- how can I keep from singing?

"What though my joys and comforts die? The Lord my Savior liveth;
What though the darkness gather round! Songs in the night He giveth:
No storm can shake my inmost calm while to that refuge clinging;
Since Christ is Lord of heaven and earth, how can I keep from singing?

"I lift mine eyes; the cloud grows thin; I see the blue above it;
And day by day this pathway smooths since first I learned to love it:
The peace of Christ makes fresh my heart, a fountain ever springing:
All things are mine since I am his-- How can I keep from singing?"

"Can we pray now?" There was considerable concern in Ellamae's questioning.

Désirée hesitated, and then said, "Yes. I am calm now."

They joined hands and closed their eyes. For a while, there was silence, finally broken by Désirée's tear-choked voice. "Lord, keep my husband safe."

The songs held new meaning to her.

Jaben said, "I think of myself as a theologian, but I do not know the answers to the questions on our hearts. Lord, hold us in your heart."

The faint echo of a gust of wind was heard in the cave.

Sarah began to hum, "I love you, Lord," and the others joined in.

"Why?" asked Désirée.

Silence.

As the time passed, the silence changed in character. It became deeper, a present silence. The faint sounds -- of air passing through the cavern, of people breathing, of cloth rubbing against cloth as people moved -- seemed louder, more audible, and yet part of the silence.

"Lord, we come to you with so many things on our hearts," Ellamae said. "In the midst of all this, I wish to thank you for the many blessings we have enjoyed. I thank you for my music, and for all my students, especially Sunny. She is such a delight, and I look forward to seeing her abilities mature. I thank you especially for Amos, for the delight he is to us, his patience, his deep laughter." Voices had been saying "Amen," and Jaben added, "for his taking teasing so well." "If this is the last we have seen of him, we thank you for allowing us to pass these brief moments with such a friend," Ellamae finished.

"Your will be done, on earth as it is in Heaven," Lilianne joined. "Lord, we come before you in confidence that you have adopted us as your children, and whatever we ask will be done. May our request be your will, drawing on your willingness, as we ask that our fellowship be restored, and our friend and brother be found." They sat for a time, continuing to hold each other's hands, crying, listening to the silence. Then a squeeze went around, and with one voice they said, "Amen."

It had been an hour. The hugs were long and lingering, and Jaben felt the kisses a little more. The six friends out of the cave and into their days' activities, their hearts deeply troubled and even more deeply at peace.

Chapter Thirteen

Ellamae had come over to Désirée's and Amos's little white house, ostensibly to help with the housework. They were washing and drying dishes and chattering when the doorbell rang.

Désirée, in the middle of scouring out a dirty pot, said, "Could you get that, honey? My hands are kind of full."

Ellamae set down the dish she was drying, and the towel. She walked over to the front door.

There was a police officer there, and something about his demeanor said that he did not bear good news.

"Mrs. Godfrey?"

"She's in the kitchen, washing dishes. Come on in."

Désirée had rinsed and dried her hands, and came into the living room. She shook the officer's hand. "Hi, I'm Désirée."

"Officer Rick. Would you be willing to sit down for a second?"

With trepidation, Désirée sat down in the armchair. Ellamae perched on the edge of the couch.

"Following up on a call, we found your husband's car in a

ditch by the roadside. The windows were broken, and the n-word was spray painted all over the sides."

Désirée brought her hand to her mouth, and her eyes filled with tears. She suddenly looked like a very small woman in a very big chair.

Ellamae closed her eyes in pain. The officer continued. "We are presently fingerprinting the car, and beginning a search of the area. We will call you if we find out anything definite. I'm sorry to bear this news."

Ellamae walked over, and wrapped her arms around Désirée. "Thank you, officer." She paused a moment, and said, "I think we need to be alone now. Sorry you had to bear this news."

The policeman said, "Yes, Ma'am," and stepped out the door.

Désirée and Ellamae stood, held each other, and wept.

Chapter Fourteen

Jaben walked up the steps of the sanctuary slowly. Sarah was standing next to him, and squeezed his hand; he touched her, but did not feel her. The friends walked into the church quietly; the other members of the congregation gave them a little more space, and a hush fell. Désirée held on tightly to Ellamae's arm.

"Blessed be God: Father, Son, and Holy Spirit," the celebrant said.

"And blessed be his kingdom, now and for ever. Amen," the congregation answered.

"Almighty God, to you all hearts are open, all desires known and from you no secrets are hid: Cleanse the thoughts of our hearts by the inspiration of your Holy Spirit, that we may perfectly love you, and worthily magnify your holy Name; through Christ our Lord. Amen," the celebrant prayed.

The processional hymn was Amazing Grace, words and notes that flowed automatically, thoughtlessly, until the fourth verse:

"The Lord has promised good to me
His word my hope secures;
He will my shield and portion be,
As long as life endures."

Jaben had been thinking, a lot, and he held onto those words as a lifeline. With them came a little glimmer of hope that his beloved friend might be OK.

"Glory to God, glory in the highest and peace to His people on earth.
Lord God, heavenly King. Almighty God and Father,

"We worship You, we give You thanks, we praise You for Your glory.

"Glory to God in the highest and peace to His people on earth.
Lord Jesus Christ, only Son of the Father, Lord God, Lamb of God,
"You take away the sin of the world, have mercy on us.
You are seated at the right hand of the Father, receive our pray'r.
For You alone are the Holy One, for you alone are the Lord.
For You alone are the most high, Jesus Christ, with the Holy Spirit, in the glory of God, the Father.

"Glory to God in the highest and peace to his people on earth.
Amen. Give glory to God.
Amen. Give glory to God.

"Amen. Give glory to God."

In the music, Jaben felt lifted up into the divine glory -- a taste of Heaven cut through his pain.

The celebrant said, "The Lord be with you."

The congregation echoed, "And also with you."

The celebrant bowed his head and said, "Let us pray.

"Almighty God, whose Son our Savior Jesus Christ came to seek out and save the lost: grant that we, looking in the divine Light you give us, and thinking in the holy wisdom you bestow on us, may succeed in the endeavors you set before us, through Jesus Christ our Lord, who lives and reigns with you and the Holy Spirit, one God, now and forever. *Amen.*"

A reader stepped up and said, "A reading from Ruth.

"But Ruth replied, 'Don't urge me to leave you or to turn back from you. Where you go I will go, and where you stay I will stay. Your people will be my people and your God my God. Where you die I will die, and there I will be buried. May the LORD deal with me, be it ever so severely, if anything but death separates you and me.'

"The Word of the Lord."

"Thanks be to God," the congregation answered.

The celebrant said, "We will read the Psalm together in unison."

The whole congregation read aloud, "O LORD, you have searched me and you know me.
You know when I sit and when I rise; you perceive my thoughts from afar.
You discern my going out and my lying down; you are familiar with all my ways.
Before a word is on my tongue you know it completely, O LORD.
You hem me in--behind and before; you have laid your hand upon me.
Such knowledge is too wonderful for me, too lofty for me to attain.
Where can I go from your Spirit? Where can I flee from your presence?
If I go up to the heavens, you are there; if I make my bed in the

depths, you are there.
If I rise on the wings of the dawn, if I settle on the far side of the sea,
even there your hand will guide me, your right hand will hold me fast.
If I say, 'Surely the darkness will hide me and the light become night around me,'
even the darkness will not be dark to you; the night will shine like the day, for darkness is as light to you.'"

Two tears slid down Lilianne's and Désirée's cheeks.

"The word of the Lord," the celebrant said.

"Thanks be to God," the congregation answered.

"A reading from Paul's first epistle to the Corinthians," another reader announced.

"For the message of the cross is foolishness to those who are perishing, but to us who are being saved it is the power of God. For it is written: 'I will destroy the wisdom of the wise; the intelligence of the intelligent I will frustrate.' Where is the wise man? Where is the scholar? Where is the philosopher of this age? Has not God made foolish the wisdom of the world? For since in the wisdom of God the world through its wisdom did not know him, God was pleased through the foolishness of what was preached to save those who believe.

"Jews demand miraculous signs and Greeks look for wisdom, but we preach Christ crucified: a stumbling block to Jews and foolishness to Gentiles, but to those whom God has called, both Jews and Greeks, Christ the power of God and the wisdom of God.

"For the foolishness of God is wiser than man's wisdom, and the weakness of God is stronger than man's strength. Brothers, think of what you were when you were called. Not many of you were wise by human standards; not many were influential; not many were of noble birth. But God chose the foolish things of the world to shame the wise; God chose the weak things of the world to shame the strong. He chose the lowly things of this world and the despised things--and the things that are not--to nullify the things that are, so that no one may boast before him. It is because of him that you are in Christ Jesus, who has become for us wisdom from God--that is, our righteousness, holiness and redemption. Therefore, as it is written: 'Let him who boasts boast in the Lord.'

"The Word of the Lord," concluded the reader.

"Thanks be to God," answered the congregation.

Jaben mulled over the texts.

The congregation rose, singing, "Alleluia! Alleluia!
Opening our hearts to Him.
Singing Alleluia! Alleluia! Jesus is our King."

"A reading from the Holy Gospel according to Luke," said the celebrant.

"Or suppose a woman has ten silver coins and loses one. Does she not light a lamp, sweep the house and search carefully until she finds it? And when she finds it, she calls her friends and neighbors together and says, 'Rejoice with me; I have found my lost coin.'

"The Gospel of the Lord."

"Praise to you, Lord Christ," answered the congregation, and sat down.

The celebrant walked behind the pulpit, and said, "There was a Baptist minister who would every Sunday stand behind the pulpit and say, 'The Lord be with you!' And every Sunday, the congregation would answer, 'And also with you.'

"One Sunday, he said 'The Lord be with you!' as usual, but the microphone was turned off, and his voice did not carry very well in the large sanctuary. The congregation did not respond.

"He tapped the microphone, and saw that there was no sound, and so he said in a loud voice, 'I think there's a problem with the mike!'

"The congregation answered, 'And also with you.'"

There was a chuckle throughout the congregation. Jaben's nose wrinkled in distaste. Jaben objected strongly to Kant's idea of Religion Within the Bounds of Reason. He was quite fond of Chesterton's statement that, among intellectuals, there are two types of people: those that worship the intellect, and those that use it. He objected even more strongly to America's idea of Religion Within the Bounds of Amusement. It wasn't that he didn't like a good joke, or having a bit of fun. It was just that he didn't confuse those things with edifying instruction in the Word of God. When his irritation wore off, he began to sink into thought.

Jaben slowly turned the Scripture passages over in his mind. Each one seemed to say something about Amos.

It was then and there that Jaben Onslow Pfau decided that he would do everything he could, whatever the cost, come Hell or high water, to rescue Amos Regem Godfrey, his dear and beloved friend and brother.

Chapter Fifteen

There was a clamor of people around the friends. A black man, standing 6'8" at just under 300 pounds, built like a brick wall, and bearing a gentle radiance, approached them, along with his little mother. The woman said, "I remember when Amos and my son were wee little boys, and there was rain after a heavy truck drove through the street. They both played in the mud, happy as pigs in a blanket!"

The man said, "If there's anything we can do to help, just tell us."

Jaben said, "As a matter of fact, Bear, yes, there is."

"Yes?" the man said eagerly.

"Could we join you for dinner? I need to think, and having more company and less work to do would help me."

"Certainly," Bear said. "It would be a pleasure," his mother added.

"What are we having?" Thaddeus said eagerly.

"Rice and gravy, fried chicken, and peach cobbler."

"Mmm, soul food," Thaddeus said, smiling. "I'll try not to drool on the way over."

"Ok," Bear said, his deep voice rumbling into an even deeper laughter.

Different people were in and out of the kitchen at different times, although Grace, Bear's mother, and Lilianne were always in. A pleasing aroma filled the house; Thad wasn't the only one who found it hard not to drool.

Bear picked Jaben up and squeezed him in a big Bear hug. Then he set him down, and, placing his arm over Jaben's shoulder, asked, "So, whatchya thinkin' about, Bro?"

Jaben closed his eyes. "I want to find Amos, if he's dead or alive. I know you're supposed to leave this to the authorities, but it is on my heart to do so. I want to do whatever it takes, whatever the cost, to find him."

Sarah walked out of the kitchen, her ears cocked. "I'm in."

"Me, too," said Lilianne's voice.

"How're you going to do that?" Bear asked, his eyebrows raised in curiosity.

"Don't bother me with details."

"I'm going with you, too," said Ellamae, and squeezed his hand.

"Do you want to use my gun?" Bear asked. His gun was legendary in the town as an elephant gun with a laser sight.

"Bear, you know I can't hit the broad side of a barn with a sniper rifle."

"I'm in," said Thaddeus, his eyes wide with interest. "Could we go out in the forest and shoot a few crabapples?"

"Just a second while I go get it." Bear disappeared up some stairs.

"Honey, you *know* I'm in," said Désirée.

Bear returned, carrying a very large rifle. He held it out to Thaddeus.

Thaddeus hefted it, and said, "Let's go."

As the two walked out the door, Thaddeus asked, "Why do you use such a massive gun, Bear? Nothing you hunt needs that kind of firepower."

A stick snapped under Bear's weight. "I don't know. It's me, I guess. Same reason I use a sixteen pound sledgehammer, or thirty-two when they'll let me bring one. Part of it is toy and... you know the saying, 'The only difference between a man and a boy is the size of the toy.'"

"How do you turn the laser sight on?" Thaddeus asked. "I've never used one."

"Here," Bear said. "Like this."

Thaddeus lowered himself to the ground, and said, "See that crabapple tree out at battlesight zero? See that crabapple that sticks out to the far left?"

"Battlesight zero for this gun is about three times what you're used to."

"Oh, yeah. Thanks. I'll adjust accordingly. Anyway, see that crabapple?" "The really little one?" Bear asked. "Uh-huh." Thaddeus grew still, his body's tiny swaying decreasing and decreasing. The tiny crababble glowed red. Then it stopped glowing, and Thaddeus closed his eyes.

Boom! A resounding, thunderous gunshot echoed all around.

The crabapple was no longer there.

Thaddeus rubbed his shoulder, and handed the gun to Bear.

"I'm sorry, Bear, but I can't use that gun. It's much too heavy for me, and the kick from that one shot is going to give me bruises. I can feel it now. I really appreciate the offer; I have for a long time longed to fire Bear's gun. But I can't use it. I need to stick with my .22."

"You are a true marksman, Thaddeus, and a good man. I hope that you don't meet anything that requires the firepower to take down a grizzly."

"Oh, that reminds me," Thaddeus said. "I heard this from Jaben. Which is better to have if you're attacked by a grizzly: a 10-gauge, or a hollow-nosed .45?"

"Ummm..." Bear hesitated.

"The shotgun, because you can use it as a club when it runs out of ammo."

Bear laughed a deep, mighty laugh, and then they walked back. That man, Bear thought, was not entirely telling an innocent joke.

Chapter Sixteen

Ring, Ring, Ring, Ring. "We're sorry, but the number you have dialed is an imaginary number. Please hang up, rotate the phone clockwise by ninety degrees, and dial again. *Beep!*"

"C'mon, Jaben. Pick up the phone." The voice paused, and reiterated, "Pick up the phone."

Jaben picked up the phone. "Leave me alone, Thad! I've talked with Bear, and he's given me time off. I need to do some thinking."

"Amos is in Mexico."

"*What?!?*"

"Amos is in Mexico."

"How do you know that? Did he call you? Is he OK?"

"No, he didn't call me. I was just... praying, and Amos is in Mexico."

"Ok. That changes my plans."

"Mine, too."

"Let's meet at the cave tonight. Could you call the others? I still need to do some processing."

"I already have called the others."

"Ok, see you there."

"See ya! Wouldn't want to be ya!"

Chapter Seventeen

Only one candle flickered, but the cave did not seem dark. The air was cool, but the Kythers were much too excited to feel cold. They were there with a mission, with a purpose.

Jaben said, "I think we should take a day to prepare, and then leave for Mexico. In a way, a day is not nearly enough time, but in another way a day may be more than we can afford. We need to use the time wisely. What will you do? I will work on securing material provisions."

Lilianne said, "I will pray. Pray and fast."

Thaddeus said, "I will talk with God."

Désirée said, "I will talk with my kin for support."

Sarah said, "I don't know what I'll do. Maybe tell loved ones goodbye for a while, I'm going on an adventure."

Ellamae said, "Plant a tree."

"What?" Sarah asked.

"Martin Luther was asked what he would do if he knew what the Lord were coming the next day. His answer was very simple: plant a tree. It was the ultimate scatological response. Instead of nonstop singing, prayer, fasting, and wailing about 'I am a worm!' he reasoned that he had been planning to plant a tree, and if that was worth doing at all, it would be worth doing when the Lord returned. So he said he would plant a tree. Apart from packing, I'm just going to spend my day normally, and then go."

"I'm with you," said Sarah.

Chapter Eighteen

Ellamae smiled at the familiar knock on the door. "Come in, Sunny," she said.

Sunny bounced in. "Teacher, teacher, I've been waiting to play for you." She jumped up on the piano bench.

"Go ahead and play," Ellamae said, looking with wonder on this little child.

Sunny began to play, and Ellamae listened with a shock. She had not taught the girl about different keys yet -- other than C and the pentatonic key of the black keys, which were plenty to start with -- and the child was confidently playing music in G minor. It sounded vaguely like Bach, at very least a set of variations on the theme of his little fugue -- and then Ellamae realized what she was listening to. Ellamae was listening to a fugue in one voice.

She realized with a start that the music had shifted to the key of E minor, and was growing fuller, richer, deeper. Many different threads were introduced, developed, and then integrated. The music rose to a crescendo and then came to a sudden and startling conclusion. There was silence.

"Do you like it?" Sunny said, a bashful smile on her face.

"Yes, I like it very much. Did it take you all week to compose?"

"I didn't compose it, Ellamae. I improvised it."

"Sunny, how would you like to take a walk?"

"A walk? Where?"

"To go visit my friend Sarah. I'll leave your mother a note, and not charge for this lesson. I'm going to look for my friend Amos, and I may not be back for a while. I love the keyboard, but I'd like to spend these last moments doing something else. Will you come with me?"

"I would love to!"

Ellamae wrote out a note, and taped it to the door of the lesson room, and then said, "C'mon, Sunny. Take my hand."

As they walked out, Sunny turned her face up to the light, and said, "The sunlight is warm today!"

Ellamae said, "It is. Perhaps feeling sunlight is better than looking at sunlight. What did you do this past week?"

Sunny said, "I don't know."

"Yes, you do," replied Ellamae.

"I got to ride a horse bareback with my Mom. That was fun. The horse was hot, and I could feel him breathing in and out, and I could feel the wind kissing my face."

"Is wind a mystery to you?"

"What do you mean?"

"Sighted people find wind to be confusing; we can see what it does, like blow leaves around, but we can't see the wind itself. Jesus said that the Holy Spirit is like wind that way."

"I don't find wind confusing. I feel it, and hear it, and hear what it does. It's like a friend, moving around me and hugging me. Is that like the Spirit? I don't find God to be confusing; he's like a friend, or a warm bowl of soup, or... I don't know what else to say, but he isn't confusing."

Ellamae pondered these words. Perhaps later the child would know the side of God that is wild and mysterious -- or was everything so wild and mysterious to her that she made her peace with them, and was not frightened at the wild mystery of God? This was a voice that could call God 'Daddy', and be completely unafraid.

"Is that like the Spirit?" Sunny repeated. "Is that like the Spirit, Teacher?"

"I don't know. I'm not a theologian. I think it is, but in a different way than Jesus meant. Maybe wind is different to blind people and sighted people. I wonder what else is--"

"What's a theo-lo-, a the-, a the-o-loge-yun?" Sunny interrupted.

"A theologian is someone who devotes his life to studying the nature of God, and faith, and hope, and love. A theologian is somebody who reads the Bible and learns deep lessons from it."

"Why aren't you a theo-logian? I think you're a theologian. I'm a theologian. Today I learned that God loves me. That's a deep lesson. I think everybody should be a theologian."

"Yes, but a theologian is somebody who does that in a special way, and is more qualified--wait, that isn't right, a theologian is--" Ellamae paused, and closed her eyes. "I don't know. I don't know what makes a theologian. Maybe you and I are theologians. I don't know."

"But I thought grown-ups knew everything!"

"Nonononononononono!" Ellamae said. "Grown-ups don't know everything. Here's a story I was told when I was a little girl like you in Sunday school.

"An Indian and a white man were standing together on a beach. The white man took a stick, and made a small circle in the sand. He said, 'This is what the Indian knows.'

"Then he made a big circle around the small circle, and said, 'This is what the white man knows.'

"The Indian took the stick, and made a really, really, really big circle around both of the other two circles, and said, 'This is what neither the Indian nor the white man knows.'"

They were walking along a primitive road, and Ellamae bent over, saying, "Give me your finger. Point with it." She drew a small circle along the dirt, and said, "This is what children know."

Then she drew a larger circle, overlapping with the former circle, but not engulfing it. "This is what grown-ups know. Grown-ups know more than children know, but we also forget a lot of things as we grow up, and some of them are important. So grown-ups know more than children, but children still know some pretty big things that grown-ups don't."

Then she walked around in an immense circle, dragging Sunny's fingertip through the sandy dirt. "This is what neither children nor grown-ups know, but only God knows. Do you see?"

Sunny's face wrinkled in concentration. "Yes. So you want to tell me the things I ask, but you don't know them."

"Yes," Ellamae said, continuing to walk along.

"What do children know that grown-ups don't?" asked Sunny.

Ellamae took a long time to answer. "You know how sometimes I say something, and you ask me a question, and I change what I said? That's because you brought up something I forgot, like singing being like dancing. There are other things. Jesus said to become like a little child to enter; children know how to believe, and how -- 'honest' is close, but not quite the right word. When a little boy says, 'I love you,' he means it. Children know how to imagine and make-believe, and how to play. Most adults have forgotten how to play, though a few remember (maybe by taking time to play, maybe by making work into play). That is sad most of all. This life is preparing us for Heaven, and what we do in Heaven will not be work or rest, but play. You live more in Heaven than most grown-ups."

Sunny listened eagerly. "But you remembered."

"Yes, but not easily. And not all of it. I am lucky to have friends who know how to play."

By this time they had reached Sarah's house, and Sarah saw them and came out to greet them. They sat down on a log, with Sunny in the middle.

"Teacher tells me that you're tickulish," Sunny said.

"Maybe I am and maybe I'm not," Sarah said.

Sunny poked Sarah in the side. Sarah squeaked.

"Sarah is not a Squeaky-Toy," Sarah said, sitting up and looking very dignified (and forgetting that Sunny was blind).

Sunny poked Sarah in the side. Sarah squeaked.

"Sarah is not a Squeaky-Toy," Sarah reiterated.

Sunny poked Sarah in the side. Sarah squeaked.

Sarah grabbed Sunny's hands. "I hear you like music."

"Yes, I like it a lot. I especially like to play piano. What's your name?"

"Sarah."

"I love you, Sarah-Squeak."

"Thank you, Sunny." She paused, debated whether or not to say "It's 'Sarah', not 'Sarah-Squeak'," and continued, "What do you think of when you play music?"

"Music stuff. Do you play music?"

"No, but I paint. Painting is kind of like music."

"What do you do when you paint?"

"Well, I take all sorts of different colors, and I use differing amounts to make different forms and shapes, and when I am done people can see through my painting what I was thinking of, if I do it well."

"I take different notes, and I use differing amounts to make different melodies, and when I am done people can hear through my music what I was thinking of, if I do it well. Yep, painting is like music."

Sarah pondered the painting of rainbow colors she had been working on. "You know, I'd like for you to do something with me sometime. I'd like for you to improvise a song for me, maybe record it so I can hear it a few times, and I'll see if I can translate it into a painting."

"What about words? Can you translate it into words?"

"I can't translate music into words. I don't know if anyone can. But maybe, if I tried hard enough and had God's blessing, I could translate it into a painting of color. Hmm, that gives me an idea of music for the deaf." She turned to Ellamae. "What about a video where each instrument or voice was a region of the screen, and the color went around the color wheel circle as the notes go around, and the light became more intense as you went up an octave? And they became bigger and smaller as the notes became louder and softer?"

"I'd like to see that. Music for the deaf," Ellamae said.

"Miss Sarah, please hold your arm out and pull up your shirt sleeve," Sunny said."

Sarah, curious, did as the child asked.

Sunny placed her fingers on Sarah's bare arm, and started to play it as if it were a piano keyboard. "*That* is music for people who can't hear," she said.

Sarah and Ellamae nodded.

Chapter Nineteen

Thaddeus slowly got out materials -- the right materials -- and started cleaning his gun. Ellamae ducked in the doorway, and said, "What's up?"

Thaddeus said, "Cleaning my gun. Taking care of details." He looked at a small box of ammunition, and said, "And you?"

"I don't think we'll be needing that," Ellamae said. "No good will come of it."

"There's more than people in Mexico. There are animals. I'd prefer to be prepared," Thaddeus said.

"No good will come of it," Ellamae said.

Chapter Twenty

Jaben thought about his visit with the Weatherbys. He called to apologize and explain why they wouldn't all be able to come then to talk in person, and they gave him -- unasked-for, undeserved -- a thousand dollars in traveller's cheques. He was very happy for the money. The friends had plenty of equipment from their other adventures, but money was tight, and he hadn't known where it was going to come from. Perhaps Bear.

When he finished packing the van, it contained:

- Children's toys: a truck, a doll, a top...
- Thaddeus's .22 competition rifle.
- A small box of ammunition.
- Gun cleaning supplies.
- A large box of MREs, military rations ("'Meal Ready to Eat' is three lies in one," a marine had told them, but they'll keep you moving).
- Books:
- The Bible, in four different translations (one Spanish, one French, and two English).
- Madeline l'Engle's *A Wind in the Door*, the very first book (besides the Bible) that he thought of to bring along. (He identified very strongly with Charles Wallace.)
- Jon Louis Bentley's *Programming Pearls*, for serious thinking about programming.
- Larry Wall's *Programming Perl*, for light and humorous reading.
- Neil Postman's *Amusing Ourselves to Death: Public Discourse in an Age of Show Business*, for pleasure, and to use road time to explain to his friends exactly *why* he believed that television was a crawling abomination from the darkest pits of Hell.
- Jerry Mander's *Four Arguments for the Elimination of Television*. When Jaben first saw this book sitting atop a television, he thought, "The author could only think of four?" For that, he found this book to be far deeper than Postman's, and (in thinking about what to pack) thought it would be a good book to help appreciate nature and Mexico.
- *A Treasury of Jewish Humor*, edited by Nathan Ausubel. Jaben found Jewish humor to be subtle, clever, and extremely funny, as did Lilianne; the others were beginning to catch on.
- Antoine de Saint-Exupéry's *Le Petit Prince*, to share with Sarah most of all.
- Charles Taylor's *Sources of the Self*, which he had read

much too quickly and wanted to peruse, at least in part, to better understand his own culture.

- Philip Johnson's *Darwin on Trial*. This book, apart from some web articles, was the first contact he had that changed the way he looked at academia. He thought there were some arguments to add to the ones in the book, but he couldn't put his finger on them.
- Oliver Sack's *An Anthropologist on Mars*, to stimulate his mind and help show him different ways of thinking.
- A small box of black pens (which had the most tremendous knack for disappearing) and a hardcover blank book to write in.
- Three climbing ropes.
- Four notebooks, three of which were half-filled with miscellaneous scrawl.
- The traveller's cheques.
- A heavy-duty, broad-ranging medical kit, including a snakebite kit.
- Lanterns.
- Kerosene.
- Various people's clothing, personal toiletries, etc.
- Three large hunting knives, one of which had a serrated back.
- A water drum.
- Tents, groundcloths, and sleeping bags.
- About 50 pounds in batteries.
- Seven lantern flashlights.
- Six canteens.
- Five Swiss Army Knives.
- Four pair of binoculars.
- Three coils of bailing wire.
- Two rolls of duct tape.
- Sarah's red bouncy ball.

Jaben packed it in as best he could; the equipment was smaller than it sounded, and they had a big van. He arranged it like furniture, and then called the others to come in. They joined hands in prayer, and hit the road at sundown.

Chapter Twenty-One

"Hello, and thank you for choosing Kything Airlines, where we not only get you there, but teach you how to pray. We will be cruising at an altitude of about fifteen to thirty-five hundred feet after hills, railroad crossings, and speed bumps, and zero feet otherwise. Our destination is Mexico City, Mexico, with an estimated time of arrival in thirty minutes. This is your copilot Jaben speaking, and our captain for this flight is Thaddeus."

"Dude," Thad said, "this van does like zero to sixty in fifteen minutes when it's loaded like this. But your point is well taken. I'll try not to speed."

"Yeah, I know. If this van were a computer, it would be running Windows now. Anyways, I'd like to take this time for a debriefing on Mexican culture," Jaben said.

"Don't we usually pray when we start off on a trip?" asked Sarah.

"Yes, but I would like to use the time to talk about Mexican culture when it will make a clear impression on people's minds," Jaben answered.

"But prayer is more important!" Sarah insisted.

"Yes, it's more important, but the more important things do not always take place first. Important and urgent are two separate things. You put your clothes on before you visit your friend, even though visiting your friend is more important," Jaben explained, although he was not satisfied with his example.

"I still think prayer is more important," Sarah said.

I'm not going to get into an argument, Jaben thought. An argument is definitely not the right way to start off this trip. "Very well, then, Sarah," he said. "Why don't you pray?"

"Me?" Sarah said with the earnest pleasure of a child. "I would love to.

"Dear Father, thank you for this trip, for all the good times we've had with Amos, even the time he named me Squeaky-Toy (even though I only let Jaben use that name). Father, I pray that you would help us find Amos, and Father, help us bring him back safely. And, oh, Father, please let him be all right. Amen."

Jaben took a couple seconds' more prayer to cool down, and let go of his angry thoughts about Sarah. Then he said, "Ok, for a primer on Mexican culture... let's see. Touch. When you enter or leave a room, you give everyone a firm handshake; if you don't, everyone will think you're rude. Kissing cheeks is OK among girls, and side hugs are OK on special occasions. In general, we'll have to back off on touch in public, and particularly avoid what would look like couples' PDA. This means both you and me, Sarah. We should talk less, and particularly avoid extended public conversations between the sexes. In general, avoid real, deep kything except when we're alone and away from eyes. Wait, that's not exactly right. Etiquette is very important, and chivalry and 'ladies first', and you stand when an elder enters. Address people by honorifics. Be formal; to quote Worf, 'Good manners are *not* a waste of time.' Mexican culture is much more community oriented than but our peculiarities in community that *can* be misunderstood in the United States, *will* be misunderstood in Mexico."

"Is Mexican culture higher-context than American culture?" Ellamae asked.

"Mmm, good question. Most cultures are less low-context than American culture; some Native American cultures are as high-context as the Japanese, and I think the Romance cultures are high-context. So by general guesswork and geneology, I would expect Mexican culture to be higher in context level. Except I don't know much about what that context is. There are some superstitious remnants of Roman Catholicism, but Rome is more a behind-the-scenes, unseen force than it is the pulsating life in the Catholics we know, especially Emerant. Like the grandmother in *Household Saints*. Um, what else... aah, yes, time. You'll fit in perfectly, Thaddeus. The rest of us, particularly me, will have to work on it. When you agree to meet someone at noon, that's noon, give or take two or three hours. Mexicans will wonder what the hurry is all about. Try not to fidget."

"How does Hispanic culture compare to black culture?" asked Désirée.

"Very similar; the two are probably closer than either is to white American culture. On, and girls, avoid eye contact with men; everybody, avoid flirting," Jaben stated.

Sarah said, "I can't wait to get to Mexico. Seeing another country will be so much fun!"

Jaben said, "Sarah, as I remember, you haven't been out of the country, right?"

"No," she said.

"Ok. A couple of tips on crossing cultures: prepare to have expectations violated that you didn't even know you had. Crossing cultures is both wonderful and terrible, and it's particularly rough the first time. Or at least I've heard it is for most people; I don't experience culture shock the same way. It will look to you like people are doing all sorts of things the wrong way, and some of them will indeed be wrong, but a great many are just different, and some of them better," Jaben said. "Try not to complain, or at least not to take a complaining attitude."

"Oh, dear!" Sarah said. "That sounds frightful."

"It is, and it isn't," Jaben said. "You'll love Mexico, and, knowing you, you'll walk away with at least twenty different paintings in your head, and be able to execute all of them perfectly. Which reminds me, did anyone bring a camera?"

There was no response.

"Good. We are not coming as shutterbug tourists, and taking a bunch of pictures wouldn't be proper. Let's see... what else... Aah. Does anyone know the Hacker's Drinking Song?"

"Nope," said Lilianne.

"Ok, let me sing the first two verses.

"Ninety-nine blocks of crud on the disk,
Ninety-nine blocks of crud,
Patch a bug and dump it again,
One hundred blocks of crud on the disk.

"One hundred blocks of crud on the disk,
One hundred blocks of crud,
Patch a bug and dump it again,
One hundred and one blocks of crud on the disk."

The others joined in with a thunderous noise:

"One hundred and one blocks of crud on the disk,
One hundred and one blocks of crud,
Patch a bug and dump it again,
One hundred and two blocks of crud on the disk..."

They continued singing noisily until the wee hours of the morning.

Chapter Twenty-Two

"Wake up," a voice said. "Wake up; the sun is high in the sky."

"Oh, hi, Lilianne, can't I sleep more?" Thaddeus said.

"No, we should get moving."

"I like to be well-rested when I drive. My reflexes are faster."

"Speaking of faster, I'd like to congratulate you on the stop you made when you decided you were too tired to drive. I didn't know this van could stop that fast," Lilianne said.

"Could I have just a half-hour more sleep?"

"I'm setting my watch."

After another half-hour of sleep, Thaddeus was indeed alert; they drove along, stopping at an IHOP for breakfast. The conversation consisted mostly of how to rearrange the equipment to be more comfortable, and breakfast was followed by about half an hour of rearrangement. The friends got in, their stiffness reduced, and felt better about sitting down. This time, Ellamae rode shotgun.

"I'm bored," Sarah said as they hit the road.

"How would you like to play riddles?" Jaben asked.

"I would love to!" said Sarah.

Jaben said,

"A man without eyes,
saw plums in a tree.
He neither ate them nor left them.
Now how could this be?"

"That's impossible!" Sarah said. "A cabin on a mountain--"

Sarah paused. "Are the eyes he doesn't have literal eyes, like you and I have?"

"Literal eyes."

"Not like the eye of a storm?"

"Not like the eye of a storm."

"And he literally saw? Did he see in a dream?"

"He literally saw, as I literally see you now."

"Exactly the same?"

Jaben closed his eyes. "There is a slight difference, that is understandable if you know a bit of biology or psychology."

"That's not a fair riddle!" Sarah said. "You know that only Ellamae knows psychology. Don't give me a riddle I can't answer!"

"You do not need to know of biology or psychology to solve this riddle. In fact, I never thought of connecting this riddle with biology or psychology until now."

"I know what the answer is," said Ellamae.

"What is it?" Jaben asked, smiling.

"The man had only one eye. He took some of the plums, but not others."

Sarah sat, silently, and then said, "Oooooooh."

Jaben said, "*Et voila!*"

"How did psychology tell you that?" Sarah asked, confused.

"Put one hand over your eye," Ellamae said. "Do you notice anything different in how things look?"

"Yeah, everything looks flat like in a picture."

"Your depth perception (things not looking flat, but having depth) is what happens when your brain takes input from both eyes (which are in slightly different positions, and see something slightly different) and puts them together. A man who had only one eye would see slightly differently from someone with two eyes -- like you did when you covered one eye with your hand."

"Ok, what's the next riddle?"

Jaben chanted in a lyrical voice,

"'Twas whispered in Heaven, 'twas muttered in Hell,
And echo caught faintly the sound as it fell;
On the confines of earth 'twas permitted to rest,
And in the depths of the ocean its presence confes'd;
'Twill be found in the sphere when 'tis riven asunder,
Be seen in the lightning and heard in the thunder;
'Twas allotted to man with his earliest breath,
Attends him at birth and awaits him at death,
Presides o'er his happiness, honor, and health,
Is the prop of his house, and the end of his wealth.
In the heaps of the miser 'tis hoarded with care,
But is sure to be lost on his prodigal heir;
It begins every hope, every wish it must bound,
With the husbandman toils, and with monarchs is crowned;
Without it the soldier and seaman may roam,
But woe to the wretch who expels it from home!
In the whispers of conscience its voice will be found,
Nor e'er in the whirlwind of passion be drowned;
'Twill soften the heart; but though deaf be the ear,
It will make him acutely and instantly hear.
Set in shade, let it rest like a delicate flower;
Ah! Breathe on it softly, it dies in an hour."

The van was silent for a minute, and then Ellamae said, "The letter 'h'."

"You have a sharp mind," Jaben said.

A light of comprehension flashed in Sarah's eyes, as she murmured parts of the riddle to herself, and then she said, "Give us a riddle that will take longer to solve, and that Ellamae won't get."

Jaben closed his eyes, thinking, waiting. Then, as if not a moment had passed, he pulled a duffel bag onto his lap, and said, "What have I got in my pocket?"

"What have I got in my pocket? What have I got in my pocket?" Sarah said, again murmuring to herself, and said, "I know! A pair of pliers!"

"No," Jaben said. "My pliers is on my knife. And it's something very specific, not my wallet."

"A picture of me!" she said, beaming.

"No, I forgot to pack that. But I usually carry a picture of you in my pocket. I like to look at you."

"Ok, I give up. What is it?"

Jaben put the duffel bag back, reached into his pocket, and pulled out an annulus, which had a metallic shimmer and yet was not of metal. He handed it to Ellamae, and said, "Hold it in the sunlight."

Ellamae smiled, and said, "The sunlight is hot, and yet the CD-ROM remains cool. On the inner edge of the central hole I see an inscription, an inscription finer than the finest penstrokes, running along the CD-ROM, above and below: lines of fire. They shine piercingly bright, and yet remote, as out of a great depth: 42 72 65 61 64 20 61 6E 64 20 74 65 6C 65 76 64 73 69 6F 6E 73. I cannot understand the fiery letters and numbers." She looked very elfin.

"No," said Jaben, "but I can. The letters are hexadecimal, of an ancient mode, but the language is that of MicroSoft, which I will not utter here. But this in the English tongue is what is said, close enough:

"One OS to rule them all, One OS to find them,
One OS to bring them all and in the darkness bind them."

Chapter Twenty-Three

The friends stopped for a picnic lunch on the grass. Thaddeus remarked that it was a cool day, although sunny, and the women protested until Jaben pointed out that Thaddeus, having lived in Malaysia and spent a lot of time with Indians, used the words 'hot' and 'cool' to distinguish weather that will melt a brass doorknob from weather that will merely make it a bit mushy. They ate MREs and talked *de tout et de rien*, of everything and nothing, and then packed up the waste and left.

As they got into the van, Jaben picked up *A Treasury of Jewish humor*, and said, "Here, from the introduction. An anti-Semite says to a Jew, 'All our troubles come from the Jews!'

"'Absolutely! From the Jews--and the bicycle riders.'

"'Bicycle riders! Why the bicycle riders?'

"'Why the Jews?'"

There was a chuckle, but Désirée said, "You know, Jaben, your jokes are good, but I think we're all kinda laughed out now. Or at least I am. Why don't we do something else?"

"Did Jaben pack *A Wind in the Door*?" Sarah asked.

Lilianne smiled. All of the Kythers had read the book cover to cover at least three or four times, and Sarah knew it by heart. It was the book from which they had taken their name, alongside a lesser and obscure document listing 100 ways of kything.

Jaben rummaged among the bags, and produced a small, battered black book. "Lilianne, why don't you read?"

Lilianne took the book gently, and said, "Since we all know *Wind* so well, I'm just going to open it at random, look until I find something good, and read it aloud, and then we can talk about it. Lessee..." she opened the book to the middle, and read silently, then said, "Aah, here. Page eighty-one. Meg and Proginoskes are talking.

"Meg says, 'Okay, I can get to the grade school all right, but I can't possibly take you with me. You're so big you wouldn't even fit into the school bus. Anyhow, you'd terrify everybody.' At the thought she smiled, but Proginoskes was not in a laughing mood.

"'Not everybody is able to see me,' he told her. 'I'm real, and most earthlings can bear very little reality.'" Lilianne closed the book.

"That's my favorite part!" Sarah said, with an animated smile. "Or one of my favorites; I like positive parts. But 'most earthlings can bear very little reality' is true. Most people, when they grow up, lose their childhood. I don't mind that they become adults. That's good. But they stop being children and that's really sad. You can't be a true adult without being a child. Some people have asked me when my interminable childhood was going to end, and I have always told them 'never'. I was surprised and happy when Jaben told me, 'You have somehow managed to blossom into womanhood without losing the beauty of a little girl.' Jaben was the first to understand me.

"Children are able to bear reality. They are so expert at bearing reality that they can even bear not-reality just as easily. Santa Claus and Easter bunny and fairies don't harm them like they'd harm an adult, because they are from the same source as a deeper reality -- faith and goodness and providence and wonder. This is why, when children pray, things happen. People are healed. Their prayers are real. This is also why Chesterton said, 'A man's creed should leave him free to believe in fairies,' or kind of. A child who looks at some leaves and sees the wee folk is wrong, but not nearly as wrong as the adult who looks at the human body and sees nothing but matter. Not only because the error is worse, but because the child knows he is a child and wants to grow up, and the adult thinks he already *is* grown up. I still want to grow up; it's a shame when a person's growth is stunted by thinking he's grown up. Anyways, God is too big and too real for us to deal with -- so is his Creation -- but most children can bear something they can't handle, and most adults can't bear much of anything they can't handle. Like death; our culture denies death, whether it is tearing the elderly and dying out of their houses and isolating them in hospitals and nursing homes, or this whole pornography of death like Arnold Schwarzenegger movies. And that philosopher Kant's -- what was it called? The book that cut faith into --"

"*Religion Within the Bounds of Reason*," Jaben said.

"Like the Jews who told Moses, 'We don't want to see the Lord. Be our prophet for us that we don't see him, so we don't die.' I count myself really, really, really lucky to have friends who can bear reality, who kythe, who touch me, who look into my paintings, who can see that I am not a ditz."

Thaddeus winked at her. "Yes, Squeaky-Toy."

"Hey!" Sarah said. "Only Jaben is allowed to call me that."

"Me rorry," Thad said affectionately.

A silence fell. Jaben began to hum a strand from a French lovesong -- <<*Elle est femme, elle est gamine,*>> and when Sarah asked what he was humming, he explained that a man was singing of his beloved, that she was both a woman and a child. Sarah smiled, not feeling the slightest hint of romantic interest. Jaben was presently undecided as to whether he wanted to live celibate or married -- presently not dating anyone, not seeking to, but not closed to the possibility -- and yet was fascinated by lovesong and love poetry. It had taken Sarah some time to understand that his collection of erotica -- from all places and all times -- was not pornographic and was perused without lust by *un chevalier parfait, sans peur et sans reproche*. She was finally persuaded, not by the force of his arguments (for she knew how often forceful arguments could be wrong), but by the passion and the purity of his heart. Jaben had memorized Baudelaire's *l'Invitation au Voyage*, and had made his own translation of the Song of Songs because, he said, politics had coerced translators into bowlderizing the English rendition and using wooden literality to obscure its meaning. Sarah had turned a very bright shade of red when Jaben explained to her the meaning of "I have entered my garden;" her skin matched her shining hair, and Jaben had revelled in her beauty. Thereafter, and after Jaben gave explanations to un-bowlderize other areas of the Bible, she always giggled at certain texts. Sarah found it quite curious that most of the sexual content in the Bible was softened considerably, but none of the violence; in her mind, it was connected not only to the behavior of many Christians -- who wouldn't touch a film with nudity (not even *Titanic*, which Sarah loved and Jaben hated), but didn't flinch at movies that were rated 'R' for violence, let alone cartoons that show how funny it is to drop an anvil on someone's head -- but to a movie ratings system that, in the words of one magazine article, found "massaging a breast to be more offensive than cutting it off."

These -- and many other things like them -- were thought about in the car. Some of them were discussed; others did not need to be said aloud, because of the common understanding between them; this gave the dialogue a unique potency and depth, and thus it remained the next day, and the day after, until when -- as they were in Texas, approaching the Mexican border -- something interesting happened.

Their radiator blew out.

Chapter Twenty-Four

"Well," Jaben said. "we just passed a town. Let's some of us stay with the van and some of us go in. Drink a goodly bit of water, he said, grabbing a canteen, "and we'll hope to be back soon." They talked amongst themselves, and Thaddeus, Jaben, and Sarah decided to go, leaving Désirée, Lilianne, and Ellamae to sit in the van's shade.

"Do you think you could ever write like Kant," Sarah said.

"Certainly," Jaben answered, "if I tried hard and studied a certain book."

"Which of Kant's books?" Sarah asked.

"Not one of Kant's books," Jaben said. "The *Handbook of Applied Cryptography*."

Sarah's eyes lit up, and then filled with perplexity. "You don't like that type of deep philosophical writing?"

Jaben said, "It is hard to think deep thoughts. It is harder still to think deep thoughts and record them faithfully. It is hardest to think deep thoughts and record them faithfully in a manner that people will understand. *That* is what I aim for."

As they walked around, they passed an abandoned 1950's truck, rusted and with one window broken. A small animal scurried behind a tire.

"Stop," Sarah said. "I want to look at this truck." They stopped, and Sarah stood, looked at the truck, tilted her head, bent over, walked a bit, and walked further. Then she finally said, "Okay. I have my picture ready," and continued talking into town as if not a moment had passed.

After stopping in a gas station, they found an auto body and repair shop, and junkyard, advertising, "Largest parts selection in fifty miles." There was a tall man who was sitting in a rocker in the shade outside the shop, and rose to greet them. "Hello, folks. May I help you?"

"Yes. Our van's radiator blew out, and we were looking for a mechanic." Jaben tried not to wince, thinking about the damage that the repairs would do to their funds.

"I wish Bear were here. He's so good with cars," said Sarah.

"You know a guy named Bear? The Bear I know is almost seven feet tall, weighs three hundred pounds--"

"--and has an elephant gun with a laser sight," Jaben finished. "How do you know him?"

"He's my cousin." Now all those present were astonished. "How do you know him?"

"He's my friend and my boss. My name's Jaben, by the way, and this is Thaddeus and Sarah."

"I'm Jim. I think I might have heard of you. What are y'all doing down here?"

Jaben's smile turned to a frown. "We are looking for our friend Amos, who has disappeared, and whose location we do not know."

Jim's jaw dropped. "Amos has disappeared? Bear said the best things about him. They used to play together as little boys, and--ooh, I'm not going to tell you that story, because Bear and Amos (if you find him) will kill me."

Jaben said, "He has, which is why we're on this adventure. It may be a fool's errand, but we want to see it through."

The mechanic looked at him with a deep, probing gaze. "Your friendship runs that deep?"

"Our friendship runs that deep," said Jaben.

The mechanic closed his eyes for a second, then said, "Come on over to my truck. I'll throw a blanket in the bed so the metal doesn't burn you, and there are a few containers of iced tea in the fridge. Y'all look like you're melting. The repair is on me. What's the make and model of your van?"

Jaben was so surprised that he forgot to tell James the requested information. Sarah ran up and gave him a hug and a kiss. Thaddeus asked, "What can we do to thank you?"

The mechanic took out a notebook, and wrote something on it. "This is my number. You can give me a call when you find Amos, or give up the chase. And, if you want to do something else, you can bring Amos by here when you find him. I've always wanted to meet him. Did Bear ever show you that gun of his?"

Thaddeus pulled his shirt collar aside to reveal several bruises. "These black and blue marks are from firing it, once. He offered to let me take his gun with us, but I can't handle a gun like that."

"Yep, that sounds like something Bear would do. He's a big man with an even bigger heart. Would you step inside? The fridge is there, and some of my tools. I've got several vans with radiators in the junkyard. Any of you handy with tools?"

Jaben raised his hand.

"All right. Here's my leather gloves; I don't want you burning your hands. Let's go."

Chapter Twenty-Five

Jim invited them to stay for the night -- which they did, unrolling their sleeping bags in the living room. In the morning the women especially were happy to have a real shower. After a breakfast of eggs and bacon, Jaben asked about where to get certain supplies, and insisted on paying for a siphon, a 12-pack of cigarette lighters with 7 left, a stack of old newspapers (*USA*

Today, Jaben was glad to see, so he wouldn't feel bad about burning them), and a couple of other odd items. They drained the water drum and refilled it afresh, and left with a hearty goodbye and thank you, hugs and a kiss from Sarah.

There seemed to be not much change on the road from Texas to Mexico; they stopped at a border town on the way to change some money, and two or three hours after crossing the border, they came on the town of Juarez and decided to stop for lunch.

The marketplace was wild, colorful, and full of smells. It had an energy about it that was lacking in American supermarkets. "Ooh, look!" Sarah said, and walked over to a vendor. There were several paintings, and she was looking intently at a small painting of a seashell on the sand. "Two hundred pesos," the vendor said.

Jaben looked at the painting, looked at the vendor, and pulled out seventy pesos. "*Este dinero es suficiente.*"

The vendor seemed slightly surprised, and took the money.

As they walked over to the fruit stands, Jaben said, "I don't mind that you bought that picture, Sarah, but we are not here as tourists, and money is tight. Please don't buy anything else we don't need."

"But Jaben, look!" Sarah said, holding the picture up.

He looked, and there was a glimmer of comprehension in his eyes. The picture was a deep picture, and he would need some more time to understand it. The artist must have been talented. "Thank you for buying it, Sarah," Jaben said slowly.

Picking up a few oranges, Jaben asked the vendor, "*Cuánto cuestan estas naranjas?*"

"*Uno peso*."

As well as the oranges, they purchased some bananas, avocados, and a chili pepper or two for Thad to munch on. The friends sat down in a corner, and talked, and watched the children play. They were kicking a rock around; their clothing was well worn and their bodies thin, and yet the children seemed to be playing in bliss. One of them walked over, and Ellamae gave the little girl half of her orange. Thaddeus pulled out a knife and was about to cut up one of the avocados, when Sarah reached into the pockets of her baggy pants, and said, "I know why I brought my red bouncy ball along!"

Jaben said, "No, wait. Sarah!"

Sarah had already rolled the ball down the street. A child kicked it, and it knocked the avocado out of Thaddeus's hand, and looked very sheepish. Then Sarah batted it back to the children, and--

Perhaps the best way to describe the ensuing chaos would be to say that it would have given Amos a headache, and that Jaben loved it. The ball was tossed around; people said things in English and in Spanish, not understanding the words and yet somehow understanding the meaning; there was dance; there was chaos. At one point, two teams formed, but they were trying to give the other team possession of the ball, and then that shifted, and then there were three teams, and then none. At one point, the friends and the children were all hopping on one foot; at another, they were all weaving a pattern in the air with their hands. There was touch; there was tickling; there was dodging. At the end of the joyous romp, Jaben sat down, exhausted; Sarah took the ball, and placed an arm over Jaben's shoulder (Jaben shifted away, and said, "Not here. Remember what I told you."), and said, "So, Jaben, how'd you enjoy your first game of Janra-ball?"

Jaben laughed. "I didn't think it was possible."

Chapter Twenty-Six

As they drove along, the desert gave way to rocky land. The friends pulled over about an hour's drive away from Mexico city, and got out to go.

Ellamae and Sarah started to head around a rocky corner -- the first words out of Sarah's mouth when they stopped were, "I really need to pee!" -- and stopped cold in their tracks. Ellamae, her voice stressed, said, "Thaddeus, come here. There's a rattlesnake raised to strike."

Jaben said, "Whatever you do, don't move a muscle. Be a statue."

Sarah said, "Still is the last thing I can be right now. I'm--"

Jaben said, "Recite to me the subjects of your last five paintings."

Sarah said, "I can't do that. I'm too scared."

Jaben calmly said, "Yes, you can. What is the first--"

Bang! A gunshot sounded. Ellamae and Sarah jumped high. The rattlesnake fell to the ground, dead.

Thaddeus was crouched on a rock, holding a smoking gun. He loaded another round, and then walked over. He drew a hunting knife. "You guys know that rattlesnake meat is considered a delicacy?"

Sarah quivered, and said, "Thank you, Thaddeus. Now if I can change my pants--"

Ellamae looked in his eyes, and said, "I'm sorry for what I said about your gun. You saved my life."

Thaddeus opened his mouth to say something, then closed it as he had nothing to say. Finally, he said, "You're welcome."

Jaben said, "Thaddeus, I've always wondered why you didn't even get a gun with a clip. Not that you have to have a semi-automatic, but..." his voice trailed off.

Thaddeus and said, "This was the only good rifle that was within my price range when I brought it, and I brought it for target practice, not for hunting. But as to the other aspect -- I just decided that I wanted to practice until my aim was good enough that I would never need to shoot twice."

Ellamae said, "Again, thank you."

They set up camp, and soon fell into a deep sleep.

Chapter Twenty-Seven

Two warriors, clad in back, holding unsheathed katanas, silently approached each other in the forest. A sliver of moonlight fell. They circled around each other, slowly, crouched, waiting.

Then one of them swung, and there was a counter. Silence.

Another swing. A flurry of motion. They circled.

They were both masters, and as they fought -- one of them swinging, the other swiftly evading the razor sharp blade -- it became apparent that one was greater than the other.

The greater swordsman lowered his weapon and closed his eyes, and in an instant the lesser struck him down.

Ellamae awoke, greatly troubled by her dream, but decided to tell no one.

As she drifted off to sleep again, Ellamae wondered who had really won the duel.

Chapter Twenty-Eight

They pulled into Mexico City early in the morning, the stench of smog only a hint of how bad it would get. Thaddeus had no difficulty finding the governmental buildings, nor Jaben in finding the appropriate bureaucrats. Getting anything useful out of them was a different matter.

As the friends sat down for lunch, Jaben said, "I'm a little disappointed at progress, but not surprised. Mexican bureaucracies are almost impossible to navigate if you don't know someone on the inside."

"That stinks!" Sarah said. "Aren't the officials supposed to help people?"

"Sarah, culture shock is difficult. It's a leading cause of suicide, right up there with divorce. There is great beauty in seeing a new country, but also great pain. I'm surprised at how well you're adapting; you're in the hardest part now," Jaben said.

"Stop talking philosophy at me!" Sarah snapped, and then repeated her question. "Aren't officials supposed to help people?"

"Yes, but in this culture you don't just see someone when you want something from them. Relationships are very important, and you cultivate a relationship with someone inside the bureaucracy before trying to get something out of them. In a way, what we are doing is rude, asking for services without taking the time to first establish a connection. Except we have to be rude, because--"

"I still think it stinks," Sarah said.

"I would rather we were dealing with an American bureaucracy, too. American bureaucracies are sluggish and Machiavellian and do things wrong, but they have a rare achievement in being responsive to the needs of strangers -- a Brazilian I know was amazed when he got a scholarship after just filling out a form, without knowing anyone on the inside. But we don't have that now; we are looking for Amos in Mexico, and therefore have to deal with a Mexican bureaucracy. I didn't expect much, but I wanted to check just in case. Being open to the wind of the Spirit blowing, eh?" Jaben answered.

"So what do we do now?" Désirée asked, rubbing her arm nervously.

"We go to Tijuana," Thaddeus stated.

"What?" several voices said in unison.

"The voice of the Spirit says to go to Tijuana."

"Ok," Désirée said.

They finished their lunch in silence, and got into the van. As they pulled out of the city, Lilianne said, "Thaddeus, I'd give your driving in Mexico City about, oh, an 8.7."

"Really?" Thaddeus said, his eyes widening. "On a scale of 1 to 10?"

"No, on the Richter scale."

Chapter Twenty-Nine

As they drove, Jaben said, "Sarah, remember that one time when you asked me what I didn't like about television, and I said, 'Sarah, I'd really like to explain it to you, but I have to go to bed some time in the next six hours?'"

"Yeah, I remember that. Why?" Sarah said.

"We're going to have a few days driving to Tijuana, and I think this would be a good time to give your question the answer it deserves," Jaben said.

"Ok," Sarah said thoughtfully. "But you still like Sesame

Street?"

"I grew up on it, but no. I do not like Sesame Street," Jaben said.

"Why not?" Sarah said, with sadness in her voice.

"I mean to give your question the answer it deserves."

Ellamae cocked her ears, attentive. So did Lilianne.

"I have a number of thoughts to give. I would like to begin by reading the foreword to Neil Postman's book, *Amusing Ourselves to Death: Public Discourse in the Age of Show Business*, the first one I read on that score:

"'We were keeping our eye on 1984. When the year came and the prophecy didn't, thoughtful Americans sang softly in praise of themselves. The roots of liberal democracy had held. Wherever else the terror had happened, we, at least, had not been visited by Orwellian nightmares.

"'But we had forgotten that alongside Orwell's dark vision, there was another--slightly older, slightly less well known, equally chilling: Aldous Huxley's *Brave New World*. Contrary to common belief even among the educated, Huxley and Orwell did not prophesy the same thing. Orwell warns us that we will be overcome by an externally imposed oppression. But in Huxley's vision, no Big Brother is required to deprive people of their autonomy, maturity and history. As he saw it, people will come to love their oppression, to adore the technologies that undo their capacities to think.

"'What Orwell feared were those who would ban books. What Huxley feared was that there would be no reason to ban a book, for there would be no one who wanted to read one. Orwell feared those who would deprive us of information. Huxley feared those who would give us so much that would be reduced to passivity and egoism. Orwell feared that the truth would be concealed from us. Huxley feared the truth would be drowned in a sea of irrelevance. Orwell feared we would become a captive culture. Huxley feared we would become a trivial culture, preoccupied with some equivalent of the feelies, the orgy porgy, and the centrifugal bumblepuppy. As Huxley remarked in *Brave*

New World Revisited, the civil libertarians and rationalists who are ever on the alert to oppose tyrrany "failed to take into account man's almost infinite appetite for distractions." In *1984*, Huxley added, people are controlled by inflicting pain. In *Brave New World*, they are controlled by inflicting pleasure. In short, Orwell feared that what we hate will ruin us. Huxley feared that what we love will ruin us.

"'This book is about the possibility that Huxley, not Orwell, was right.'"

Jaben closed the book.

Chapter Thirty

Jaben said, "Let's see. The first part of *Amusing* talks about how different media impact the content of discourse. Somewhat overstated, I think, but an extremely important point."

Sarah asked, "You mean there's a difference between reading something in a book and reading it on the web?"

Jaben replied, "Yes, there is. The web appears -- and in some ways is -- an author's dream come true. It is a kind of text where you can read about a surgical procedure and click on a link to see an MPEG of it being performed, or have transparent footnotes that actually pull up the document quoted. All of this has wonderful potential, but there is a dark side. For starters, a book has to be purchased or picked up at the library, which means that you have to invest something to get it, and if you're reading it, you have to get up and walk to put the book away and get another one. This makes for some commitment to the present document, which is not present on the web. Furthermore, putting color pictures in books is prohibitively expensive. This makes it more likely that a book which draws people's attention will do it with substance. But images are far cheaper on the web, and images grab attention much faster than books do. So if you'll look at a corporate website, you will find sound bites and flashy pictures, and almost nothing thought-provoking. *The web has potentential to be far better than books, but it also has a strong tendency to be much worse.*"

"You mean with all the porn that's out there?" Sarah asked.

"Well, that's a part of it. But even apart from that -- have you ever gone to look for some information on the web, and found yourself clicking all sorts of silly links, and looked at your watch and realized that an hour had gone by, completely wasted?"

"Well, yeah, but I thought that was just me."

"It's not just you. It's the Web."

Sarah pondered this in silence.

"Technology -- some more than others -- is something I treat like a loaded gun, or like alcohol. It can be beneficial, very beneficial, but you should never lay the reins on the horse's neck, and never treat it as something neutral. It has a sort of hidden agenda. Have you heard of the Sorceror's Bargain?" Jaben explained.

"No, what's that?"

"In the Sorceror's Bargain, the Devil says, 'I will give you power if you will give me your soul.' But there's a problem -- obviously, you lose your soul, and less obviously, it isn't really you that has the power at all. All that has really happened in the exchange is that you've lost your soul. You haven't gained anything."

"That stinks," Sarah said.

"It does, and something of that is what happens with technology. Mammon and Technology are twin brothers, and I think I see part of why Jesus said, 'No man can serve two masters. Either he will love the one and hate the other, or else hate the one and love the other. You cannot serve both God and Mammon.' What I find fascinating is that he did not refer to money as a slave, but as a master. With technology -- have you noticed that I use e-mail for all sorts of technical and intellectual matters, but never for personal matters? That I walk over and talk with you in person?"

"Yes, and it means a lot to me," Sarah said.

"Technologies have an obvious benefit, and a less obvious, insidious cost; there is always a cost, and with some it is worse than others. With--"

"Are you a Luddite?" Sarah asked.

"I am at present riding in a van; one of my hobbies is writing computer programs; I have a massive collection of books; I eat prepared foods, wear clothes, telephone people, and speak language. All of these are technologies, and I use them in clean conscience. Someone said of war, 'I don't think we need more hawks or more doves. I think we need more owls.' I don't want to be a hawkish technology worshipper or a Luddite dove. I want to be an owl.

"As I was saying, television has an incredible darkside. It is a sequence of moving images that stimulates the senses and makes brain cells atrophy. I fervently believe that, since the beginning of time, the twilight hours have belonged to the teller of tales and the weavers of songs. You know I like music, and role play, and listening to Désirée tell stories, and all sorts of things. But television is among pass-times what nihilism is among philosophy, what Bud Lite is among beers. That is why, I think, the author of the 100 ways of kything said, 'Television is a crawling abomination from the darkest pits of Hell. It is a pack of cigarettes for the mind. It blinds the inner eye. It is the anti-kythe. A home without television is like a slice of chocolate cake without tartar sauce.'"

Chapter Thirty-One

Jaben said, "The second half of the book deals with how television is impacting public life, how everybody is always expecting to be amused. A good place to start is," he said, flipping through the text, "let's see..."

After some more flipping, he started fiddling with the folded sheet of paper being used as a bookmark. "I'm not sure that there's a good, concise place to begin, and the problem may get worse with *Four Arguments for the Elimination of Television*."

"The author could only think of four?" Ellamae asked.

Jaben idly opened the sheet of paper, and then his eyes

widened. "This'll do nicely. It must have been left as a bookmark by the previous patron to check the book out. It's a seminar announcement:

"The Middle School PTA is sponsoring a free parent education seminar -- Why are we slowing down?"

"We're being pulled over," Thaddeus said.

Jaben reached into his wallet and pulled out 70 pesos, handing them forward to the front.

They stopped, and Thaddeus unrolled the window. "*Buenos dias, señor.*" He held out the money; the officer took it, said "*Gracias*," and walked back.

Jaben put his foot on the petal and rolled up the window at the same time.

"It's really cool that in Mexico you can pay a speeding ticket on the spot without having to go into an office. That would have cost us so much time," said Sarah.

"Why are you smiling, Jaben?" Sarah asked, after a moment had passed.

"That wasn't exactly paying a ticket, Sarah."

"Well what was it then."

"A little bit of grease on his palm."

"You bribed a police officer?" Sarah asked, incredulous.

"Yes, Sarah. It's not the same as in America." Jaben said, folding the paper, sticking it in the book, and closing the book.

"I can't believe you did that!" Sarah said. "Does breaking the law only count in the United States, not in Mexico? There is no authority except from God, and Romans 13 and all."

"Sarah, do you know why the cop pulled us over?"

"Because Thad thinks that he's in Malaysia."

"Uh, ok. You have a point there. But do you know why else he pulled us over?"

"Yes, he was going to write a ticket."

"No, the cop had no intention whatsoever of writing a ticket."

Sarah closed her eyes in concentration for a minute. "Are you saying he pulled us over in the hope of receiving a bribe?"

"No, I'm saying he pulled us over in the *certainty* of receiving a bribe."

"Well, if a corrupt cop pulls us over, why don't we go in and report him?"

"Sarah, do you know what would happen if we did that?"

"Yes, they'd put him under discipline."

"Not exactly."

"Ok, I give up. What would happen?"

"We'd be laughed out of court," Jaben said.

Sarah opened her mouth, then closed it.

"Police officers are paid much too little, like the majority of other Mexicans, and it's an accepted part of the culture. In our country, bribes are associated with corruption and subversion of justice, but in Mexico they do not have that meaning. It's just an informal income distribution system with very little overhead. The outrage you are experiencing is culture shock."

"So there's nothing wrong with Mexico? All there is is difference? You can critique American culture, but Mexican culture is off limits?"

"No; there are a great many things wrong with Mexican culture, some of which make me sick. It's a macho culture, but women hold all the power --"

"Go, women!" Sarah cheered. Jaben decided not to recite Ambrose Bierce's definition of 'queen', and continued, "--and it's an unhealthy, manipulative power that they hold. If you were my wife, you might get me drunk and steal money from my wallet. The phenomenon exists in the United States; it's just not so stark. It's why there were all those bumper stickers saying, 'Impeach President Clinton and her husband.' In many families, the husband's off doing his own thing, drinking with his buddies, and the wife is meeting her emotional needs with her children, especially her oldest son. It's not incestuous, but it's very unhealthy. In contradistinction to our own culture's exaggeration of 'leave and cleave', a man will choose his mother and sister over his wife and children. They have the opposite error. Mexican culture emphasizes family and community, but certain aspects of familial community are very unhealthy. Their culture is as much marked by the Fall as our own."

Sarah sat in thought, and said, "Why do you condemn these things, but condone bribing an officer?"

Jaben said, "Later, I'd like to talk with you about implications of fundamental beauty. But for now, just trust me on this."

"Ok," Sarah said slowly. "I'll trust you."

Chapter Thirty-Two

"The Middle School PTA," Jaben read, "is sponsoring a free parent education seminar by So-and-so, a highly sought after seminar leader who combines practical strategies with a high energy 'you can do it' approach to parenting middle schoolers. So-and-so has been a professional communicator for over 20 years as a parent, teacher, clinical counselor, author and professor at the Adler School of Professional Psychology. She has addressed school districts, corporations and community organizations throughout the Chicago area on the subject of parenting. Noted for her ability to get audiences involved using a highly interactive humorous format, she has consistently received the highest level ratings for her warm, knowledgeable and practical presentations.

"So-and-so will tackle how to help your child develop attitudes and skills essential to withstanding peer pressure. She will also provide concrete ways to encourage building self-esteem in both our children and ourselves through practical techniques *that actually work*. Drawing on her years of experience in working with teenagers, So-and-so shares proven ideas you can use immediately. Don't miss this lively, inspiring and humorous session!" Jaben folded the sheet of paper, set it in the book, and closed it.

"What's wrong with that?" Désirée asked.

"Well, it doesn't distinguish between the presenter being entertaining and her being an expert in dealing with adolescents," Ellamae said.

Jaben said, "On one televangelist's show that Postman addresses, the saved get to play themselves before and after, and, Postman says, they are saved twice: by being brought into the presence of Jesus, and made a movie star. To the uninitiate, Postman says, it is hard to tell which is the higher estate." They discussed a bit more; Jaben did not say much of anything additional, beyond encouraging the others to sit down and read the book, and that a week of careful television watching and attending consumer oriented services (for which he recommended a perusal of *Why Catholics Can't Sing*), listening to people, and otherwise examining American life would reveal a lot to a perceptive mind. Asked about Jerry Mander's *Four Arguments for the Elimination of Television*, he said, "That's another discussion for another day."

Chapter Thirty-Three

Sarah said, "What was that about fundamental beauty?"

Jaben said, "There is a trinity of the good, the true, and the beautiful, in which we must neither confound the elements nor divide the substance. Those three words describe the same -- being, but in different ways. And there is something I have called 'fundamental beauty', for lack of a better term in any language, to refer to something that is fundamental and is of the character of beauty that is shared between different things, things that may look different on the surface. My favorite example is singing and dancing -- in one sense, they are not very much alike at all -- one is sound, the other is motion, and (my physics training notwithstanding) the two are not the same. But in another, deeper way, there is something very much the same about them. They are both beautiful in the same way. *They share the same fundamental beauty.*

"The Chinese character for 'metaphor' is a compound character, a little like an English word like 'doughnut', and the constituent characters are 'hidden' and 'analogy'; there can be a hidden analogy, a shared fundamental beauty, between two objects that may look very different. A recognition of shared fundamental beauty seems to me to lie at the heart of all metaphor, and the more striking and poetic the metaphor the more disparate on the surface the two things are, and the more closely they share a fundamental beauty. When a poet compared a woman to a red, red rose, the comparison was not anatomical in character, nor along any other literal lines; he was rather seeing a shared fundamental beauty.

"The present grandmaster of ninjutsu, Masaaki Hatsumi, wrote in *Essence of Ninjutsu* about talking with a photographer who took pictures of horses, and had to deal with a basic problem: horses know when they're being watched, and stiffen up. When she takes a picture, she stands with her back to the horse, waits until the horse relaxes, and then swiftly turns around and snaps a shot before the horse can tense up. He commented that it is like the ninjutsu 5th degree black belt test, where the master stands with an unsheathed katana over the disciple, and then sometime in the next thirty minutes gives a shout and brings the sword down. The disciple has to get out of the way. The grandmaster saw a likeness between the two disciplines at that point; you might say that he saw the same fundamental beauty, and commented that two disciplines, no matter how far apart, will share something in common. This kind of point of connection might also be why Musashi wrote in *A Book of Five Rings*, 'You must study the ways of all professions.' If so, it is most definitely *not* a lesson which should be confined to martial artists.

"What I realized in our discussion about bribing cops is that, not only is it possible for two different-looking things to share the same fundamental beauty, but it is possible for two similar-looking things to have very different fundamental beauties. I hesitate to use the term 'beauty' in reference to bribing a cop, but the fundamental essence of bribing an American cop and bribing a Mexican cop are different. They look the same, but the heart is different, just as ninjutsu and horse photography look quite different, but at that one point are very similar."

Sarah looked pensive for a few minutes, and said, "I see,

Jaben. I really see. I'm glad I trusted you on this one."

By this point, it was getting very late, and so they pulled over and got ready to set up camp.

Chapter Thirty-Four

They stopped in the rocks, and began to unload the groundcloths, sleeping bags, and tents. They were unpacking, when they heard a rustle. "What's that?" Ellamae said. Immediately, Thaddeus had his gun aimed at the sound.

Five bandits stepped out from behind the rocks, followd by more. They were armed with rifles. "Drop your gun," the leader said, in a thick but understandable accent.

Thaddeus casually cast aside his rifle.

"Give us your money, your women."

"No," Thaddeus said, stepping forward. "It will not help you."

"We will kill you," said the leader.

"No," Thaddeus said.

"Give now!"

"No," Thaddeus said.

The angry leader aimed his gun, grinned wickedly, and pulled the trigger.

Click. The gun jammed.

The leader angrily shook the gun, struck it against the rock, and successfully fired three shots into the air. Then he took aim once again, and pulled the trigger.

Click.

"My God is bigger than your gun," said Thaddeus.

The man threw down his gun, and drew a wicked-looking knife. He started advancing.

Thaddeus had the knife with a serrated back, but did not draw it.

Thaddeus looked intently into his eyes.

The brigand slowed his pace.

Thaddeus kept his intense, probing gaze.

The brigand stopped.

Thaddeus closed his eyes for a moment, and then looked with all the more focus.

The brigand stood still, returning his gaze.

"*Te amo*," Thaddeus said in broken Spanish, praying with his whole heart that it wouldn't be misunderstood.

The brigand sheathed his knife, took his gun, and walked away.

One by one, each of his thirty companions followed, leaving the six friends alone.

"Thanks be to God," Ellamae said.

Thaddeus collapsed in fear, relief, and exhaustion.

Chapter Thirty-Five

Packing away the equipment after eating another round of MREs, the friends got into the van. Désirée rode shotgun, and the others got into the back. "And the *Four Arguments*?" Ellamae said, looking at Jaben.

"I'm not going to treat them all; there's a reason why those arguments are given in a long book. It's necessary for a fair treatment. I'm only going to mention, for example, the argument that 'the programming is the packaging, and the advertising is the content', and advertising's role in harmful manipulation. But I do want to treat Mander's argument of artificial unusualness, in conjunction with a transposed argument from Bloom's *The Closing of the American Mind*.

"Television is inherently boring," Jaben began.

"Tell us something new," Désirée said from up front.

"No, really. Even more than you think. Have you ever had a professor tape a class session, and be bored silly with the videotape even though your professor was an engaging speaker? Television has lousy picture quality, and the viewing area is only a tiny portion of your visual field, and the sound is terrible. It's a sensory medium, but its stimulation is second rate at best.

"When a person has a handicap, he can sometimes find

ways to work around it, and become far stronger than a normal person would be. You know how weak I was in gradeschool. This happened with television; they found a number of unnatural ways of making material *artificially unusual*, kind of like taking a dull technical document and making it appear interesting by italicizing lots of text and putting an exclamation point at the end of each sentence. They do things like camera changes, or moving the camera, or adding music, or putting in computer graphics. These things are called technical events, and the rate of technical events seems to be going up; when Mander wrote his *Four Arguments*, he claims that the average rate of technical events was one every ten seconds; Postman wrote a few years later, and said that the average rate of technical events was one every three and a half seconds; last time I watched television and counted technical events, it was toeing the line of one technical event per second. This is why, if you go to Blockbuster and rent an old movie -- even an old color movie -- it appears boring. The number of technical events to keep you stimulated is much lower, and it doesn't meet your threshold for interesting. It makes an interesting experiment to watch ten minutes of regular programming (doesn't matter whether it's sitcoms, tabloids, X-files, news, or other mindless entertainment), ten minutes of commercials, ten minutes of PBS, ten minutes of a movie from this decade, and then ten minutes of some 1960's movie, and monitor both the number of technical events, and how excited or bored you are. This, incidentally, ties in to sex and violence in TV and movies; it's not just that some of the producers have questionable morals, but also that a bit of skin flashing across the screen is stimulating in a way that wholesome shows cannot be. Two people respectfully talking through a disagreement doesn't have nearly the same camera appeal as a bit of a fistfight.

"This is where Allan Bloom comes in. In *The Closing of the American Mind*, he talks about different things that are crippling American students -- interestingly, though he is not writing from a moralistic perspective, he is concerned about many of the same things we are, such as promiscuity and divorce of parents. He could be quoted in a sermon to argue that sin is harmful and that, in fact, God has given us moral law, not for *his* own good, but for *our* own good, just as the Bible says. One of the things he says in particular as a crimp on American students is drugs. The argument is terrifying, and if it were believed by our youth, it would keep them away from narcotics like no 'do drugs, do time' posters ever could.

"The argument is very simple. Once you have done drugs -- once you have cheaply and for nothing experienced the godlike heights of pleasure associated with the greatest successes -- a heroic victory in battle, or the consummation of a marriage -- what, in your day to day life, could you *possibly* experience to compete with that? What can possibly compare? Suddenly, everything is bleak, dull, grey, boring. Everything.

"It would be like -- remember that time when we were in the cave, our eyes comfortably adjusted to the candlelight, and Sarah thought that Désirée and Amos looked so cute snuggling, and whipped out her pocket camera and snapped a picture? There was an instantaneous and tremendously bright flash of light, and then none of us could see *anything*, not even the candles' flames. This is why, by the way, I never use a flashlight when I am outside; I regard it as an implement of blindness rather than an implement of sight, because it brightly illuminates one area but prevents you from seeing the others. That's why, when Lilianne offered me a flashlight that one time, I said, 'No thanks, I want to see.' If you have to use a flashlight, you will never step out from a cabin into brilliant summer moonlight, and I don't know how to tell you -- fair is the sunlight, fairer still the moonlight, fairest of all is the light of thy face --

"Television, video games, movies, are things that embody the same fundamental ugliness as drugs. Non-chemical narcotics, you might call them. The strength of this is hard to recognize if you've used them enough to get inured to them, but I remember the first time I watched that one James Bond movie, with 007 and 006 and that Georgian pilot... I was on the edge of my seat with lust after the usual James Bond opening of half-naked women -- I believe the proper term for that is 'artistic pornography' -- and it still quickens my pulse to remember how my heart was pounding when James Bond was free falling and climbing into the free falling airplane. If you've seen the movie, you probably didn't experience it that way. Hollywood needs to build a stronger and stronger brew to have the same effect on people, and I was much more strongly affected by the movie than most other people would -- just like I would be extremely affected by what would be to a drug addict just a little bit to tide him over until he needed more.

"After you've watched TV, where all the men have high-paying jobs and all the women look sexy in their tight clothes, and there's a camera change every second, and there is music and perhaps a laugh track, and every conversation is exciting and witty -- just what, exactly what, in your normal experience is going to compete with that? Talking with your friends has lulls in the conversation, and not everything is a witty retort; running provides you with something like the same camera change, but the people who go for long runs aren't the people who sit in front of a television. A book, however profound, is not stimulating enough to even lose a competition with television. So people watch television, at, what, six hours a day? Television is kind of like alcohol; a little bit can be good (or, in the case of television, tolerable), a lot at once induces a stupor, and a lot over time rots the brain."

The discussion that followed was vivid and animated. Sarah was disappointed to learn that Sesame Street had been created by a group of former advertisers, and listened with interest to Jaben's argument that advertising embodies the same fundamental ugliness as pornography: "It arouses desires that cannot have a righteous fulfillment, in this case spending money on material possessions beyond even what natural greed would produce. This is, incidentally, why a television is the most expensive household appliance you can buy; it deducts from your pocketbook for long after you've paid it off." Lilianne was particularly interested in this claim; her way of believing (each believer, she said, who is in full orthodoxy has very much his own way of believing) placed a particular emphasis on living simply. "What should I do with my television, then?" asked Lilianne, who felt that she would never look at a television again in the same way. Jaben's reply was simple: "Give it to Thad. He could always use a new target."

Chapter Thirty-Six

It was not long before they arrived in Tijuana, and searched everywhere. They searched high and low, in the resorts and in the slums; they prayed; Lilianne said glumly, "We're looking for a needle in a haystack." After a week of searching, Jaben said, "This city is too noisy. I need to go out into the countryside to think."

The friends drove aimlessly, and pulled over for a lunch of MREs. Each person grabbed one, and they sat down on the edge of a cornfield.

"So what do we do now?" Sarah asked.

"I don't know," Thaddeus said. "I felt positive that the Spirit was pulling us to Tijuana."

"At least we tried to be faithful," Ellamae said.

Jaben pulled out the Windows CD-ROM, placed it on the tip of his index finger, and ran his thumb along the edge. "I wonder. I think--"

"Why is the ground trembling?" Sarah asked.

The friends dropped their food and staggered to their feet.

There, not fifty feet away, molten rock was spewing into the air. A chunk landed ten feet away.

The heat was incredible.

Jaben hurled the annulus into the lava, where it disappeared in a burst of lambent flame. "Let's run!"

They did run, and this time Thaddeus's driving was estimated to be about a 9.5 on the Richter scale. They drove and drove, and after a time realized they were lost.

"We're approaching a small village," Lilianne said. "Maybe they'll be able to tell us where we are, or how to get to the nearest city."

"We'd better not," said Jaben.

"Men! Always refusing to ask directions," Sarah said.

"It's not that, Sarah. You know I ask directions at home," Jaben said.

"Which is why you should do it here, too," Sarah said, crossing her arms and nodding her head.

"It's standard procedure in Mexico, if you don't know where something is, to make up directions. They could give us driving directions to Brazil," Jaben said.

"They could hardly leave us more lost than we are now," Lilianne said.

Jaben said, "Slow down. I want to get out."

Thaddeus stopped the van.

Jaben got out, and walked to the doorway of the nearest hovel. "*Por favor,*" he asked, "*disez cómo encontrar--*"

"Jaben?" a faint voice queried from the darkness within.

"*Amos!*"

Chapter Thirty-Seven

Amos was weak and slightly emaciated, but hardly ever had the friends seen so beautiful a sight as he -- Désirée had never been so happy. They gathered around him, and laid hands in prayer; healing flowed through Ellamae's fingers, and Amos stood up, strengthened.

"*Por favor, dinez con nosotros,*" the peasant said.

It was a simple meal; the friends were each given a few corn tortillas.

"This isn't much food," Sarah said. "How much do they have?"

"Eat it," Jaben said. "This is more than they can spare. The family will go hungry tonight."

"I know!" Sarah said. "We could give them some of our MREs."

"No," Jaben said. "I'd be happy to give them, but to a great many Mexicans, corn is food and food is corn. Our own ancestors had difficulty finding food in a New England whose waters were teeming with lobster. Each culture has its own baggage, and these simple folk are giving us the only food they know. A gift of MREs would not do them much good."

Sarah wasn't the only one to wipe a tear from her eyes.

The meal was mostly quiet; Amos explained how he had been abducted, beaten, and left for dead in a field, and how the peasants had taken him in and slowly nursed to health. "Will this make it hard for you not to hate white people?" Jaben asked.

"Very hard," Amos said. "But you're worth it."

The peasant family consisted of a grandmother, a mother, a father, a teenaged son, a preteen daughter, two little boys, and a baby girl. They were all thin, and lines of suffering were etched on all but the youngest of faces, but at the same time there was a real joy, a glow, about them. "I would like to go to mass with them, if they go to mass, but we should really be going back," Jaben thought. "I need to get back to work." Still, he did not wish in the least to haste this moment.

After the meal, they said goodbye, gave *abrazos*, and then Jaben reached into the sheath on his left hip and pulled out a thick Swisschamp Swiss Army Knife, showed them every one of its twenty-seven features (the children liked the magnifying glass), and then ceremoniously handed it to the father. The man's eyes lit up.

Sarah stared at Jaben; she knew what that knife meant to him, where he had taken it. Then she ran to the van, and ran back, and threw her red bouncy ball to the children, gave them each a kiss, and departed.

Chapter Thirty-Eight

Jaben said, "Amos, you're the guest of honor. Would you like to make the reading selection? We have *Darwin on Trial*, *An Anthropologist on Mars*, *A Wind in the Door*, *Four--*"

"*A Wind in the Door*," Amos said.

Jaben handed him the small volume. Amos opened it, flipped one way, flipped another way, closed the book, opened it, turned a few pages, and said, "Aah, here. Page 82." He read terrifying words as Proginoskes showed Meg a moment when stars had been murdered -- Xed.

"I've had a lot of time to think, and to feel, and I've realized something. It is a chilling feeling -- un-Named, Xed -- to know that someone hates you. Their brutality, their words, their blows hurt, but not nearly as badly as the real knowing that there was hate. My stomach hurt so much when they were done beating me, but the pain was nothing. Désirée, remember the time when we were dating, and I got my thumb in your eye? I know that hurt, but it only hurt physically. With hate it is different. It is a hurt of the spirit, and it is worse. Terribly worse.

"I am drawn to *Wind*, as you are, for its bliss and beauty. But it shows as very real the power of evil, and this passage was the one my heart was drawn to. I never knew how real the story was until I knew that there were men who could kill me. Hate is a very real power, and I have come to appreciate that, in the end, Proginoskes gave everything he had to give to stop the Echthroi. He gave until there was nothing left to give. Hate is so evil, that sometimes it costs that much."

Amos opened his mouth, then closed it, then began to weep. Ellamae and Sarah crawled across the baggage; Ellamae was first, kissing him on the forehead, and Sarah wrapped her arms around him. Their tears began to mingle with his, and soon all but Thad (who was with them in spirit) joined in the embrace; no one offered him anything to say, because they saw his pain was so great. And they stayed together for hours.

Chapter Thirty-Nine

There was healing in Ellamae's touch, and that of the others -- restoration not only for Amos's wounded body, but for his broken soul. Their love was a healing balm, and after a day of weeping and eating MREs as fast as he could keep them down,

Amos graced them with his deep, rich smile, and a day later he called for a rousing chorus of "99 bottles of beer," sung very loudly and very off-key, sometimes in several keys at once. This was one of Amos's favorite traditions, and it had surprised more than a couple of people who knew how truly good his baritone voice was. They were in Texas, approaching Jim's village, when something interesting happened.

Their radiator blew.

Jaben and Amos walked into the village, although by the end of the walk they had each drunk a canteen dry, and were thirsty and sorefooted when they reached Jim's shack. Jim rose to greet them, and said, "Hi, Jaben, and is this Amos? Why the sheepish grin, Jaben?"

Jaben shuffled, cleared his throat, and said, "I'm embarrassed to say this, but could we impose on you for another radiator?"

Jim laughed, and said, "Sure. I just got another van of your make and model in this week. I thought your new radiator had a bit more life in it. Would come with me to the yard? I'll step inside for my tools."

Jim was pleased to make Amos's acquaintance, and it was mostly those two who were talking as Jim and Jaben worked on the radiator ("You'd make a great mechanic," Jim said -- "I might try that when my present position ends," Jaben replied). It wasn't that long before the friends' van had a new radiator, and it wasn't long after that that they were sitting at Jim's regular table, with the card table pulled up, eating collard greens and smothered pork chops.

Sarah opened the conversation, by saying, "I'm grateful to you, Jim, and I trust you."

Jim smiled, and said, "Thank you. Out of curiosity, why do you trust me?"

"Your touch is that of a trustworthy man."

"How can you tell that from touch?"

"You know when two strangers are sitting next to each other on the bus, and their legs are touching? Their bodies are touching, but their spirits aren't touching. They aren't really touching.

"I've had hugs that felt like handshakes, and handshakes that felt like hugs; what most people know is that a touch means different things depending on how much of the body is touching and where, but what most people don't know is that a touch also is different depending on how much of the spirit is touching and where. Children's hugs can be the best, because when they're touching you, they aren't doing anything else, not anything; you're their whole universe, and you're wrapped in their trusting arms. There is something in the touch of a child who has not yet learned to draw back, just like there is something in the words of a child who has not yet learned guile. I don't mean that young children can't lie, or pull back -- but a child who will transparently lie about stealing cookies still doesn't know how to put guile into real and honest communication, and a child who draws back and says 'I don't want to hug you' still doesn't know how to draw back when he's touching someone. I --"

"So that's why your hug reminded me of a child," interrupted Jim.

Sarah began to blush, and continued. "You can tell a lot about a man by the way he touches. Kind of like what you can tell by whether and how he looks you in the eyes -- eye con*tact* is a form of touch -- only moreso. Your touch has a lot of strength -- even apart from your calloused hands, I can tell that you spend a lot of time applying force when you fix things -- but it is a strength with complete control and gentleness. You are strong, but I do not fear you. And it is a touch that draws me into your heart. You have a big heart. If you were a man whom I couldn't trust, you would be holding something back; you can tell when a person's holding back, and his touch says, 'There is something about me that I don't want you to know.' But your touch doesn't say that. It's transparent. Even when you gave me a handshake, when I touched your hand, I felt your heart."

Jim sat, with his mouth open. "What else do you know about me?"

"Not much," Sarah said. "I'm not an astrologer."

"You saw more of Sarah than she usually shows at first glance. Most people think she's a ditz," Lilianne said.

Jaben got up, and gently pulled Sarah's hair aside, so he could see part of her scalp.

"What are you doing?" Sarah asked.

"What an odd tattoo," Jaben said. "It says, 'Do not exceed 65 PSI.'"

Sarah hit Jaben, and he sat down.

Amos said, "It's so good to have your friendship, your community, your banter.

Désirée said, "It's so good to have you back, Amos. Our communion is restored; our fellowship is complete."

Amens circled round the table. They joined hands over the meal:

Praise God from whom all blessings flow.
Praise him all creatures here below.
Praise him above, ye heavenly host.
Praise Father, Son, and Holy Ghost.
Amen.

They dug in, and for a time people were silent as they enjoyed the meal. Then Thad said, "I had a mystical experience when we were driving out of Tijuana. It was my first mystical experience while driving."

Jim raised his eyebrows, and said, "A mystical experience while driving? I thought they came in church, and deep meditation, and things like that. I've never had one. I'm too ordinary."

Thaddeus smiled, and said, "Those moments are gifts from God, that come quite often unexpected. The biggest qualification you can have is a sense of need before God. And there is something ordinary about the mystical -- no, that's not quite right, or maybe there is. There is something mystical about the ordinary. Mysticism is not this strange and remote thing; it is very near to us, and you may know more mystics than you think. Every child is born a mystic. The problem is how to keep him that way."

Jim said, "So how do you become a mystic? Do you read a book, or spend a lot of time praying, or whatever?"

Thaddeus said, "I don't know. I don't know how I became a mystic. It's not something you can achieve by doing the right things; it's a gift from God. It's kind of like asking what we did to achieve being given two radiators; the answer is that we did, quite properly, nothing; we cooperated with your gift and God's, but it was given. Prayer can be helpful, but if you try praying six hours a day to make yourself a mystic --

"To borrow from a Zen koan:

"A master observed that a novice was very diligent in prayer; he prayed an hour a day more than anyone else, and could shut out all distractions. One day, the master asked the novice, 'What are you doing?'

"The novice said, 'I am praying hard to make myself a mystic.'

"The master took a tile, set it before the novice, and began to polish it vigorously. 'What are you doing?' the novice asked.

"'I am polishing this tile to make it into a mirror,' the master answered.

"'You can't make a tile into a mirror by polishing it!' the novice protested.

"'And neither can you make yourself into a mystic by prayer,' the master answered.

"Prayer is a fundamental part of mysticism, and there are good books -- I can think of *Experiencing God* and, let's see, *Tales of a Magic Monastery*, which is my personal favorite. But if you go to a book and say, 'This will make me a mystic,' you are setting yourself up for failure."

"What was your last mystical experience like? How did you manage to drive and have a mystical experience at once? How much more often do they come when you become an experienced mystic?" James asked.

"I don't know how to describe it. I was driving, and I was with God, and I was suddenly very aware of his presence and love for me, in, under, and through everything around me. I was also intensely aware of my surroundings; it helped me drive, if anything. But I would not too much dwell on mystical experiences; they are a blessing, but there are far greater blessings, those that non-mystics think are dull next to mysticism. It's hard to explain," Thaddeus answered.

James said, "I am still listening with interest."

Thaddeus said, "I feel like I'm in a bind, like I can only explain these things to someone who needs no explanation -- and, in saying this, I probably sound otherworldly and mysterious and an initiate of circles you cannot hope to probe. It is not like that at all. Perhaps my best advice is this: if you value mysticism, forget completely about being a mystic, and seek God with your whole heart. God will make you a mystic if he wants."

Jim said, "I am already doing that."

Thaddeus said, "Then I have nothing to add to you."

Ellamae held her plate, and said, "Could you give me a pork chop?" and then, receiving the food, said, "I think you were following God when you gave us the radiator. It helped us receive our friend back. And the story about that --"

"What is the story about you finding him? Were the Mexican police much help?"

An animated recounting of the story's events followed, and lasted long into the night. They stayed the night, showered, packed up, and headed on the road home.

Chapter Forty

Jaben said, "Ellamae, why don't you choose our Bible reading today? It's been a while since we read the *sacra pagina*."

Ellamae said, "I'd like to read the extended commentary on the words 'The just shall walk by faith,' as found in Hebrews chapter eleven. It's my favorite passage of Scripture."

Jaben handed a Bible and a flashlight to Lilianne, and said, "Lili, will you do the honors?"

Lili took the book reverently, opened it, flipped a few

pages, and began, "Faith is the realization of what is hoped for and evidence of things not seen. Because of it the ancients were well attested. By faith we understand that the universe was ordered by the word of God, so that what is visible came into being through the invisible. By faith Abel offered to God a sacrifice greater than Cain's. Through this he was attested to be righteous, God bearing witness to his gifts, and through this, though dead, he still speaks. By faith Enoch was taken up so that he should not see death, and 'he was found no more because God had taken him.' Before he was taken up, he was attested to have pleased God. But without faith it is impossible to please him, for anyone who approaches God must believe that he exists and that he rewards those who seek him. By faith Noah, warned about what was not yet seen, with reverence built an ark for the salvation of his household. Through this he condemned the world and inherited the righteousness that comes through faith.

"By faith Abraham obeyed when he was called to go out to a place that he was to receive as an inheritance; he went out, not knowing where he was to go. By faith he sojourned in the promised land as in a foreign country, dwelling in tents with Isaac and Jacob, heirs of the same promise; for he was looking forward to the city with foundations whose architect and maker is God. By faith he received power to generate, even though he was past the normal age -- and Sarah herself was sterile -- for he thought that the one who had made the promise was trustworthy. So it was that there came forth from one man, himself as good as dead, descendants as numerous as the stars in the sky and as countless as the sands on the seashore.

"All those died in faith. They did not receive what had been promised but saw it and greeted it from afar and acknowledged themselves to be strangers and aliens on the earth, for those who speak thus show that they are seeking a homeland. If they had been thinking of the land from which they had come, they would have had the opportunity to return. But now they desire a better homeland, a heavenly one. Therefore, God is not ashamed to be called their God, for he has prepared a city for them.

"By faith Abraham, when put to the test, offered up Isaac, and he who had received the promises was ready to offer his only son, of whom it was said, 'Through Isaac descendants shall bear your name.' He reasoned that God was able to raise even from the dead, and he received Isaac back as a symbol. By faith regarding the things still to come Isaac blessed Jacob and Esau. By faith Jacob, when dying, blessed each of the sons of Joseph and 'bowed in worship, leaning on the top of his staff.' By faith Joseph, near the end of his life, spoke of the Exodus of the Israelites and gave instructions about his bones.

"By faith Moses was hidden by his parents for three months after his birth, because they saw that he was a beautiful child, and they were not afraid of the king's edict. By faith Moses, when he had grown up, refused to be known as the son of Pharoah's daughter; he chose to be ill-treated along with the people of God rather than enjoy the fleeting pleasure of sin. He considered the reproach of the Anointed greater wealth than the treasures of Egypt, for he was looking to the recompense. By faith he left Egypt, not fearing the king's fury, for he persevered as if seeing the one who is invisible. By faith he kept the Passover and sprinkled the blood, that the Destroyer of the firstborn might not touch them. By faith they crossed the Red Sea as if it were dry land, but when the Egyptians attempted it they were drowned. By faith the walls of Jericho fell after being encircled for seven days. By faith Rahab the harlot did not perish with the disobedient, for she had received the spies in peace.

"What more shall I say? I have not the time to tell of Gideon, Barak, Samson, Jephthah, of David and Samuel and the prophets, who by faith conquered kingdoms, did what was righteous, obtained the promises; they closed the mouths of lions, put out raging fires, escaped the devouring sword; out of weakness they were made powerful, became strong in battle, and turned back foreign invaders. Women received back their dead through resurrection. Some were tortured and would not accept deliverance, in order to obtain a better resurrection. Others endured mockery, scourging, even chains and imprisonment.

They were stoned, sawed in two, put to death at sword's point; they went about in skins of sheep or goats, needy, afflicted, tormented. The world was not worthy of them. They wandered about in deserts and on mountains, in caves and in crevices in the earth.

"Yet all these, though approved because of their faith, did not receive what had been promised. God had foreseen something better for us, so that without us they should not be made perfect."

Lilianne closed the book.

Sarah said, "That's awesome."

Ellamae said, "The part I like best about this is that there was no distinction made between those who were miraculously saved and those who died in faith. None whatsoever. In Daniel, the three men, Shadrach, Mechach, and Abednego say, 'Our God can save us, but even if he does not, know, O king, that we will not bow down.' Some manuscripts even say, 'if he cannot.' It reminds me of--

"Thaddeus, when you were looking down the barrel of that brigand's gun, what was going through your mind?" she asked

"My heart was completely at peace," Thaddeus said.

"Did you know that the gun was going to jam?"

"No."

"Did you pray that the gun would jam?"

"No."

At this, Ellamae was surprised. "What did you pray?"

"I prayed that God's will would be done."

There was silence for a second, and then Jaben said, "I like how the text says that we are strangers and aliens, that this world is not our home: we look for a better country, a heavenly one. I fit in better in French culture than American culture, but not even very well there; no culture on earth is a home. Each culture is a cave, as Bloom reminds us, and I can't wait for the day when I will climb *out* of the caverns and behold the sun in all its glory."

Amos said, "The chapter reminds me of the words, 'Here I stand, ready to live, ready to die."

Ellamae said, "'My name is Aragorn, son of Arathorn. If by

life or death I may serve you, that I shall.'"

Jaben said, "Jewish tradition holds that the prophet Isaiah was sawn in two."

"Interesting," Lilianne said. "What was the story?"

"I don't know. I haven't spent nearly as much time studying the Talmud and Jewish tradition as I should. Maybe reading the Babylonian Talmud will be my next project."

"All things in this chapter point to the King of the Jews," Ellamae said. "Every righteous man was a shadow of the One who was to come. And there is more -- I cannot say it."

The conversation went on for hours, days. Before they knew it, the friends pulled into a driveway...

Chapter Forty-One

It was dusk as the van pulled out, finally at home, and slowed down. Everybody got out, yawning, Thaddeus still, out of habit, carrying his rifle slung over his shoulder. They closed the van doors and walked along, silently, when --

a roaring sound was heard

"Look out, a bear!"

the Spirit moved in Thaddeus's heart like rapid fire. "Shoot it."

Thaddeus, bewildered, was pushed into a dimension beyond time, out of ordinary time, and automatically took what seemed an eternity slowly aiming the gun into the bear's mouth, frozen open, hoping by some providence to sever part of the time

fired

a resounding, thunderous gunshot echoed

the bear staggered

Thaddeus looking at his smoking .22 in confusion

BOOM! another gunshot echoed

the bear staggered

BOOM! another gunshot echoed

the bear staggered

BOOM! another gunshot echoed

the bear fell

a stick snapped

a massive man, holding a massive gun, walked out of the forest

the gun still aimed at the dying bear

"Bear!" Désirée said. "Boy, are you a sight for sore eyes!"

"You're back. Is that Amos I see? How are you, Amos?"

"Happy."

Bear drew a few paces back from the grizzly's body, cautiously set his smoking gun down, still pointing at the grizzly, and then drew all seven friends into his enormous, thick, strong, gentle arms. "Good to have y'all back, folks. Good to have ya back."

Chapter Forty-Two

It was good to be back in church. The seven friends filed into the sanctuary and sat down.

"Blessed be God: Father, Son, and Holy Spirit," the celebrant said.

"And blessed be his Kingdom now and forever. Amen," the congregation answered.

"Almighty God, to you all hearts are open, all desires known and from you no secrets are hid: Cleanse the thoughts of our hearts by the inspiration of your Holy Spirit, that we may perfectly love you, and worthily magnify your holy Name; through Christ our Lord," the celebrant said, joined by the congregation in saying, "Amen."

Then came the opening hymn:

"Here in this place new light is streaming,
Now is the darkness vanished away,
See in this space our fears and our dreamings,
Brought here to you in the light of this day.
Gather us in-- the lost and forsaken,
Gather us in-- the blind and the lame;

Call to us now, and we shall awaken,
We shall arise at the sound of our name.

"We are the young-- our lives are a myst'ry,
We are the old-- who yearn for your face,
We have been sung throughout all of hist'ry,
Called to be light to the whole human race.
Gather us in-- the rich and the haughty,
Gather us in-- the proud and the strong;
Give us a heart so meek and so lowly,
Give us the courage to enter the Song.

"Here we will take the wine and the water,
Here we will take the bread of new birth.
Here you shall call your sons and your daughters,
Call us anew to be salt for the earth.
Give us to drink the wine of compassion,
Give us to eat the bread that is you;
Nourish us well, and teach us to fashion
Lives that are holy and hearts that are true.

"Not in the dark of buildings confining,
Not in some heaven, light-years away,
But here in this place the new light is shining,
Now is the Kingdom, now is the day.
Gather us in and hold us forever,
Gather us in and make us your own;
Gather us in-- all peoples together,
Fire of love in our flesh and our bone."

Then all the voices stepped into the timeless, eternal song:

"Glory to God in the highest and peace to his people on earth.
Lord God, heavenly King, Almighty God and Father,
we worship You, we give You thanks, we praise You

for your glory.
Glory to God.

"Lord Jesus Christ, only Son of the Father, Lord God,
Lamb of God.
You take away the sin of the world, have mercy on us.
You are seated at the right hand of the Father:
receive our prayer, receive our prayer.

"For You alone are the Holy One, You alone are the
Lord.
You alone are the Most High. Jesus Christ, with the
Holy Spirit
In the glory of God the Father, in the glory of God the
Father. Amen. Amen."

"The Lord be with you," the celebrant said.

"And also with you," answered the congregation.

"Let us pray," the celebrant began.

"Almighty and everlasting God, increase in us the gifts of faith, hope, and charity; and, that we, the redeemed, may obtain what you promise, make us work with you the work of your redemption; through Jesus Christ our Lord, who lives and reigns with you and the Holy Spirit, one God, for ever and ever." The congregation joined in, "Amen."

"A reading from the book of First Kings," the reader said.

"Some time later the son of the woman who owned the house became ill. He grew worse and worse, and finally stopped breathing. She said to Elijah, 'What do you have against me, man of God? Did you come to remind me of my sin and kill my son?' 'Give me your son,' Elijah replied. He took him from her arms, carried him to the upper room where he was staying, and laid him on his bed.

"Then he cried out to the Lord, 'O Lord my God, have you brought tragedy also upon this widow I am staying with, by causing her son to die?' Then he stretched himself out on the boy three times and cried to the Lord, 'O Lord my God, let this boy's life return to him!' The Lord heard Elijah's cry, and the boy's life returned to him, and he lived. Elijah picked up the child and carried him down from the room into the house. He gave him to his mother and said, 'Look, your son is alive!' Then the woman said to Elijah, 'Now I know that you are a man of God and that the word of the Lord from your mouth is the truth.'"

"The Word of the Lord," the reader said.

"The psalm will be read with the women on the even numbered verses, and the men on the odd numbered verses."

The women began, "I will declare your name to my brothers; in the congregation I will praise you."

The men answered, "You who fear the Lord, praise him! All you descendants of Jacob, honor him! Revere him, all you descendants of Israel!"

"For he has not despised or disdained the suffering of the afflicted one; he has not hidden his face from him but has listened to his cry for help."

"From you comes the theme of my praise in the great assembly; before those who fear you will I fulfill my vows."

"The poor will eat and be satisfied; they who seek the Lord will praise him-- may your hearts live forever!"

"All the ends of the earth will remember and turn to the Lord, and all the families of the nations will bow down before him,"

"for dominion belongs to the Lord and he rules over the nations."

"All the rich of the earth will feast and worship; all who go down to the dust will kneel before him-- those who cannot keep themselves alive."

"Posterity will serve him; future generations will be told about the Lord."

"They will proclaim his righteousness to a people yet unborn--for he has done it."

"A reading from the book of Acts," the reader said.

"Meanwhile, Saul was still breathing out murderous threats

against the Lord's disciples. He went to the high priest and asked him for letters to the synagogues in Damascus, so that if he found any there who belonged to the Way, whether men or women, he might take them as prisoners to Jerusalem.

"As he neared Damascus on his journey, suddenly a light from heaven flashed around him. He fell to the ground and had a voice say to him, 'Saul, Saul, why do you persecute me?'

"'Who are you, Lord?' Saul asked. 'I am Jesus, whom you are persecuting,' he replied. 'Now get up and go into the city, and you will be told what to do.'"

"The word of the Lord," the reader said.

"Thanks be to God," answered the congregation.

The congregation rose, singing:

"Alleluia, alleluia! Give thanks to the risen Lord,
Alleluia, alleluia! Give praise to his name!"

"The holy Gospel of our Lord Jesus Christ, according to St. Luke," the celebrant said.

"Glory to You, Lord Christ," the congregation answered.

"Now one of the Pharisees invited Jesus to have dinner with him, so he went to the Pharisee's house and reclined at the table. When a woman who had lived a sinful life in that town learned that Jesus was eating at the Pharisee's house, she brought an alabaster jar of perfume, and as she stood behind him at his feet weeping, she began to wet his feet with her tears. Then she wiped them with her hair, kissed them and poured perfume on them.

"When the Pharisee who invited him saw this, he said to himself, 'If this man were a prophet, he would know who is touching him and what kind of woman she is--that she is a sinner.' Jesus answered him, 'Simon, I have something to tell you.' 'Tell me, teacher,' he said. 'Two men owed money to a certain moneylender. One owed him five hundred denarii, and the other fifty. Neither of them had the money to pay him back, so he canceled the debts of both. Now which of them will love him more?'

"Simon replied, 'I suppose the one who had the bigger debt canceled.' 'You have judged correctly,' Jesus said. Then he turned toward the woman and said to Simon, 'Do you see this woman? I came to your house. You did not give me any water fro my feet, but she wet my feet with her tears and wiped them with her hair. You did not give me a kiss, but this woman, from the time I entered, has not stopped kissing my feet. You did not put oil on my head, but she has poured perfume on my feet. Therefore, I tell you, her many sins have been forgiven--for she loved much. But he who has been forgiven little loves little.' Then Jesus said to her, 'Your sins are forgiven.' The other guests began to say among themselves, 'Who is this who even forgives sins?' Jesus said to the woman, 'Your faith has saved you; go in peace.'"

"The Gospel of the Lord," the celebrant said.

"Praise to You, Lord Christ," the congregation answered.

"'There is a Redeemer,'" the preacher began, "'Jesus, God's own son,' begins one song. I'm not going to inflict my singing voice on you, but that's how the song begins. Today I want to talk to you about the message of redemption in the Gospel, in the whole Bible. This is one of the most important messages in Scripture.

"Forgive and forget. Forgive and forget. That's what our culture says, and I don't agree with that. I've thought and prayed, and I really don't agree with that. If you forgive, you don't forget. If you forget, you don't forgive. God takes evil, and makes it better than if nothing had gone wrong. The New Jerusalem will be better than Eden ever could have been -- that's how powerful a God we serve. "*Eloi, Eloi, lama sabachthane?* My God, my God, why have you forsaken me? These were the words that Christ cried in agony on the cross, and they were not new. He was quoting, and more specifically he was quoting the first verse of the twenty-second psalm. In those days, people emphasized memory a bit more than we do now. They didn't memorize Bible verses; they memorized the whole Bible. To those who were looking on, the Pharisees leering at him, Jesus was quoting the whole psalm, the Psalm of the Cross: I can count all my bones.

They look, they stare at me. They divide my clothing among them; for my garments they cast lots. They pierced my hands and my feet. These words, and others, foretold the exact way and manner of Christ's death, and in quoting them, Jesus was saying, 'Look, you who have pierced me. This prophecy is fulfilled this day in your midst.'

"The beginning of psalm twenty-two is a psalm of lament, but the end is a psalm of triumph, and those are the verses we read earlier in the service. The cross is the balance point of the story, but not its end. God's strength at work is very powerful, and they take the cross, because it was the most evil moment, the hour when darkness reigned, and placed it at the heart of his triumph. Christ trampled death by death, and when he rose from the dead, the power of death was forever broken, like the stone table in C.S. Lewis's *The Lion, the Witch, and the Wardrobe*. And not only can death not hold *him* any longer, but death is now too weak to hold those who believe. When the body dies, the spirit is held in God's heart until the resurrection we await, when the dead in Christ shall rise first, and the body will surge with power and be reunited with the spirit. That is how God has redeemed death.

"I want to tell you something important. God isn't just trying to restore Eden, he has a whole, new, bigger project. He can redeem me; he can redeem you. He redeemed the sinful woman in our Gospel reading, and not only left her with a new beauty but left behind one of the most beautiful stories in the whole Bible -- and that story was very widely circulated among the ancient Church. The point of saving us, Lewis tells us, is to make us into little Christs. The whole purpose of becoming a Christian is simply nothing else. God is transforming us so that we may become gods and goddesses to reign with him forever in the holy City. Let me repeat that. God is transforming us so that we may become gods and goddesses to reign with him in the holy City.

"I would like to tell you a story. I prayed, and hesitated now -- Lord, I pray, bind me from saying anything that would harm these little ones, bind the power of the Evil One, and keep me in your heart. But I'll tell the story, with a warning that I don't agree with all of it. When I told it to one young man, he asked me, 'So, do you really believe that God created man just to prove a point?' I stepped back and said, 'No. I don't believe that. That's not why I told the story at all; it's just that I don't know how to tell the story without it looking that way.' So I ask you to excuse my weakness, and I pray that you will see what in this story I mean to tell: God's power and wisdom as manifest in his redemption.

"In the very beginning, before God created the heavens and the earth, he created angels, stars of light to shine in the light of glory. He created one star higher and holier than any of the others, and named him Lucifer, the Light-Bearer.

"Lucifer saw his own wisdom, majesty and glory, and told God, 'I want you to give me my rightful place, as head of you as well as head of the angels. I am wiser than you.'

"God could have zapped Lucifer then and there, and that would have established his power. But not his wisdom. So God decided on something very different.

"'Very well, then,' God said, 'Prove it. I'll unfold my plan, and you'll unfold yours.'

"The great Dragon shouted in rebellion, and swept the sky with his tail, and flung down a third of the stars, and a third of the stars chose to become dragons, vipers, worms.

"Then God created Heaven and earth; he set the stars, in their courses, and created glory after glory after glory: no two blades of grass alike, thousands upon thousands of species of beetles, and as the crowning glory man, created godlike in his image, pure, holy, spotless.

"Then the Dragon appeared in the form of a serpent, and beguiled the woman, and the woman pulled the man down with her. The whole creation became accursed, and began to rot, with poison seeping in a wound.

"'Well, then,' the Dragon said, 'Who is wiser now?' And God wept.

"Then God pointed to one person and said, 'You see that man?'

"'Yes,' the Devil said.

"'Hey, there!' God said to the man. 'You in the desert. Build a huge boat.'

"And the man did. When the wind and rain came, the man and his household were saved.

"Then the Devil walked on the earth, and said, 'I see not one who is righteous,' and God said, 'Have you considered my servant Job?' And Job, bewildered, saw his children and his property taken away, and then his health -- and cried in agony, cursing the day of his birth, but refusing to curse God like the Serpent said he would. In the midst of his misery, Job said, 'I know that my redeemer liveth, and in my flesh I shall see God. Though he slay me, yet shall I praise him.'

"The story unfolded, and God sent a prophet to give his people Law. When they strayed, he sent prophets, never tiring of loving them. Finally, in the fullness of time, he sent his Son, to become a man.

"This man was a stranger in a strange land, and passed through the world like a flame. The Serpent spoke beguiling words into the ear of one of his disciples, and he was betrayed, and nailed to a piece of wood, and left to die. And darkness reigned.

"'Surely you will acknowledge,' said the Serpent, 'that I am wiser?'

"God raised his Son from the dead, in a new and incorruptible life, surging with power. And the Devil trembled with fear.

"His Spirit filled those who were his Son's disciples, and they burst forth with new life. The Serpent tried everything to stop them -- even making some of the people God had called to persecute them. God was not discouraged; he called one of the persecutors to join in the new life." The preacher took off his glasses, and said, "I'd like to read to you now from one of the letters written by that persecutor:

"'Although I am less than the least of all God's people, this grace was given me: to preach to the Gentiles the unsearchable riches of Christ, and to make plain to everyone the administration of this mystery, which for ages past was kept hidden in God, who created all things. His intent was that now, through the church, the manifold wisdom of God should be made known to the rulers and authorities in the heavenly realms, according to his eternal purpose which he accomplished in Christ Jesus our Lord.'

"The Church -- I mean you and me, not just people who wear a white collar -- stands as a family for Christ, his brother and sister and mother, as children for God the Father, as God's *magnum opus*, as a servant to the world, as a witness to the world, as a mother and family to those who believe, and lastly as a warrior against Satan. This is the secret God has concealed in his bosom, and his many-sided wisdom is displaying so that all of the angels and even all of the demons, Satan himself, can look and see the wisdom of God's plan.

"Christ came once; he will come again, and then every knee shall bow. Then the redeemed shall stand holy, spotless, pure, and perfect, gods and goddesses, sons and daughters of God, to enter into his eternal paradise. Then the Dragon will look and see beyond any question or doubt that God's plan is wiser. Then, and *only* then, will Satan and all his minions be cast into the lake of eternal fire.

"I'd like to conclude by saying that Heaven is off in the future, but it is also here now. We can, and should, bring Heaven down to earth. Each time we forgive, each time by God's grace we work good out of evil, there is Heaven. When we arrive at the Holy City, we will see that Heaven has always been very close. Let's pray.

"Lord, thank you for being the Redeemer, and calling us out of our sin, out of our filth. Thank you for calling me out of my slavery to the bottle and my worship of alcohol. Help us to be co-workers and co-redeemers with you, with hearts that are holy and lives that are true. In Jesus' name, amen.

"Will you please stand?"

The congregation rose, and said with one voice,

"I believe in one God, the Father, the Almighty,
Maker of Heaven and earth, of all that is, seen and unseen.

"I believe in one Lord, Jesus Christ,
the only Son of God, eternally begotten of the Father,
God from God, Light from Light, true God from true God,
begotten, not made, of one Being with the Father.
Through him all things were made.
For us and for our salvation he came down from Heaven:
by the Holy Spirit he became incarnate from the Virgin Mary, and was made man.
For our sake he was crucified under Pontius Pilate;
he suffered death and was buried.
On the third day he rose again in accordance with the Scriptures;
he ascended into Heaven
and is seated at the right hand of the Father.
He will come again in glory to judge the living and the dead,
and his kingdom will have no end.

"I believe in the Holy Spirit, the Lord, the giver of life,
who proceeds from the Father and the Son.
With the Father and the Son he is worshiped and glorified.
He has spoken through the Prophets.
I believe one holy Catholic and apostolic Church.
I acknowledge one baptism for the forgiveness of sins.
I look for the resurrection of the dead,
and the life of the world to come.
Amen."

A deacon said aloud, "Father, we pray for your holy Catholic Church;"

The congregation answered, "That we all may be one."

"Grant that every member of the Church may truly and humbly serve you;"

"That your Name may be glorified by all people."

"We pray for all bishops, priests, and deacons;"

"That they may be faithful ministers of your Word and Sacraments."

"We pray for all who govern and hold authority in the nations of the world;"

"That there may be justice and peace on the earth."

"Give us grace to do your will in all that we undertake;"

"That our works may find favor in your sight."

"Have compassion on those who suffer from any grief or trouble;"

"That they may be delivered from their distress."

"Give to the departed eternal rest;"

"Let light perpetual shine on them."

"We praise you for your saints who have entered into joy;"

"May we also come to share in your heavenly kingdom."

"Let us pray for our own needs and those of others."

A time of silence ensued.

The celebrant said, "Let us confess our sins against God and our neighbor."

The friends knelt in silence.

"Most merciful God," the celebrant began, joined by the people,

"We confess that we have sinned against you
in thought, word, and deed,
by what we have done,
and by what we have left undone.
We have not loved you with our whole heart;
we have not loved our neighbors as ourselves.
We are truly sorry and we humbly repent.

For the sake of your Son Jesus Christ,
have mercy on us and forgive us;
that we may delight in your will,
and walk in your ways,
to the glory of your Name.
Amen.

The celebrant raised his hand, and said, "Almighty God have mercy on you, forgive you all your sins through our Lord Jesus Christ, strengthen you in all goodness, and by the power of the Holy Spirit keep you in eternal life. Amen.

"The peace of the Lord he always with you."

"And also with you," the congregation answered.

The friends exchanged the Kiss of Peace; Jaben placed his lips on Sarah's cheek and planted a kiss. It was not romantic, erotic, or sexual, but it was very much real. Their bodies touched; their spirits touched. Jaben gave the kiss his whole attention; he wasn't doing anything else, not anything. This is why--Sarah thought afterwards--the Kiss of Peace between friends should not just be a handshake, but a hug, or even better a kiss. And why I like Jaben's kisses best of all.

The kiss bore the same fundamental beauty as singing
dancing
a small white feather in the air
a placid lake
deep green seaweed swaying under the ocean
a glass of dry white wine
silence
stillness
moonlight
starlight
crystalline ice
a fire of roses
a child falling asleep in its mother's arms
agape
life.

Someone said that, when thinking of singing Alleluia, one should not so much think of "We start and stop this song," as, "There is a song which always has been going on and always will go on, and when we sing, we step into it for a time."

This kiss was not a momentary kythe, but a moment stepping into the Eternal Kythe.

It lasted less than a second, but it filled eternity.

The offering plates were passed around, and the voices joined together singing the doxology:

"Praise God from whom all blessings flow.
Praise him, all creatures here below.
Praise him above, ye heavenly host.
Praise Father, Son, and Holy Ghost.
Amen."

The celebrant said, "The Lord be with you."

"And also with you," answered the congregation.

"Lift up your hearts," the celebrant said.

"We lift them to the Lord." the congregation answered.

The celebrant said, "Let us give thanks to the Lord our God."

The congregation answered, "It is right to give him thanks and praise."

The celebrant said, "It is right and a good and joyful thing, always and everywhere to give thanks to you, Father Almighty, Creator of Heaven and earth. For by water and the Holy Spirit you have made us a new people in Christ Jesus our Lord, to show forth your glory in all the world. Therefore, we praise you, joining our voices with Angels and Archangels and with all the company of Heaven, who for ever sing this hymn to proclaim the glory of your Name:"

The eternal Song arose like incense:

"Holy, holy, holy Lord, God of pow'r and might.
Heaven and earth are filled with your glory.

"Holy, holy, holy Lord, God of pow'r and might.
Heaven and earth are filled with your glory.

"Hosanna! Hosanna in the highest.
Hosanna! Hosanna in the highest.

"Blessed, blessed is He who comes in the name of the Lord.
Hosanna in the highest.

"Blessed, blessed is He who comes in the name of the Lord.
Hosanna in the highest."

The celebrant said, "Holy and gracious Father: In your infinite love you made us for yourself; and, when we had fallen into sin and become subject to evil and death, you, in your mercy, sent Jesus Christ, your only and eternal Son, to share our human nature, to live and die as one of us, to reconcile us to you, the God and Father of all.

"He stretched out his arms upon the cross, and offered himself in obedience to your will, a perfect sacrifice for the whole world.

"On the night he was handed over to suffering and death, our Lord Jesus Christ took bread; and when he had given thanks to you, he broke it, and gave it to his disciples, and said, 'Take, eat: This is my Body, which is given for you. Do this for the remembrance of me.'

"After supper he took the cup of wine, and when he had given thanks, he gave it to them, and said, 'Drink this, all of you. This is my Blood of the new Covenant, which is shed for you and for many for the forgiveness of sins. Whenever you drink it, do this for the remembrance of me.'

"Therefore we proclaim the mystery of faith:"

The whole congregation said, with one voice,

"Christ has died.
Christ is risen.
Christ will come again."

The celebrant said, "We celebrate the memorial of our redemption, O Father, in the sacrifice of praise and thanksgiving. Recalling his death, resurrection, and ascension, we offer you these gifts.

"Sanctify them by your Holy Spirit to be for your people the Body and Blood of your Son, the holy food and drink of new and unending life in him. Sanctify us also that we may faithfully receive this holy Sacrament, and serve you in unity, constancy, and peace; and at the last day bring us with all your saints into the joy of your eternal kingdom.

"All this we ask through your Son Jesus Christ. By him, and with him, and in him, in the unity of the Holy Spirit all honor and glory is yours, Almighty Father, now and forever. Amen.

"And now, as our Savior Christ has taught us, we are bold to say:"

Celebrant and congregation joined voices in a natural, almost chantlike recital:

"Our Father
which art in Heaven,
hallowed be thy name.
Thy Kingdom come,
thy will be done,
on earth as it is in Heaven.
Give us this day our daily bread,
and forgive us our trespasses,
as we forgive those who have trespassed against us.
Lead us not into temptation,
but deliver us from evil,
for thine is the Kingdom,
and the power,
and the glory forever.

Amen."

The celebrant said, "Alleluia! Christ our Passover is sacrificed for us;"

"Therefore let us keep the feast! Alleluia!" the congregation answered.

All said in unison,

"Most merciful Lord,
your love compels us to come in.
Our hands were unclean,
our hearts were unprepared;
we were not fit even to eat the crumbs from under
your table.
But you, Lord, are the God of our salvation,
and share your bread with sinners.
So cleanse and feed us with the precious body and
blood of your Son,
that he may live us and we in him;
and that we, with the whole company of Christ,
may sit and eat in your Kingdom.
Amen."

The celebrant held up the elements, and said, "The gifts of God for the People of God. Take them in remembrance that Christ died for you, and feed on him in your hearts by faith, with thanksgiving."

The congregation was seated for a moment, and then rose with the power and energy of a song:

"The heavens are telling the glory of God,
and all creation is shouting for joy.
Come, dance in the forest, come, play in the field,
and sing, sing to the glory of the Lord.

"Praise for the sun, the bringer of day,

He carries the light of the Lord in his rays;
The moon and the stars who light up the way
Unto your throne.

"The heavens are telling the glory of God,
and all creation is shouting for you.
Come, dance in the forest, come, play in the field,
and sing, sing to the glory of the Lord.

"Praise for the wind that blows through the trees,
the sea's mighty storms, the gentlest breeze;
They blow where they will, they blow where they please
To please the Lord.

"The heavens are telling the glory of God,
and all creation is shouting for joy.
Come, dance in the forest, come, play in the field,
and sing, sing to the glory of the Lord.

"Praise for the rain that waters our fields,
And blesses our crops so all the earth yields;
From death unto life her myst'ry revealed
Springs forth in joy.

"The heavens are telling the glory of God,
and all creation is shouting for joy.
Come, dance in the forest, come, play in the field,
and sing, sing to the glory of the Lord.

"Praise for the fire who gives us his light,
The warmth of the sun to brighten our night;
He dances with joy, his spirit so bright,
He sings of you.

"The heavens are telling the glory of God,

and all creation is shouting for joy.
Come, dance in the forest, come, play in the field,
and sing, sing to the glory of the Lord.

"Praise for the earth who makes life to grow,
The creatures you made to let your life show;
The flowers and trees that help us to know
The heart of love.

"The heavens are telling the glory of God,
and all creation is shouting for joy.
Come, dance in the forest, come, play in the field,
and sing, sing to the glory of the Lord.

"Praise for our death that makes our life real,
The knowledge of loss that helps us to feel;
The gift of yourself, your presence revealed
To lead us home.

"The heavens are telling the glory of God,
and all creation is shouting for joy.
Come, dance in the forest, come, play in the field,
and sing, sing to the glory of the Lord.
Sing, sing to the glory of the Lord."

As they came up to receive communion, Jaben thought, "The body and blood of Christ. Real food and real drink."

Thaddeus thought, "The body of Christ, the Church. I am mystically united with the whole body of Christ, across all ages and all nations, and -- what I hold more special still -- I drink the divine life."

Désirée thought, "United again with my husband; made one in two ways now."

Amos thought, "United again with my wife; made one in two ways now."

Lilianne thought, "Here is a magic beyond anything in my

daydreams, anything I can dream of."

Ellamae thought, "This chalice holds a fluid more precious than ichor. This cup is the Holy Grail."

Sarah thought, "God descends to meet my senses, and oh, how I appreciate that taste, that touch. He goes Within me."

They sat in silence after returning to their seats.

"Let us pray," the celebrant said.

The congregation joined him in saying,

"Eternal God, heavenly Father,
you have graciously accepted us as living members
of your Son our Saviour Jesus Christ,
and you have fed us with spiritual food
in the Sacrament of his Body and Blood.
Send us now into the world in peace,
and grant us strength and courage
to love and serve you
with gladness and singleness of heart;
through Christ our Lord.
Amen."

The celebrant raised his hand in blessing, and said, "To him who is able to keep you from falling and to present you before his glorious presence without fault and with great joy--to the only God our Savior be glory, majesty, power and authority, through Jesus Christ our Lord, before all ages, now and forevermore! May the blessing of God Almighty, the Father, the Son, and the Holy Spirit, be upon you and remain with you for ever.", and the congregation said, "Amen."

They sang a recessional filled with joy:

"For the beauty of the earth
For the glory of the skies,
For the love which from our birth
Over and around us lies.

"Lord of all, to Thee we raise,
This our hymn of grateful praise.

"For the beauty of each hour,
Of the day and of the night,
Hill and vale, and tree and flower,
Sun and moon, and stars of light.

"Lord of all, to Thee we raise,
This our hymn of grateful praise.

"For the joy of human love,
Brother, sister, parent, child,
Friends on earth and friends above,
For all gentle thoughts and mild.

"Lord of all, to Thee we raise,
This our hymn of grateful praise.

"For Thy church, that evermore
Lifteth holy hands above,
Offering upon every shore
Her pure sacrifice of love.

"Lord of all, to Thee we raise
This our hymn of grateful praise."

"For Thyself, best Gift Divine,
To the world so freely given,
For that great, great love of Thine,
Peace on earth and joy in heaven.

"Lord of all, to Thee we raise
This our hymn of grateful praise."

The celebrant raised his right hand in benediction, this time lowering his ring finger to meet his thumb. "Go forth into the world in peace, rejoicing in the power of the Spirit."

The congregation answered, "Thanks be to God."

Chapter Forty-Three

Jaben was awoken by a phone call. "Be at Mortmain's Cove at 6:00 PM, and bring your friends along." He set the phone back on the receiver, and looked at his clock. 3:43 AM. Jaben scratched his head in puzzlement, and then drifted off to sleep.

Chapter Forty-Four

The friends' van pulled around the corner, and they piled out. "I wonder what this could be about," Désirée murmured.

Jaben put his arm over Ellamae's shoulder, and said, "Ellamae, there's this one joke I've got to tell you. You'll laugh so hard, your breasts will fall off."

Then he glanced down at her chest for a moment, and said, "Oh, wait. You've already heard it."

Ellamae did not immediately react, then her mouth opened with a most delicious expression of "I can't believe I just heard what I thought I heard," and started laughing, and hit him in the arm. "Naughty, naughty," she said.

Thad said, "Ok. You are in a field. There is a clown suit, a crowbar, and a laptop here. Above are ominous clouds."

"I go west," Amos said.

"I do not recognize the verb 'I'."

"Take clown suit."

"Taken."

"Wear clown suit."

"The clown suit is about three sizes too small for you, and its colors clash with each other and your skin. Definitely you. You see--"

"Hullo, what's this?" said Ellamae.

Another van came up. It had no license plates.

Four men in white sheets stepped out. Two of them were

carrying shotguns, and one of them was holding a box, about a fifteen by fifteen by six inches. The last one stepped out, and said, "Which of you is Jaben?"

Jaben stepped forward and said, "Me."

"Jaben," the Klansman said with a sneer. "Don't you think that when we get rid of one of *them*, it is with good reason?"

"We have rescued our friend," Jaben said calmly. "Is that not good reason?"

"No. You are ashamed of being white, and you are a disgrace to our race."

"I am very proud of being white," Jaben said. "I am proud of all the paintings and philosophy and poetry my race has produced. And I believe that loving others of your race comes before loving people not of your race."

"You do?" the Klansman asked with some surprise.

"Most definitely. But I don't think race defines the end of love. I believe in loving myself, my kin, my race, all of humanity, in an ever expanding circle of love. Your love of your kindred helps you love whites who are not your relations; my love of whites helps me love men who are not white. I am the richer for the friendships I have had with people who are not white, most of all Amos and Désirée. You would be the richer if you could expand your circle of love as well."

The Klansman snorted. "I did not come here to discuss philosophy with you. I came to challenge you to a duel." He opened the box to reveal two silver handguns. "Each of these is a . 45."

"I don't believe in fighting. You can as much win a duel as win an earthquake."

Another Klansman fired a warning shot into the air. The echo resounded. "You will enter this duel, or we will mow down you and your friends, starting with the two of *them*."

Jaben closed his eyes, and prayed silently. His friends -- not touching him, not moving -- prayed with him. Then he opened his eyes, and said, "Ok."

Ellamae looked at him in absolute shock.

Jaben said -- loud enough for the Kythers to hear -- "Trust me," and walked over, and whispered something in Ellamae's ear.

Ellamae gulped.

Jaben walked over to the Klansmen, took one of the pistols. He stepped to the side, pointed the gun up, and turned his back.

The Klansman took the other pistol, and stood back to back with Jaben.

"One. Two. Three. Four. Five. Six. Seven. Eight. Nine. Ten."

Jaben turned, fired a shot into the air, and dropped his gun to the ground. "My brother!" he cried, facing his adversary.

The Klansman turned, took aim, and shot him through the heart.

Chapter Forty-Five

Ellamae was the first to reach him, and caught him before he reached the ground. She knelt down and held him, his hot blood coursing over her shirt. She kissed him on the forehead, and Jaben smiled. Then the life left his eyes.

The others gathered around, for one last embrace. Thaddeus closed Jaben's eyes, which were still open, vacant, empty. Ellamae's voice once again rose in a song that was high, clear, pure. It was immediately joined by Sarah's voice, Thaddeus's, Lilianne's, Désirée's, and Amos's.

> "When peace, like a river, attendeth my way,
> When sorrows like sea billows roll;
> Whatever my lot, Thou hast taught me to say,
> It is well, it is well with my soul.
> It is well, it is well,
> With my soul, with my soul,
> It is well, it is well with my soul.
>
> "Though Satan should buffet, though trials should come,

Let this blest assurance control,
That Christ hath regarded my helpless estate,
And hath shed His own blood for my soul."

Amos could not sing. His voice was choked with tears.

"It is well, it is well,
With my soul, with my soul,
It is well, it is well with my soul.

"My sin! O the bliss of this glorious thought,
My sin! not in part, but the whole,
Is nailed to the Cross and I bear it no more,
Praise the Lord, praise the Lord, O my soul!
It is well, it is well,
With my soul, with my soul,
It is well, it is well with my soul.

"And, Lord, haste the day when my faith shall be made sight,
The clouds be rolled back as a scroll,
The trump shall resound and the Lord shall descend,
Even so, it is well with my soul.
It is well, it is well,
With my soul, with my soul,
It is well, it is well with my soul."

They sang a second time.

"When peace, like a river, attendeth my way,
When sorrows like sea billows roll;
Whatever my lot, Thou hast taught me to say,
It is well, it is well with my soul.
It is well, it is well,
With my soul, with my soul,
It is well, it is well with my soul.

"Though Satan should buffet, though trials should come,
Let this blest assurance control,
That Christ hath regarded my helpless estate,
And hath shed His own blood for my soul.
It is well, it is well,
With my soul, with my soul,
It is well, it is well with my soul.

"My sin! O the bliss of this glorious thought,
My sin! not in part, but the whole,
Is nailed to the Cross and I bear it no more,
Praise the Lord, praise the Lord, O my soul!
It is well, it is well,
With my soul, with my soul,
It is well, it is well with my soul.

"And, Lord, haste the day when my faith shall be made sight,
The clouds be rolled back as a scroll,
The trump shall resound and the Lord shall descend,
Even so, it is well with my soul.
It is well, it is well,
With my soul, with my soul,
It is well, it is well with my soul."

Amos choked back tears long enough to say, "Let's sing it a third time."

This time, they sang more slowly:

"When peace, like a river, attendeth my way,
When sorrows like sea billows roll;
Whatever my lot, Thou hast taught me to say,
It is well, it is well with my soul.
It is well, it is well,
With my soul, with my soul,

It is well, it is well with my soul.

"Though Satan should buffet, though trials should
come,
Let this blest assurance control,
That Christ hath regarded my helpless estate,
And hath shed his own blood for my soul."

Here they all stopped, and for a time there was only a sound of tears. Then the song continued, loudly, powerfully, mightily.

"It is well, it is well,
With my soul, with my soul,
It is well, it is well with my soul.

"My sin! O the bliss of this glorious thought,
My sin! not in part, but the whole,
Is nailed to the Cross and I bear it no more,
Praise the Lord, praise the Lord, O my soul!
It is well, it is well,
With my soul, with my soul,
It is well, it is well with my soul.

"And, Lord, haste the day when our faith shall be
made sight,
The clouds be rolled back as a scroll,
The trump shall resound and the Lord shall descend,
Even so, it is well with my soul.
It is well, it is well,
With my soul, with my soul,
It is well, it is well, with my soul.

"Amen."

Lilianne looked up, and looked around. The Klansmen had all fled in terror.

The Kythers had been so deeply enraptured in the song that they had not even heard the sound of the van.

"The gun!" Sarah said. "We still have a gun with their fingerprints on it. Maybe the police can trace whoever it was, and bring them to justice."

Ellamae picked up the gun with two fingers, as if she were holding a dead fish, and moved it a few paces away. Then she went into their van, took out a container and a cigarette lighter, poured some kerosene on the gun, and lit it.

"No," she said. "That is not the way."

She looked at Sarah, and said, sadly, "An eye for an eye only ends by making the whole world blind."

Chapter Forty-Six

"I can't believe he's gone," Désirée said. "Or that his life was cut so short."

"I don't believe that he's gone," Lilianne said. "Or that his life was cut short."

"Explain," Désirée said, raising her eyebrows.

"You know Hebrews chapter 11, that great chapter cataloging all the heroes of faith? After that, Paul writes, 'Therefore, since we are surrounded by such a great cloud of witnesses, let us throw off everything that hinders and the sin that so easily entangles, and let us run with perserverance the race marked out for us.'

"The image is that of a stadium, where all those who have completed the race and received their laurel wreaths are standing around, excited, cheering on those who are still running. I may never hear from Jaben again this side of Heaven, but that doesn't mean he isn't here with us, watching us, praying, smiling on us. Jaben only lived a few years, but he managed in his own special way to cram more living into the scant years that he did live, than many people would live in a hundred years. I don't know how to explain it, but his life was complete."

The conversation gave way to a deep and powerful silence,

a silence on which Jaben smiled.

Chapter Forty-Seven

Friends and family gathered inside the church, weeping. The pastor began,

> "I am the Resurrection and the Life, says the Lord.
> Anyone who believes in me, even though that person dies, will live
> and whoever lives and believes in me
> will never die.
>
> "I know that I have a living Defender
> and that he will rise up last, on the dust of the earth.
> After my awakening, he will set me close to him,
> and from my flesh I shall look on God.
> He whom I shall see will take my part:
> my eyes will be gazing on no stranger.
>
> "For none of us lives for himself
> and none of us dies for himself;
> while we are alive, we are living for the Lord,
> and when we die, we die for the Lord:
> and so, alive or dead,
> we belong to the Lord.
>
> "Blessed are those
> who die in the Lord
> Blessed indeed, the Spirit says;
> now they can rest for ever after their work."

"The Lord be with you," the pastor said softly.

"And also with you," answered the congregation, even more softly.

"Let us pray."

There was a deep, still, empty silence, a wounded, grieving silence, that after a time took the form of the celebrant's words:

"O God of grace and glory, we remember before you this day our brother Jaben. We thank you for giving him to us, his family and friends, to know and to love as a companion on our earthly pilgrimage. In your boundless compassion, console us who mourn. Give us faith to see in death the gate of eternal life, so that in quiet confidence we may continue our course on earth, until, by your call, we are reunited with those who have gone before; through Jesus Christ our Lord."

"Amen," all said together.

"Most merciful God," the celebrant said, "whose wisdom is beyond our understanding: Deal graciously with Amos, Désirée, Lilianne, Ellamae, Thaddeus, Sarah, Wallace, Elizabeth, and Bear in their grief. Surround them with your love, that they may not be overwhelmed by their loss, but have confidence in your goodness, and strength to meet the days to come; through Jesus Christ our Lord."

An Amen filled the church.

"A reading from the Song of Songs," said the reader.

"Set me as a seal on your heart,
as a sigil on your arm.
For love is stronger than death,
more relentless than Hades.
Its flame is a flash of fire,
a flame of Yahweh himself.
Many waters cannot quench love,
neither can floods drown it.

"The Word of the Lord," the reader said.

"Thanks be to God," the congregation answered.

"A reading from Paul's first letter to the Corinthians.

"What you sow must die before it is given new life; and what you sow is not the body that is to be, but only a bare grain, of wheat I dare say, or some other kind; it is God who gives it the sort of body that he has chosen for it, and for each kind of seed its own kind of body.

"Not all flesh is the same flesh: there is human flesh; animals have another kind of flesh, birds another and fish yet another. There are heavenly bodies and earthly bodies; the heavenly have a splendor of their own, and the earthly a different splendor. The sun has its own splendor the moon another splendor, and the stars yet another splendor; and the stars differ among themselves in splendor. It is the same too with the resurrection of the dead: what is sown is perishable, but what is raised is imperishable; what is sown is contemptible but what is raised is glorious; what is sown is weak, but what is raised is powerful; what is sown is a natural body, and what is raised is a spiritual body.

"The Word of the Lord," the reader said.

"Thanks be to God," the congregation echoed.

All rose, and the pastor said, "The Holy Gospel of our Lord Jesus Christ according to John."

The congregation answered, "Glory to you, Lord Christ."

"'Do not let your hearts be troubled.
You trust in God, trust also in me.
In my Father's house there are many places to live in;
otherwise I would have told you.
I am going now to prepare a place for you,
and after I have gone and prepared you a place,
I shall return to take you to myself,
so that you may be with me
where I am.
You know the way to the place where I am going.'

"Thomas said, 'Lord, we do not know where you are going, so how can we know the way?' Jesus said:

'I am the Way; I am Truth and Life.
No one can come to the Father except through me.'"

The pastor closed the Bible, saying, "The Gospel of the Lord."

The congregation answered, "Glory to you, Lord Christ."

The pastor paused, and began, "A conservative, someone said, is someone who interprets the book of Jonah literally and the Song of Songs figuratively. A liberal is someone who interprets the book of Jonah figuratively and the Song of Songs literally." He paused, and then continued. "I'm not sure where that would place Jaben; I don't know how Jaben interpreted Jonah, but I do know that he interpreted the Song of Songs on at least three levels: a literal level, a figurative level, and a level of human relationships. He explained to me the last one by saying that if marriage is the crowning jewel of human relationships, as the Bible leads us to believe, then we should expect a book devoted to marriage to not only be a book about marriage, but a book about every human relationship. 'Catch for us the foxes, the little foxes, that wreak havoc on our vineyards' means to deal with the little problems that wreak havoc on a relationship, and that is sound advice for a marriage and sound advice for any other friendship.

"The Song of Songs was Jaben's favorite book, so much so that he made his own translation -- that and, he said, the fact that existing translations are highly bowlderized. Remind me to tell you sometime later what happened when the scholars working on the NIV made mistake of translating the greatest Song well. What you have in your Life Application Bible isn't what the translators--

"I normally read from the King James at funerals, but Jaben would not have liked that. The King James, he said, is a wonderful monument of Elizabethan prose that should respectfully be permitted to rest in peace. So other readings in the service were taken from the New Jerusalem Bible, the most current English equivalent to the French *Bible de Jérusalem* that Jaben read, but the passage from the Song of Songs was from Jaben's own translation. I would read other passages, but there are children listening.

"I thought about having 'His Banner Over Me Is Love' sung at this service, but I decided not to, for two reasons. The first reason is that it is a bouncy song, and does not very much sound like a dirge. And the second and most important reason? Jaben would have rolled over in his grave. The ultimate emasculation of an erotic text, he said, is to take a woodenly literal translation that obscures its meaning, and make it into a children's song. Come to think of it, I will tell you of one portion of Jaben's translation. He translated 'His banner over me is love' as 'He is gazing on me with desire.'

"Jaben was a brilliant man; he spoke four languages fluently, received a bachelor's degree in physics, and did things with computers I can't begin to understand. He was also quite a joker. I'll never forget the time he was talking with a senior political science major who was looking for a job, put an arm around his shoulder, and said, 'What did the computer science graduate say to the humanities graduate?' 'What?' 'I'll have the burger and fries, please.'

"And yet, as I think about him, not his humor, nor even his intelligence, strike me as most important about him. To explain exactly what *was* most important, I will in a moment tell you about his death.

"Jaben believed in living counterculturally. He believed in working to establish a culture of life in the midst of a culture of death. He always, always had time for people, from the youngest to the oldest. He would play with children, and sit at the feet of the aged and listen to their stories. He wouldn't have anything of disposable relationships--he kept up correspondence with his friends in France, and made a conscious decision to stay with his friends here until death. God alone knew how soon that death would come.

"His friend Amos was abducted, and I have never seen friendship so deep as in that seven-stranded cord of friends. He and the other friends left, and traveled through Mexico to find Amos, and at last came back as seven friends, singing loudly and off-key. That is quite a story, to be told another time. But when he came back--

"Amos was abducted out of hate, a hate that is real and not only white against black. Amos is struggling hard not to be consumed by the same hate that consumed his adversaries, and I ask you, brothers and sisters, to pray for him. He bears a heavy burden. The men who left Amos to die in Mexico were enraged that he be brought back alive, and insisted on a duel -- their way. Jaben was not allowed to choose the place and weaponry as used to be the etiquette when duels were fought. The place was Mortmain's Cove and the weapon was a magnum .45. Jaben deliberately fired into the air, and then his opponent shot him through the heart.

"His last words, spoken to his murderer just before his death, were, 'My brother!'

"His next to last words, whispered into Ellamae's ears as he faced death, were, '*Tell my brothers and sisters that I love them.*'

"To understand the full extent of these words, let me tell you something. *Jaben was an only child.*

"When he said, 'Tell my brothers and sisters that I love them,' he was talking about you. And me. He loved us, and loves us still.

"When Jesus knew that his hour was approaching, he said over and over again, 'Love one another' -- the heart of Christian ethics -- and 'There is no love like this, that a man lay down his life for his friends.' That is exactly what Jaben did. He gave his life as a ransom for Amos and the others. He decided to try to rescue Amos, whatever the cost -- even his life.

"He gave more than money or time. He gave himself, his life. He lived well. He died well. We have before us the body of a man, of a hero. He is no longer with us. But his love remains.

"Let us pray.

"Lord, thank you for the scintillating light that shone in your servant Jaben. We stand bereaved; his candle burned short, but it blazed. Grant that each of us may learn from him and carry him in our hearts, and that you would enfold him in your own heart. Draw us into your heart. In Jesus' name, Amen."

The congregation began to rise, as the pastor said, "In the assurance of eternal life given at Baptism, let us proclaim our faith and say,"

One united voice said,

"I believe in God, the Father almighty,
creator of heaven and earth.

"I believe in Jesus Christ, his only Son, our Lord.
He was conceived by the power of the Holy Spirit
and born of the Virgin Mary.
He suffered under Pontius Pilate,
was crucified, died, and was buried.
He descended to the dead.
On the third day he rose again.
He ascended into heaven,
and is seated at the right hand of the Father.
He will come again to judge the living and the dead.

"I believe in the Holy Spirit,
the holy Catholic Church,
the communion of saints,
the forgiveness of sins,
the resurrection of the body,
and the life everlasting.
Amen."

The pastor said, "Lord, help us to be like you, just as your servant Jaben was like you. Let us be shaped in your image, in preparation for that day when we shall ever be changing from glory to glory, in your presence even more fully than he is in your presence. Help us to know that we are strangers, we are aliens, we are not of this world, even as Jaben was not of this world, and is in it no longer. Draw us all into your eternal home, with its many dwelling places, in your eternal heart. Amen."

The pastor stood in silence for a full minute, the silence

breathing life into the prayer. Then he closed his eyes, and said, "Lord Jesus Christ, we commend to you our brother Jaben, who was reborn by water and the Spirit in Holy Baptism. Grant that his death may recall to us your victory over death, and be an occasion for us to renew our trust in your Father's love. Give us, we pray, the faith to follow where you have led the way; and where you live and reign with the Father and the Holy Spirit, to the ages of ages." The congregation joined him in saying, "Amen."

The pastor and the others ordained walked over to the coffin, and prayed, "Give rest, O Christ, to your servant with your saints,"

The people joined him, saying,

"where sorrow and pain are no more,
neither signing, but life everlasting."

"You alone are immortal," the pastor continued, "the creator and maker of mankind; and we are mortal, formed of the earth, and to earth shall we return. For so did you ordain when you created me, saying, "You are dust, and to dust you shall return." All of us go down to the dust; yet even at the grave we make our song: Alleluia, alleluia, alleluia."

All said in unison,

"Give rest, O Christ, to your servant with your saints,
where sorrow and pain are no more,
neither sighing, but life everlasting."

The pastor turned to the body, and said, "Into your hands, O merciful Savior, we commend your servant Jaben. Acknowledge, we humbly beseech you, a sheep of your own fold, a lamb of your own flock, a sinner of your own redeeming. Receive him into the arms of your mercy, into the blessed rest of everlasting peace, and into the glorious company of the saints in light." And all the people said, "Amen."

The pastor raised his hand in benediction, and said, "The peace of God, which passes all understanding, keep your hearts and minds in the knowledge and love of God, and of his Son Jesus Christ our Lord; and the blessing of God Almighty, the Father, the Son, and the Holy Spirit, be among you, and remain with you always," and the congregation joined him in saying, "Amen."

"Let us go forth in the name of Christ," the pastor said.

"Thanks be to God," the people answered.

As the body was carried out from the church, the people chanted:

"Christ is risen from the dead,
trampling down death by death,
and giving life to those in the tomb.

"Into paradise may the angels lead you.
At your coming may the martyrs receive you,
and bring you into the holy city Jerusalem."

Chapter Forty-Eight

Désirée said, "Remember Sarah's first time making hamburgers? She put raw meat on top of hamburger buns, and then put them in the oven at 550. When someone smelled smoke, the buns and the outside were burnt to a crisp, and the inside of the burgers was still raw. We scraped off the charred buns, and put fresh ones, and Amos said, 'Jaben, would you return thanks for this meal?'

"And Jaben folded his hands, and bowed his head, and began, 'Lord, bless the hands that repaired this meal...'"

A chuckle moved among the friends.

"Or remember," Désirée said, "the time when Bear ate a steakhouse out of shrimp, and the time after that that Jaben outate Bear? I never saw Bear stare like that. Or you, Amos, dear." She gave her husband a squeeze.

"Or remember that time on the internet when Jaben advertised free, automated technical support for all versions of Windows, and created a CGI that would read in a user's question, and then display a page that said, 'Your computer appears to be infected with a piece of malicious code known as Windows. To remedy this problem, try upgrading to the most recent version of Debian or Redhat.' Man, some of the flames he got after that!

"Or remember the time Jaben installed a Blue Screen of Death screensaver on Bear's laptop? I never seen Bear so mad.

"Or remember the time when he went into a bike shop, and opened the entire supply of locks the store had around a bar, and walked up to the front counter, and said, 'These aren't very effective, are they?'

"Or remember the time when Sarah was working on a paper, and called out, 'How do you spell "Approximately?"' And Jaben answered, 'Q-F-R-3.' And Sarah said, 'No, really. I want a real spelling of a real word,' and Jaben answered, 'A-L-M-O-S-T?'

"Or remember that one last time when he called his medical insurance, waited for thirty minutes listening to music, and then said, 'Hello. I'm calling to inquire as as to whether mental health will pay for singing lessons for the voices in my head?'"

The six friends were holding hands in a circle, laughing, weeping. Ellamae wiped a tear from her eye, and then softly whispered, "Fare thee well, Jaben. Adieu."

Chapter Forty-Nine

Jaben looked. "Aah, Pope Gregory. There is something I'd like a theologian's feedback on."

"Yes?"

"My theories of prophecy. When I have asked people on earth to look at it, they have said that the theories are too deep to comment on."

"Aah, yes," the Pope said with a twinkle in his eyes. "They are great favorites in this realm. It serves to continually astonish us how someone so intelligent, so devout, and so open to the Spirit's leading could be so completely wrong."

Jaben looked, then smiled, then laughed, then laughed harder, then roared with laughter. His whole form shimmered with mirth. His laughter echoed throughout Heaven, and shook the foundations of Hell. Finally, he stopped laughing, and said, "That's the funniest thing I've ever heard."

He paused a second, and asked, "Will you introduce me to the folk here?"

"Mary!"

"Welcome, child," smiled the lady. "I have been waiting for you for ages."

"What news do you have to tell me?"

"Désirée is with child, though she does not know it, and will give birth to a man-child who will be no ordinary child."

"What will his name be?"

"His name shall be called Jaben."

"And what do you have to tell me of yourself?"

"Only this: I love you." She held him to herself as a little child.

Jaben asked Gregory, "Who was the greatest saint of all? Paul? Francis of Assisi? Theresa of Avila?"

"Come, let me show you to her." He introduced her to a little girl. "This child's name is Roberta. She lived in fourteenth century Italy, and you have not heard of her. She died at the age of seven in an epidemic, and she was not particularly attractive or bright -- she was slightly retarded -- she worked no miracles, and she was very easy to ignore (and most everyone did ignore her). She certainly wasn't canonized. If you were to find an earthly account of her life, it would strike you as that of an ordinary and somewhat dull child. But here, we look at things a little differently. God saw into her heart, and saw faith, hope, and love such as never has occurred in mere man before and will never occur again."

"Hi, Mister," the child said. "May I please hold your hand?"

They walked along, and saw three men talking. "Who are

these?" he asked Gregory.

"These are Peter, Augustine, and Aquinas."

Jaben felt a moment of awe, and said, "May I join your theological discussion?"

"What a funny idea!" Aquinas said. "We weren't discussing theology. There is no need for that here. You don't need a picture of a friend when you can see his face. We were doing something far holier -- telling jokes."

"Aah, wonderful. May I tell you my favorite joke? It involves you three."

"Certainly. Sit down."

"There is a seminary student who is about to finish his studies, when he is killed in a car accident. He goes and waits outside the Pearly Gates.

"Peter asks the first person in line, 'Who are you?' And then Augustine replies, 'I'm Augustine.' 'Prove it,' Peter says. So you talk for a time about the *Civitas Dei*, and Peter lets him in, saying, 'Welcome to Heaven, my dear friend.'

"Then Peter asks the next person in line, 'Who are you?' And Thomas replies, 'I'm Thomas Aquinas.' 'Prove it,' Peter says. So the two talk for a time about how Aristotle's *Nicomachean Ethics* can enlighten our understanding of the Natural Law. And he says to Aquinas in turn, 'Welcome to Heaven, my dear friend.'

"Finally, it's the seminary student's turn, and so you ask him, 'Who are you?' He replies, 'Well, I'm, like, Nabal, and I was, like, studying all this really cool stuff in seminary about how we can bring together the best in, like, Christianity and New Age and other religions, and how it's OK to honor the goddess in our worship, and then this car, like, creams me, and so here I am.'

"Peter pauses a second, and says, 'Very well, then. You'll have to prove who you are, just like Augustine and Aquinas.'

"'Augustine? Aquinas? Like, dude, man, who are they?'

"'Welcome to Heaven, my dear friend.'"

They were swept up with a merry, joyful mirth, and then, another voice called out, "Come! Sing the great song! Dance the great dance!"

He was swept away in a tempest of fire and wind and motion -- wholly wild, wholly uncontrollable, wholly good. Song was over it and in it and through it. Notes flowed in and out to something beyond notes, and this incredible unfathomable motion was somehow also perfect peace. It was neither work nor rest, but play -- pure, unending, awesome, wondrous play.

At last he found himself before a throne of seven stones.

"Daddy! I have been so longing to meet you!"

"Why, child? You have known me from childhood."

"But oh, Daddy, how I long to touch your face."

"Blessed are you who long to touch my face, for that you shall. Come. Touch."

After a time, the Father said, "What else is on your heart, child?"

"Many things, but only one thing."

"Yes?" "My friends, and the men who murdered me. I want them to know each other, to be reconciled, and I want them all to be with me in the New Jerusalem. Oh, Daddy, will you give me that?"

"Absolutely."

With that, Jaben sunk into the Father's heart of love, never again to leave.

soli deo gloria
marana tha

www.ingramcontent.com/pod-product-compliance
Lightning Source LLC
Chambersburg PA
CBHW030818310726
48980CB00006B/536/J

* 9 7 8 0 6 1 5 2 0 2 1 8 1 *